ENCOUNTER WITH AN ENEMY

'Come on the Kestrels!' Drinkwater's scream cracked into a croak but about him there was a hefting of pikes, a re-gripping of cutlasses and then they were surging forward, driving the Dutch before them. Over a larboard gun leapt Short, a maniacal laugh erupting from him as he pitched a man overboard, then drove two more before him into the larboard quarter. They were disarmed and with his pike Short tossed them both over the shattered transom like stooks on to a rick.

With careless swathes of the hanger Drinkwater slashed aft. A Dutch officer came on guard in front of him and instinct made him pause and come into the same pose, but he was passed by Short, his face a contorted mask of insane delight, his pike levelled at the officer. A pistol ball entered Short's eye and took the back of his skull off. Still the boatswain's mate lunged and the Dutch lieutenant crashed to the deck, pierced by the terrible weapon with Short's twitching corpse on top of him.

Drinkwater stepped aside and faced the man who had fired the pistol.

It was Edouard Santhonax.

A King's Cutter

RICHARD WOODMAN

SPHERE BOOKS LIMITED

SPHERE BOOKS LTD

Penguin Books Ltd, 27 Wrights Lane, London W8 5TZ (Publishing and Editorial)
and Harmondsworth, Middlesex, England (Distribution and Warehouse)
Viking Penguin Inc., 40 West 23rd Street, New York, New York 10010, USA
Penguin Books Australia Ltd, Ringwood, Victoria, Australia
Penguin Books Canada Ltd, 2801 John Street, Markham, Ontario, Canada L3R 1B4
Penguin Books (NZ) Ltd, 182–190 Wairau Road, Auckland 10, New Zealand

First published in Great Britain by John Murry (Publishers) Ltd 1982
Published by Sphere Books Ltd 1984
Reprinted 1987

Publisher's Note

This novel is a work of fiction. Names, characters, places and incidents are either the product of
the author's imagination or are used fictitiously, and any resemblance to actual persons, living
or dead, events, or locales is entirely coincidental.

Made and printed in Great Britain by
Richard Clay Ltd, Bungay, Suffolk
Set in V-I-P Times

Contents

For the crew of the cutter
KESTREL

Author's Note

The exploits of Nathaniel Drinkwater during the period 1792 to 1797 are based on fact. The services of cutters for all manner of purposes were, in the words of the contemporary historian William James, 'very effectually performed by British cruisers even of that insignificant class.'

A man named Barrallier did escape from France to build ships for the Royal Navy while, shortly before the collapse of the Nore mutiny, eight men disappeared in a ship's boat. Until now their destination was a mystery. During the mutiny scare wild tales circulated about mysterious strangers traversing the lanes of Kent and French subversion was popularly supposed to lie behind the trouble at the Nore.

Many of the characters that appear actually existed. Apart from the admirals, Warren and h famous frigate captains and the commanders of Duncan's ships, Captain Schank was inventively employed at this time. Captain Anthony Calvert and Jonathan Poulter did indeed destroy the Thames buoyage to prevent the mutineers escaping.

The precise reason why De Winter sailed is still open to question. Both his fleet and the considerable number of troop and storeships that lay with him in the Texel were clearly intended to form part of a grand expedition and Ireland seems the likely destination. Wolfe Tone was with De Winter during part of 1797 as he had been with De Galles at Bantry the year before. It has also been suggested that the Dutch sailed to destroy Duncan who was supposed to command an unreliable force, or that they sallied to restore Dutch prestige. In fact De Winter retired before contacting Duncan. Yet, when battle was inevitable, his fleet fought with great ferocity. Perhaps the parts played by Drinkwater and Edouard Santhonax in a campaign disastrous to the Dutch fleet explain some of the tension of that desperate year.

PART ONE

The English Channel

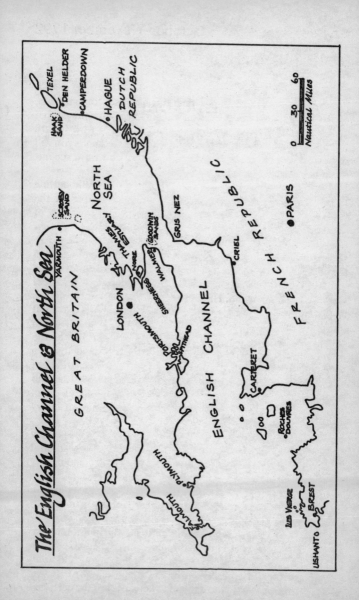

The English Channel & North Sea

Chapter One   October–November 1792

The Puppet's Hand

'You will be,' said Lord Dungarth, lifting his hands for emphasis, 'merely the hand of a puppet. You will not know what the puppet master intends, how the strings are manipulated or why you are commanded to do the things that you will do. Like hands you will simply execute your instructions efficiently. You were recommended for your efficiency, Nathaniel . . .'

Drinkwater blinked against the reflected sunlight silhouetting the two earls. Beyond the windows the dark shapes of the Channel Fleet were anchored in the sparkling waters of Spithead. Beneath his feet he felt the massive bulk of the *Queen Charlotte* trim herself to the tide. For a second or two he revolved the proposition in his head. After six years as second mate in the buoy yachts of Trinity House he was at least familiar with the Channel, even if the precise purpose of the armed cutter *Kestrel* was obscured from him. He had held an acting commission as lieutenant eleven years earlier when he had expected great things from it, but he was more experienced now, married and almost too old to consider probable the dazzling career the Royal Navy had once seemed to offer him. He had found a satisfying employment with the Trinity House but he could not deny the quickened heartbeat as Dungarth explained he had been selected for special service aboard a cutter under direct Admiralty orders. The implications of that were given heavy emphasis by his second interviewer.

'Well, Mr Drinkwater?' Earl Howe's rich voice drew Drinkwater's attention to the heavy features of the admiral commanding the Channel Fleet. He must make his mind up.

'I would be honoured to accept, my lords.'

Lord Dungarth nodded with satisfaction. 'I am much pleased, Nathaniel, much pleased. I was sorry that you lost your promotion when Hope died.'

'Thank you my lord, I have to admit to it being a bitter blow.' He smiled back trying to bridge the years since he and Dungarth had last met. He wondered if he had changed as much as John Devaux, former first lieutenant of the frigate *Cyclops*. It was more than the succession to a title that had affected the earl; that

3

alone could not have swamped the ebullient dash of the man. It might have produced his lordship's new introspection but not the hint of implacability that coloured his remarks. That seemed to stem from his mysterious new duties.

A month later Drinkwater had received his orders and the acting commission. His farewell to his wife had affected him deeply. Whatever her own misgivings in respect of his transfer from buoy yachts to an armed cutter, Elizabeth kept them to herself. It was not in her nature to divert his purpose, for she had loved him for his exuberance and watched it wither with regret when the navy had failed him. But she could not disguise the tears that accompanied their parting.

His arrival on board the cutter had been as secret as anyone could have wished. A late October fog had shrouded the Tilbury marshes as he searched for a boat, stumbling among the black stakes that rose out of the mud oozing along the high water mark. Patches of bladder wrack and straw, pieces of rotten wood and the detritus of civilisation ran along the edge of the unseen Thames. Somewhere in the region of Hope he had found a man and a boat and they had pushed out over the glass-smooth grey river, passing a mooring buoy that sheered and gurgled in the tide. A cormorant had started from the white stained staves and overhead a pale sun had broken through slowly to consume the nacreous vapour.

The cutter's transom had leapt out of the fog, boat falls trailing in the tide from her stern davits. He had caught a brief glimpse of a carved taffrail, oak leaves and her name: *Kestrel*. Then he had scrambled aboard, aware of a number of idlers about the deck, a huge mast, boom and gaff and a white St George's ensign drooping disconsolately aft. A short, active looking man bustled up. About forty, with beetling eyebrows and a brusque though not impolite manner. He conveyed an impression of efficiency.

'Can I help you, sir?' The blue eyes darted perceptively.

'Good morning to you. My name's Drinkwater, acting lieutenant. D'you have a boat down?' he nodded aft to the vacant davits.

'Aye, sir. Jolly boat's gone to Gravesend. We was expecting you.'

'My chest is at Tilbury fort, please to have it aboard as soon as possible.'

4

The man nodded. 'I'm Jessup, sir, bosun. I'll show you to your cabin.' He rolled aft and hopped over the sea-step of a companionway. At the bottom of the ladder Drinkwater found himself in a tiny lobby. Behind the ladder a rack of Tower muskets and cutlasses gleamed dully. Leading off the space were five flimsy doors. Jessup indicated the forward one. 'Main cabin, cap'n's quarters . . . he's ashore just now. This 'ere's your'n sir.' He opened a door to starboard and Drinkwater stepped inside.

The after-quarters of *Kestrel* were situated between the hold and the rudder trunking. The companionway down which they had come left the deck immediately forward of the tiller. Facing the bottom of the ladder was the door to the main cabin extending the full width of the ship. The four other doors opened on to tiny cabins intended by a gracious Admiralty to house the officers of the cutter. The after two were tapering spaces filled with odds and ends and clearly unoccupied. The others were in use. His own was to starboard. Jessup told him the larboard one was 'for passengers . . .' and evaded further questioning.

Drinkwater entered his cabin and closed the door. The space was bare of a chair. A small bookshelf was secured to the pine bulkhead. A tiny folding table was fitted beneath the shelf, ingeniously doubling as the lid of a cabinet containing a bucket for night soil. A rack for a carafe and glass, both of which articles were missing, and three pegs behind the door completed the cabin's fittings. He went on deck.

The visibility had improved and he could see the low line of the Kent coast. He walked forward to enquire of Jessup whether the boat had returned.

'Aye, sir, been and gone. I sent it to Tilbury for your dunnage.'

Drinkwater thanked him, ignoring the scrutiny of the hands forward. He coughed and said, 'Perhaps you would be kind enough to show me round the deck.' Jessup nodded and went forward.

The huge bowsprit came inboard through the stemhead gammon iron and was housed in massive timbers that incorporated the windlass barrel. Abaft this was a companionway to the fo'c's'le, a large dark space extending beyond the mast which rose from the deck surrounded by its fiferails, belaying pins, lead blocks and coils of cordage.

'How many men do we bear, Mr Jessup?'

'Forty-eight full complement, forty-two at present . . . here's the hatch, sir, fitted with a platform, it ain't a proper 'tween deck ... used as 'ammock space, sail room an' 'old.' Jessup ran his hand along the gunwale of the larboard gig chocked on the hatch as they continued aft. Drinkwater noted the plank lands were scuffed and worn.

'The boats see hard service, then?'

Jessup gave a short laugh. 'Aye, sir. That they do.'

Abaft the hatch were the galley funnel, the cabin skylight and the companionway surmounted by a brass binnacle. Finally the huge curved tiller dominated the after-deck, its heel secured in the brassbound top of the rudder stock, its end terminating in the carved head of the falcon from which the cutter took her name.

Jessup ran his hand possessively over the proud curve of the beak and nodded to a small padlocked hatch let into the stern cant and surrounded by gratings.

'Magazine 'atch.' He turned forward pointing at the guns. 'Mounts twelve guns, sir. Ten three-pounders and two long brass fours forrard, throws a broadside of nineteen pounds. She's seventy-two feet on the gun deck, nigh on one 'undred and twenty-five tons . . .' he trailed off, still suspicious, weighing up the newcomer.

'You been in cutters before, sir?'

Drinkwater looked at him. It did not do to give too much away, he thought. Jessup would know soon enough. He thought of the buoy-yacht *Argus*. It was his turn to look enigmatic.

'Good heavens yes, Mr Jessup. I've served extensively in cutters. You'll not find me wanting there.'

Jessup sniffed. Somehow that indrawn air allowed him the last word, as if it indicated a secret knowledge that Drinkwater could not be a party to. Yet.

'Here's the boat, sir, with your traps.' Jessup walked over to the side to hail it. To seal the advantage he had over the newcomer he spat forcefully into the gliding waters of the Thames.

Shortly before noon the following day the captain had come on board. Lieutenant Griffiths removed his hat, ran a searching eye over the ship and sniffed the wind. He acknowledged Drinkwater's salute with a nod. The lieutenant was tall and stoopshouldered, his sad features crowned by a mane of white hair that lent his sixty-odd years a patriarchal quality. A Welshman of untypical silences he seemed to personify an ancient purpose that might have been Celtic, Cymric or perhaps faerie. Born in Caernarfon he had served as mate in Liverpool slavers before being pressed into the navy. He had risen in the King's service by sheer ability and escaped that degree of intolerance of his former messmates that disfigured many of his type. Lord Howe had given him his commission, declaring that there was no man fitter to rise in the navy than Madoc Griffiths who was, his lordship asserted in his curious idiom, an ornament to his profession. Whatever the idiosyncracies of his self-expression 'Black Dick' was right. As Drinkwater subsequently learnt there was no facet of the cutter's activities of which Griffiths was not master. A first, superficial impression that his new commander might be a superannuated relic was almost instantly dispelled.

Drinkwater's reception had been guarded. In a silence that was disconcerting Griffiths examined Drinkwater's papers. Then he leaned back and coolly studied the man in front of him.

A week short of twenty-nine, Drinkwater was lean and of medium height. A weathered complexion told of continuous sea service. The grey eyes were alert and intelligent, capable of concentration and determination. There were hints of these qualities in the crowsfeet about the eyes and the pale thread of a scar that puckered down from the left eye. But the furrows that ran down from the straight nose to the corners of a well-shaped mouth were prematurely deep and seemed to constrain more than a hint of passion.

Was there a weakness there? Griffiths pondered, appraising the high forehead, the mop of brown hair drawn back into a black ribboned queue. There was a degree of sensitivity, he thought, but not sensuousness, the face was too open. Then he had it; the passion of temper lurked in the clamped corners of that mouth, a temper born of disappointment and disillusion, belied by the level eyes but recognisable to a Welshman. There was something suppressed about the man before him, a latent energy that Griffiths, in isolating, found reassuring. '*Duw* but this man's a terrible fighter,' he muttered to himself and relaxed.

'Sit you down, Mr Drinkwater.' Griffiths's voice was deep and quiet, adding to the impression of otherworldliness. He enunciated his words with that clarity of diction peculiar to some of his race. 'Your papers do you credit. I see that your substantive rank is that of master's mate and that you held an acting commission at the end of the American War . . . it was not confirmed?'

7

'No sir. I was given to understand the matters had been laid before Sir Richard Kempenfelt but . . .' He shrugged, remembering Captain Hope's promise as he left for the careening battleship. Griffiths looked up.

'The *Royal George* was it?'

'Yes sir. It didn't seem important at the time . . .'

'But ten years is a long while to keep a sense of proportion.' Griffiths finished the sentence for him. The two men smiled and it seemed to both that a hurdle had been crossed. 'Still, you have gained excellent experience in the Trinity Yachts, have you not?'

'I believe so, sir.' Drinkwater sensed his commander's approval.

'For my personal satisfaction, *bach*, I require your oath that no matter discussed between us is repeated beyond these bulkheads.' Griffiths's tone was soft yet uncompromising and his eyes were briefly cold. Drinkwater closed his imagination to a sudden vision of appalling facts. He remembered another secret learned long ago, knowledge of which had culminated in death in the swamps of Carolina. He sighed.

'You have my word, as a King's officer.' Drinkwater stared back. The shadow had not gone unnoticed by Griffiths. The lieutenant relaxed. So, he thought, there was experience too. *'Da iawn,'* he muttered.

'This cutter is under the direct orders of the Admiralty. I, er, execute an unusual office, do you see. We attend to certain government business on the French coast at certain times and at certain locations.'

'I see, sir.' But he did not. In an attempt to expand his knowledge he said, 'And your orders come from Lord Dungarth, sir?'

Griffiths regarded him again and Drinkwater feared he had been importunate. He felt the colour rising to his cheeks but Griffiths said, 'Ah, I had forgotten, you knew him from *Cyclops*.'

'Yes, sir. He seems much changed, although it is some years since I last spoke to him.'

Griffiths nodded. 'Aye, and you found the change intimidating, did you?'

Drinkwater nodded, aware that again Griffiths had exactly expressed his own feelings. 'He lost his wife, you know, in child-bed.'

Drinkwater did not keep pace with society gossip but he had been aware of Dungarth's marriage with Charlotte Dixon, an

India merchant's daughter of fabled wealth and outstanding beauty. He had also heard how even Romney had failed to do her likeness justice. He began to see how the loss of his countess had shrivelled that once high-spirited soul and left a ruthless bitterness. As if confirming his thoughts Griffiths said, 'I think if he had not taken on the French republic he would have gone mad . . .'

The old man rose and opened a locker. Taking two glasses and a decanter he poured the sercial and deftly changed the subject. 'The vessel is aptly named, Mr Drinkwater,' he resumed his seat and continued. '*Falco tinnunculus* is characterised by its ability to hover, seeking out the exact location of its prey before it stoops. It lives upon mice, shrews and beetles, small fry, Mr Drinkwater, *bach*, but beetles can eat away an oak beam . . .' He paused to drain and refill his glass. 'Are you seeing the point of my allegory?'

'I, er, I think so, sir.' Griffiths refilled Drinkwater's glass.

'I mention these circumstances for two reasons. Lord Dungarth spoke highly of you, partly from your previous acquaintance and also on the recommendation of the Trinity House. I trust, therefore, that my own confidence in you will not prove misplaced. You will be responsible for our navigation. Remonstrations on lee shores are inimical to secret operations. Understand, do you?'

Drinkwater nodded, aware of the intended irony and continuing to warm to his new commander.

'Very well,' Griffiths continued. The second reason is less easy to confess and I tell you this, Mr Drinkwater, because there is a possibility of command devolving upon you, perhaps in adverse circumstances or at an inconvenient time . . .' Drinkwater frowned. This was more alarming than the previous half-expected revelations. 'Many years ago on the Gambian coast I contracted a fever. From time to time I am afflicted by seizures.'

'But if you are unwell, sir, a, er . . .'

'A replacement?' Griffiths raised an indignant eyebrow then waved aside Drinkwater's apology. 'Look you, I have lived ashore for less than two years in half a century. I am not likely to take root there now.' Drinkwater absorbed the fact as Griffiths's face became suddenly wistful, an old man lost in reminiscence. He finished his glass and stood up, leaving the commander sitting alone with his wine, and quietly left the cabin.

Overhead the white ensign cracked in the strong breeze as the big cutter drove to windward under a hard reefed mainsail. Her topsail yard was lowered to the cap and the lower yard cockbilled clear of the straining staysail. Halfway along her heavy bowsprit the spitfire jib was like a board, wet with spray and still gleaming faintly from the daylight fading behind inky rolls of cumulus to the westward. The wind drove against the ebb tide to whip up a short steep sea, grey-white in the dusk as it seethed alongside and tugged at the boat towing close astern. The cutter bucked her round bow and sent streaks of spray driving over the weather rail.

Acting Lieutenant Nathaniel Drinkwater huddled in his tarpaulin as the spume whipped aft, catching his face and agonising his cheek muscles in the wind-ache that followed.

He ran over the projected passage in his mind yet again, vaguely aware that an error now would blight any chances of his hoped-for promotion. Then he dismissed the thought to concentrate on the matter in hand. From Dover to their destination was sixty-five miles, parallel with the French coast, a coast made terrible by tales of bloody revolution. In the present conditions they would make their landfall at low water. That, Drinkwater had been impressed, was of the utmost importance. He was mystified by the insistence laid upon the point by Lieutenant Griffiths. Although the south-westerly wind allowed them to make good a direct course Griffiths had put her on the larboard tack an hour earlier to deceive any observers on Gris Nez. The cape was now disappearing astern into the murk of a wintry night.

Drinkwater shivered again, as much with apprehension as with cold; he walked over to the binnacle. In the yellow lamplight the gently oscillating card showed a mean heading of north-west by west. Allowing for the variation of the magnetic and true meridians that was a course of west by north. He nodded with satisfaction, ignoring the subdued sound of conversation and the chink of glasses coming up the companionway. The behaviour of his enigmatic commander and their equally mysterious 'passenger' failed to shake his self-confidence.

He walked back to the binnacle and called forward, summoning the hands to tack ship. A faint sound of laughter came up from below. After his interview, Griffiths had withdrawn, giving the minimum of orders, apparently watching his new subordinate. At first Drinkwater thought he was being snubbed, but swiftly realised it was simply characteristic of the lieutenant. And the man who had boarded at Deal had not looked like a spy. Round, red faced and jolly he was clearly well-known to Griffiths and released from the Welshman an unexpected jocularity. Drinkwater could not imagine what they had to laugh about.

'Ready sir!'

From forward Jessup's cry was faintly condescending and Drinkwater smiled into the darkness.

'Down helm!' he called.

Kestrel came up into the wind, her mainsail thundering. Drinkwater felt her tremble when the jib flogged, vibrating the bowsprit. Then she spun as the wind filled the backed headsails, thrusting her round.

'Heads'l sheets!'

The jib and staysail cracked until tamed by the seamen sweating tight the lee sheets.

'Steadeeee . . . steer full and bye.'

'Full an' bye, sir.' The two helmsmen leaned on the big tiller as *Kestrel* drove on, the luff of her mainsail just trembling.

'How's her head?'

'Sou' by west, sir.'

That was south by east true, allowing two points for westerly variation. 'Very well, make it so.'

'Sou' by west it is, sir.'

The ebb ran fair down the coast here and the westing they had made beating offshore ought to put them up-tide and to windward of the landing place by the time they reached it, leaving them room to make the location even if the wind backed. Or so Drinkwater hoped, otherwise his commission would be as remote as ever.

Towards midnight the wind did back and eased a little. The reefs were shaken out and *Kestrel* drove southwards, her larboard rail awash. Drinkwater was tired now. He had been on deck for nine hours and Griffiths did not seem anxious to relieve him.

Kestrel was thrashing in for the shore. Drinkwater could sense rather than see the land somewhere in the darkness ahead. It must be very near low water now. Drinkwater bit his lip with mounting concern. With a backing wind they would get some lee from the cliffs that rose sheer between Le Tréport and Dieppe and it would be this that gave them the first inkling of their proximity. That and the smell perhaps.

In the darkness and at this speed *Kestrel* could be in among the breakers before there was time to go about. Anxiously he strode forward to hail the lookout at the crosstrees. 'Who's aloft?'

'Tregembo, zur.' The Cornishman's burr was reassuring. Tregembo had turned up like a bad penny, one of the draft of six men from the Nore guardship that had completed *Kestrel*'s complement. Drinkwater had known Tregembo on the frigate *Cyclops* where the man had been committed for smuggling. He was still serving out the sentence of a court that had hanged his father for offering revenue officers armed resistance. To mitigate the widow's grief her son was drafted into the navy. That he had appeared on the deck of *Kestrel* was another link in the chain of coincidences that Drinkwater found difficult to dismiss as merely random.

'Keep a damned good lookout, Tregembo!'

'Aye, aye, zur.'

Drinkwater went aft and luffed the cutter while a cast of the lead was taken. 'By the mark, five.' *Kestrel* filled and drove on. There was a tension on deck now and Drinkwater felt himself the centre of it. Jessup hovered solicitously close. Why the devil did Griffiths not come on deck? Five fathoms was shoal water, but it was shoal water hereabouts for miles. They might be anywhere off the Somme estuary. He suppressed a surge of panic and made up his mind. He would let her run for a mile or two and sound again.

'Breakers, zur! Fine on the lee bow!'

Drinkwater rushed forward and leapt into the sagging larboard shrouds. He stared ahead and could see nothing. Then he saw them, a patch of greyness, lighter than the surrounding sea. His heart beat violently as he cudgelled his memory. Then he had it, Les Ridins du Tréport, an isolated patch with little water over it at this state of the tide. He was beginning to see the logic of a landfall at low water. He made a minor adjustment to the course, judging the east-going stream already away close in with the coast. They had about three miles to go.

'Pass word for the captain.' He kept the relief from his voice.

The seas diminished a mile and a half offshore and almost immediately they could see the dark line of the land. Going forward again and peering through the Dollond glass he saw

12

what he hardly dared hope. The cliffs on the left fell away to a narrow river valley, then rose steeply to the west to a height named Mont Jolibois. The faint scent of woodsmoke came to him from the village of Criel that sheltered behind the hill, astride the river crossing of the road from Tréport and Eu to Dieppe.

'*Da iawn*, Mr Drinkwater, well done.' Griffiths's voice was warm and congratulatory. Drinkwater relaxed with relief: it seemed he had passed a test. Griffiths quietly gave orders. The mainsail was scandalised and the staysail backed. The boat towing astern was hauled alongside and two men tumbled in to bale it out. Beside Drinkwater the cloaked figure of the British agent stood staring ashore.

'Your glass, sir, lend me your glass.' The tone was peremptory, commanding, all trace of jollity absent.

'Yes, yes, of course, sir.' He fished it out of his coat pocket and handed it to the man. After scrutinising the beach it was silently returned. Griffiths came up.

'Take the boat in, Mr Drinkwater, and land our guest.'

It took a second to realise his labours were not yet over. Men were piling into the gig alongside. There was the dull gleam of metal where Jessup issued sidearms. 'Pistol and cutlass, sir.' There was an encouraging warmth in Jessup's voice now. Drinkwater took the pistol and stuck it into his wiastband. He refused the cutlass. Slipping below, screwing his eyes up against the lamplight from the cabin, he pushed into his own hutch. Behind the door he felt for the French *épée*. Buckling it on he hurried back on deck.

Mont Jolibois rose above them as the boat approached the shore. To the left Drinkwater could see a fringe of white water that surged around the hummocks of the Roches des Muron. He realised fully why Griffiths insisted they land at low water. As many dangers as possible were uncovered, providing some shelter and a margin of safety if they grounded. Forward the bowman was prodding overside with his boathook.

'Bottom, sir!' he hissed, and a moment later the boat ran aground, lifted and grounded again. Without orders the oars came inboard with low thuds and, to Drinkwater's astonishment, his entire crew leapt overboard, holding the boat steady. Then, straining in a concerted effort that owed its perfection to long practice, they hove her off the sand and hauled her round head to sea. Drinkwater felt foolishly superfluous, sitting staring back the way they had come.

'Ready sir.' A voice behind him made him turn as his passenger rose and scrambled on to the seaman's back. The boat lifted to a small breaker and thumped back on to the bottom. The seaman waded ashore and Drinkwater, not to be outdone, kicked off his shoes and splashed after them with the agent's bag. Well up the beach the sailor lowered his burden and the agent settled his cloak.

'Standard procedure,' he said with just a trace of that humour he had earlier displayed. He held out his hand for the bag. 'Men with dried salt on their boots have a rather obvious origin.' He took the bag. 'Thank you; *bonsoir mon ami*.'

'Goodnight,' said Drinkwater to the figure retreating into the threatening darkness that was Revolutionary France. For a second Drinkwater stood staring after the man, and then trudged back to the boat.

There was a perceptible easing of tension as the men pulled back to the waiting cutter. As though the shadow of the guillotine and the horrors of the Terror that lay over the darkened land had touched them all. Wearily Drinkwater clambered on board and saluted Griffiths.

The lieutenant nodded. 'You had better get some sleep now,' he said. 'And Mr Drinkwater . . .'

'Sir?' said Drinkwater from the companionway.

'*Da iawn*, Mr Drinkwater, *da iawn*.'

'I'm sorry sir, I don't understand.' He wrestled with fatigue.

'Well done, Mr Drinkwater, well done. I am pleased to say I do not find my confidence misplaced.'

Chapter Two

First Blood

Not all their operations went as smoothly. There were nights that seemed endless when a rendezvous was missed, when the guttering blue lights shown at the waterline spat and sizzled interminably achieving nothing. There were hours of eye strain and physical weariness as the cutter was laboriously kept on a station to no purpose, hours of barely hidden bad temper, hunger and cold. Occasionally there was brief and unexpected excitement as when, in thick weather, *Kestrel* disturbed a mid-Channel rendezvous of another kind. The two boats that parted in confusion did so amid shouts in French and English; slatting lugsails jerked hurriedly into the wet air and the splash of what might have been kegs was visible in the widening gap between the two vessels. *Kestrel* had fired her bow chasers at the retreating smugglers to maintain the illusion of being the revenue cruiser she had been taken for.

Then there had been an occasion of dubious propriety on their own part. Griffiths sent two boats to creep for barricoes off St Valery while *Kestrel* luffed and filled in the offing, Griffiths handling her with patient dexterity. Sitting in one of the boats Drinkwater continually verified their position, his quadrant horizontal, the images of two spires and a windmill in alternating sequence as he made minute adjustments to the index. His voice cracked with shouting instructions to the other boat, his eyes streamed at the effort of adjusting to look for Jessup's wave before refocusing on the reflected images of his marks. The two boats trailed their grapnels up and down the sea bead for hours before they were successful. What was in the little barrels Drinkwater never discovered for certain. Griffiths merely smiled when he eventually reported their success. It crossed his mind it might, quite simply, be cognac; that Griffiths as a man entrusted with many secrets might have capitalised on the advantages his position offered. After all, thought Drinkwater, it was in the best traditions of naval peculation and there was the matter of a few loose gold coins he had himself acquired when he retook the *Algonquin* in the last war. Somehow it was reassuring

15

to find Griffiths had some human failings beyond the obvious one of enjoying his liquor. Certainly *Kestrel* never lacked strong drink and Griffiths never stinted it, claiming with a mordant gleam in his eye, that a good bottle had more to offer a man than a good woman.

'A woman, look you, never lets you speak like a bottle does, boy-o. She has the draining of you, not you her, but a bottle leaves your guts warm afterwards . . .' He finished on a long sigh.

Drinkwater smiled. In his half-century at sea poor Griffiths could only have experienced the fleeting affection of drabs. Hugging his own knowledge of Elizabeth to him Nathaniel had felt indulgent. But he had not refused the cognac that made its appearance after the day off St Valéry.

Certainly Griffiths was unmoved by the presence of women which always sent a wave of lust through the cutter when they transferred fugitives from French fishing boats. The awkward bundles of women and children, many in bedraggled finery, who clambered clumsily over the stinking bulwarks into the boats to the accompanying grins of the Frenchmen, never failed to unsettle the exemplary order of the cutter. Griffiths remained aloof, almost disdainful, and obviously pleased when they had discharged their passengers. While their duties became this desperate business of strange encounters and remote landings Drinkwater patiently worked at his details. The tides, distances and the probabilities of unpredictable weather occupied him fully. Yet his curiosity and imagination were fed by these glimpses of fear and the glint of hatred that mingled with that of avarice in the fishermen's eyes as they handed over their live cargoes. 'We may stink of fish,' a giant Malouin had laughed as his lugger drew off, 'but you stink of fear . . .'

As time passed, by a gradual process of revelation, Drinkwater slowly acquired knowledge beyond the merely digital duty of his own part of the puppet's hand. From an apparently mindless juggling with the moon's phases and southing, with epacts and lunitidal intervals, a conspiratorially winking Jessup one day showed him a lobster pot containing pigeons. The bosun silently revealed the small brass cylinder strapped to a bird's leg. 'Ah, I see,' said Drinkwater, as pleased with the knowledge as the demonstration of trust bestowed by Jessup. Another link in the mysterious chain was added when he saw the pot hidden in the fishwell of a boat from Dieppe.

Greater confidence came from Griffiths on an afternoon of polar air and brilliant December sunshine when the gig landed them on the shingle strand below Walmer castle. Within its encircling trees the round brick bastions embraced the more domestic later additions. Lord Dungarth was waiting for them with two strangers who talked together in French. He led them inside. Drinkwater spread the charts as he was bid and withdrew to a side table while Dungarth, Griffiths and the livelier of the two men bent over them.

Drinkwater turned to the second Frenchman. He was sitting bolt upright, his eyes curiously blank yet intense, as though they saw with perfect clarity not Drinkwater before him, but a mirrored image of his own memories. The sight of the man sent a chill of apprehension through Drinkwater. He restrained an impulse to shiver and turned to the window by way of distraction.

Outside the almost horizontal light of a winter afternoon threw the foreground into shadow; black cannon on the petal-shaped bastions below, the trees, the remains of the moat and the shingle. Out over the Downs sunlight danced in a million twinkling points off the sparkling sea, throwing into extraordinary clarity every detail of the shipping. Beyond the dull black hull and gleaming spars of *Kestrel* several Indiamen got under way, their topsails bellying, while a frigate and third-rate lay in Deal Road. A welter of small craft beat up against the northerly wind, carrying the flood into the Thames estuary. The sharp-peaked lugsails of the Deal punts and galleys showed where the local longshoremen plied their legal, daylight, trade. In the distance the cliffs of France were a white bar on the horizon.

Raised voices abruptly recalled Drinkwater's attention. The three men at the table had drawn upright. Griffiths was shaking his head, his eyes half closed. The stranger was eagerly imploring something. From the rear Drinkwater found the sudden froglike jerks of his arms amusing as the man burst into a torrent of French. But the atmosphere of the room extinguished this momentary lightening of his spirit. The silent man remained rigid.

Dungarth placated the Frenchman in his own tongue, then turned to Griffiths. The lieutenant was still shaking his head but Dungarth's look was sharply imperative. Drinkwater caught a glimpse of the old Devaux, not the ebullient first lieutenant, but a distillation of that old energy refined into urgent compulsion. Griffiths's glance wavered.

'Very well, my lord,' he growled, 'but only under protest and providing there is no swell.'

Dungarth nodded. 'Good, good.' The earl turned to the window. 'There will be no swell with the wind veering north-east. You must weigh this evening . . . Mr Drinkwater, how pleasant to see you again, come join us in a glass before you go. Madoc, pray allow Drinkwater here to send his mail up with yours, I'll have it franked gratis in the usual way, *messieurs* . . .' Dungarth addressed the Frenchmen, explaining the arrangements were concluded and Drinkwater noted a change in the seated man's expression, the merest acknowledgement. And this time he could not repress a shudder.

Neither the wine nor the facility of writing to Elizabeth eased his mind after he and Griffiths returned to *Kestrel*. The sparkling view, the shadowing castle, the frantic desperation of the Frenchman, the haunted aura of his companion and above all the misgivings of Griffiths had combined with a growing conviction that their luck must run out.

Kestrel must be known to the fanatical authorities in France and sooner or later they would meet opposition. Drinkwater had no need of Griffiths's injunction that as a British officer his presence on a French beach was illegal. An enquiry as to the fate of his predecessor had elicited a casual shrug from the lieutenant.

'He was careless, d'you see, he neglected elementary precautions. He died soon after we landed him.'

Drinkwater found his feeling of unease impossible to shake off as *Kestrel* carried the tide through the Alderney Race, the high land of Cap de la Hague on the weather quarter. The sea bubbled under her bow and hissed alongside as the steady north-easterly wind drove them south. The Bay of Vauville opened slowly to larboard and, as the night passed, the low promontory of Cap Flammanville drew abeam.

Judging by his presence on deck Griffiths shared his subordinate's uneasiness. Once he stood next to Drinkwater for several minutes as if about to speak. But he thought better of it and drew off. Drinkwater had heard little of the conversation at Walmer. All he really knew was that the night's work had some extra element of risk attached to it, though of what real danger he had no notion.

The night was dark and moonless, cold and crystal clear. The stars shone with a northern brilliance, hard and icy with blue fire. They would be abeam of the Bay of Sciotot now, its southern extremity marked by the Pointe du Rozel beyond which the low, dune-fringed beach extended six miles to Carteret. The wide expanse of sand was their rendezvous, south of the shoals of Surtainville and north of the Roches du Rit. 'On the parallel of Beaubigny,' Griffiths had said, naming the village that lay a mile inland behind the dunes. 'And I pray God there is no swell,' he added. Drinkwater shared his concern. To the westward lay the ever-restless Atlantic, its effect scarcely lessened by the Channel Islands and the surrounding reefs. There must almost always be a swell on the beach at Beaubigny, pounding its relentless breakers upon those two leagues of packed sand. Drinkwater fervently hoped that the week of northerlies had done their work, that there would be little swell making their landing possible.

He bent over the shielded lantern in the companionway. The last few sand grains ran the half hour out of the glass and he turned it, straightening up with the log slate he looked briefly at his calculations. They must have run their distance now. He turned to Griffiths.

'By my reckoning, sir, we're clear of the Surtainville Bank.'

'Very well, we'll stand inshore shortly. All hands if you please.'

'Aye, aye, sir.' Nathaniel turned forward.

'Mr Drinkwater . . . check the boats, now. I'll sway out the second gig when you leave. And Mr Drinkwater . . .'

'Sir?'

'Take two loaded scatter guns . . .' Griffiths left the sentence unfinished.

Drinkwater paced up and down the firm wet sand. In the starlight he could see the expanse of beach stretching away north and south. Inland a pale undulation showed where the dunes marked the beginning of France. Down here, betwixt high and low water, he walked a no-man's-land. Behind him, bumping gently in the shallows, lay the waiting gig. Mercifully there was no swell.

'Tide's making, zur.' It was Tregembo's voice. Anxious. Was

19

he a victim of presentiment too?

It occurred to Drinkwater that there was something irrational, ludicrous even, in his standing here on a strip of French beach in the middle of the night not knowing why. He thought of Elizabeth to still his pounding heart. She would be asleep now, little dreaming of where he was, cold and exposed and not a little frightened. He looked at the men. They were huddled in a group round the boat.

'Spread out and relax, it's too exposed for an ambush.' His logic fell on ears that learned only that he too was apprehensive. The men moved sullenly. As he watched he saw them stiffen, felt his own breath catch in his throat and his palms moisten.

The thudding of hooves and jingle of harness grew louder and resolved itself into vague movement to the south. Then suddenly, running in the wavelets that covered its tracks a small barouche was upon them. The discovery was mutual. The shrill neighing of the horses as they reared in surprise was matched by the cries of the seamen who flung themselves out of the way.

Drinkwater whirled to see the splintering of the boat's gunwale as a hoof crashed down upon it. The terrified horse stamped and pawed, desperately trying to extricate itself. With the flat of his hanger Drinkwater beat at it, at the same time grabbing a rein and tugging the horse's head round clear of the gig.

A man jumped down from the barouche. '*Êtes-vous anglais?*'

'Yes, *m'sieur*, where the hell have you been?'

'*Pardon?*'

'How many? *Combien d'hommes?*'

'*Trois hommes et une femme*, but I speak English.'

'Get into the boat. Are you being followed?'

'*Oui*, yes . . . the other man, he is, er, *blessé* . . . he struggled with the English.'

'Wounded?'

'That is right, by Jacobins in Carteret.'

Drinkwater cut him short, recognising reaction. The man was young, near collapse.

'Get in the boat,' he pointed towards the waiting seamen and gave orders. Two figures emerged from the barouche, a man and a woman. They stood uncertainly.

'The boat! Get in the boat . . .' They began to speak, the man turning back to the open door. Angry exasperation began to replace his fear and Drinkwater called to two seamen to drag the wounded man out of the carriage and pushed the dithering fugitive towards the gig. *'Le bateau, vite! Vite!'*

He scooped the woman up roughly, surprised at her lightness, ignoring the indrawn breath of outrage, the stiffening of her body at the enforced intimacy. He dumped her roughly into the boat. A waft of lavender brought with it a hint of resentment at his cavalier treatment. He turned to the men struggling with the wounded Frenchman. 'Hurry there!' and to the remainder, 'the rest of you keep this damned thing afloat.' They heaved as a larger breaker came ashore, tugging round their legs with a seething urgency.

'Damned swell coming in with the flood,' someone said.

'What about the baggage, *m'sieur*?' It was the man from the carriage who seemed to have recovered some of his wits.

'To hell with the baggage, sit down!'

'But the gold . . . and my papers, *mon Dieu*! my papers!' He began to clamber out of the boat. 'You have not got my papers!' But it was not the documents that had caught Drinkwater's imagination.

'Gold? What gold?'

'In the barouche, *m'sieur*,' said the man shoving past him.

Drinkwater swore. So that was behind this crazy mission, specie! A personal fortune? Royalist funds? Government money? What did it matter? Gold was gold and now this damned fool was running back to the carriage. Drinkwater followed. He pushed to the door and looked in. Two iron bound boxes lay on the floor, just visible in the gloom.

'Tregembo! Poll! Get this box! You *m'sieur, aidez-moi*!'

They staggered under the weight, the breath rasping in their throats as they heaved it aboard the gig. The boat was lifting now, thumping on hard sand as larger waves ran hissing up the beach. Then from the direction of Carteret they heard shouts. The sand vibrated under the thunder of many horses' hooves; a troop of dragoons!

'Push the boat off! Push it off!' He ran back to the barouche, vaguely aware of the Frenchman struggling to get a canvas folio into the gig. Drinkwater stretched up and let off the brake. Running to the horses' heads he dragged them round then swiped the rump of the nearer with his   hanger. There was a wet gleam of blood and a terrified neigh as the horse plunged forward. Drinkwater jumped clear as the carriage jerked into motion.

He ran splashing to the boat which was already pulling out, its bow parting a wave that curled ashore. The water sucked and gurgled round Drinkwater's thighs as he fell over the transom. A splinter drove into the palm of his hand and he remembered the plunging hoof as the nausea of pain shot through him. For a moment he lay gasping, vaguely aware of shouts and confusion where the barouche met its pursuers. Then a ball or two whined overhead and from seaward came a hail from the other boat asking if they required help. Drinkwater raised his head to refuse but a seaman stood and fired one of the blunderbusses beside his ear. Drinkwater twisted round and looked astern. Not ten yards away rearing among the breakers a horse threw its rider into the sea. Both were hit by the langridge in the gun.

'A steady pull now lads. We're all right now.' But a flash and roar contradicted him. The six-pounder ball ricochetted three yards away. Horse artillery!

'Pull you bastards! Pull!' They had no need of exhortation. The oar looms bent under the effort.

Another bang and a shower of splinters. Shouts, screams and the boat slewed to starboard, the woman standing and shrieking astern, her hands beating her sides in fury. They were firing canister and ball and the starboard oars had been hit. The boat was a shambles as she drifted back into the breakers.

Then from seaward there was an answering flash and the whine of shot passing low overhead as *Kestrel* opened fire. A minute later the other boat took them in tow.

Drinkwater threw his wet cloak into a corner of the main cabin. He was haggard with exhaustion and bad temper. His inadequacy for the task Griffiths had given him filled him with an exasperation brittle with reaction. Two dead and three wounded, plus the Frenchman now lying across the cabin table, was a steep price to pay for a handful of fugitives and two boxes of yellow metal.

'Get below and see to the wounded,' Griffiths had said, and then, in a final remark that cut short Drinkwater's protest, 'there's a case of surgical instruments in the starboard locker.'

Drinkwater dragged them out, took up a pair of tweezers and jerked the splinter from the palm of his hand. His anger evaporated as a wave of pain passed through him, leaving him shaking, gradually aware of the woman's eyes watching him from the shadows of her hood. Under her gaze he steadied, grateful for her influence yet simultaneously resentful of her presence, remembering that hint of enmity he had caught as he passed her into the gig. Two men stumbled into the cabin slopping hot water from basins. Drinkwater took off his coat and rolled up his shirt sleeves, taking a bottle of brandy from the rack.

Drinkwater braced himself. The swinging lantern threw shadows and highlights wildly about as *Kestrel* made north on a long beat to windward. He bent over the Frenchman aware that the others were watching him, the woman standing, swaying slowly as they worked offshore, as if unwilling to accept the sanctuary of the cutter. The two men watched from the settee, slumped in attitudes of relieved exhaustion.

'Here, one of you, help me . . . *m'aidez!*'

Drinkwater found a glass and half filled it with cognac. He swallowed as the elder man came forward. Drinkwater held out the glass and the man took it eagerly.

'Get his clothes off. Use a knife . . . d'you understand?' The man nodded and began work. Drinkwater invoked the memory of Surgeon Appleby and tried to remember something of what he had been told, what he had seen a lifetime earlier in the stinking cockpit of *Cyclops*. It seemed little enough so he refilled the tumbler, catching the woman's eyes and the hostility in them. The fiery liquid made him shudder and he ignored the woman's hauteur.

He bent over the Frenchman. 'Who the devil is he?' he asked.

'His name, *m'sieur*,' said the elder Frenchman working busily at the seam of the unconscious man's coat, 'is Le Comte de Tocqueville; I am Auguste Barrallier, late of the Brest Dockyard . . .' He pulled the sleeve off and ripped the shirt. 'The young man beside you is Etienne Montholon; *mam'selle* is his sister Hortense.' From the woman came an indrawn breath that might have been disapproval of his loquacity or horror as Barrallier revealed the count's shoulder, peeling the coat and shirt off the upper left breast. De Tocqueville groaned, raised his head and opened his eyes. Then his head lolled back. 'Lost a lot of blood,' said Drinkwater, thankful that the man was unconscious.

Barrallier discarded the soaked clothing. Drinkwater swabbed the wound clean and watched uncertainly as more blood oozed from the bruised, raw flesh.

'The Arabs use a method of washing with the wine *m'sieur*,' offered Barrallier gently, 'perhaps a little of the cognac might be spared, yes?' Drinkwater reached for the bottle.

'He was shot ...' The young man, standing now next to Barrallier, spoke for the first time. He stated the obvious in that nervous way the uncertain have. Drinkwater looked up into a handsome face perhaps twenty years old.

Drinkwater slipped his hand beneath the count's shoulder. He could feel the ball under the skin. Roughly he scraped the wound to remove any pieces of clothing and poured a last measure of cognac over the mess. He searched among the apothecary's liniments and selected a pot of bluish ointment, smearing the contents over the wound, covering it with a pledget and then a pad made from the count's shirt.

'Hold that over the wound while we turn him over.' Drinkwater nodded to Barrallier who put out his bloody hands, then he looked at Montholon. 'Hold his legs, *m'sieur*, if you would. Cross them over, good. Now, together!'

Bracing themselves against *Kestrel*'s windward pitch they rolled De Tocqueville roughly over. Drinkwater was feeling more confident, the brandy was doing its work well. An over-active part of his brain was emerging from reaction to the events of the last hours, already curious about their passengers.

'Your escape was none too soon.' He said it absently, preoccupied as he rolled the tip of his forefinger over the blue lump that lay alongside the count's scapula. He did not expect the gasp to come with such vehemence from the woman, cutting through the thick air of the cabin with an incongruous venom that   distracted him into looking up.

She had thrown back the hood of her cloak and the swinging lantern caught copper gleams from the mass of auburn hair that fell about her shoulders. She appeared older than her brother with strong, even features heightened by the stress she was under. She stared at Drinkwater from level grey eyes and again he felt her hostility. Her lack of gratitude piqued him and he thought of the two dead and three wounded of *Kestrel*'s crew that had been the price of her escape.

Angry, he bent again over the count's shoulder, picking up the scalpel and feeling its blade rasp the scapula. A light-headed feeling swept over him as he encountered the ball.

'Hold the lantern closer,' he said through clenched teeth. And she obeyed.

The musket ball rolled bloodily on to the table.

24

Drinkwater grunted with satisfaction as he bound a second pledget and passed a linen strip round the count's shoulder. They strapped his arm to his side and heaved him on to the settee. Then they turned to the seamen with the splinter wounds.

Daylight was visible when Drinkwater staggered on deck soaked in perspiration. The chill hit him as he lurched to the rail and, shuddering, vomited the cognac out of his stomach. He laid his head on the rail. Hortense Montholon lay in his cot and he sank down beside the breeching of a four-pounder and fell asleep. Tregembo brought blankets and covered him.

Standing by the tiller Lieutenant Griffiths looked at the inert form. Although no expression passed over his face he was warm with approval. He had not misjudged the qualities of Nathaniel Drinkwater.

Chapter Three   December 1792–February 1793

A Curtain Rising

The incident at Beaubigny had ended *Kestrel*'s clandestine operations. Temporarily unemployed the cutter rolled in the swell that reached round Penlee Point to rock her at her anchor in Cawsand Bay.

Perspiring in his airless cabin Drinkwater sat twirling the cheap goosequill in his long fingers. Condensation hung from the deckhead, generated by the over-stoked stove in Griffiths's cabin next door. Drinkwater was fighting a losing battle against drowsiness. With an effort he forced himself to read over what he had written in his journal.

It was a matter of amazement to me that M. De Tocqueville survived my butchery. His debility was occasioned by loss of blood due to a severe grazing of the axillary artery which fortunately did not rupture entirely. The pectoral muscle was badly torn by the angle of entry of the ball but it seems we had the only chip of bone out of him. If it does not yet putrefy he will live.

He had been mildly interested in the medical details for it had been an old friend who had looked over his rudimentary surgery. Mr Appleby, appointed surgeon to the frigate *Diamond* then fitting in the Hamoaze, had been ordered aboard *Kestrel* to check the wounded. He had been complimentary about Nathaniel's unschooled suturing but had not let him escape without a lecture on the count's injuries.

Drinkwater smiled at the recollection. It had been an odd passage home. Of all the refugees *Kestrel* had brought out of France that last quartet had left an indelible impression. The feverish nobleman muttering incoherently in his delirium and the attentively ineffectual young Etienne Montholon were a contrast to their fellow travellers. The garrulous and enthusiastic Barrallier was a lively and amusing companion who let no detail of *Kestrel* escape his criticism or admiration. He seemed to cut himself off from the others, turning his back on France, as if desperate to be seen as anglophile in all things. Markedly different from the men, Hortense remained aloof; cold and contemptuous in the isolation of her sex. Her beauty caused a whispering, wondering admiration among the hands and a vague disquiet among the officers with whom she was briefly accommodated.

Drinkwater was not alone in his relief at their disembarkation at Plymouth with their specie and the folio of plans, but they left in their wake a sense of unease. Like many of his contemporaries who had served in the American War, Drinkwater found a wry amusement in the visitation of republican revolution on the French. Many of those who had served under Rochambeau and La Fayette, men who had drawn the iron ring around Cornwallis at Yorktown and professed admiration for liberty, now ran like rats before the Jacobin terriers.

But there was also a strand of sympathy for the revolution in Nathaniel's heart, born of a sympathy for the oppressed awakened years earlier on the stinking orlop of *Cyclops*. He could not entirely condemn the principles of revolution, though he baulked at the method. Despite the sanctuary given the émigrés, Englishmen of liberal principles and many naval officers of independent mind saw with eyes uncluttered by party interest. Drinkwater was no pocketed Whig nor heedless Tory adherent and he had precious little 'interest' to tie him to principles of dubious propriety.

He lay down his pen and snapped the cap on his inkwell, transferring himself to the cot. He picked up the creased newspaper that Griffiths had left him. The print danced in front of his eyes. In the light of recent events Mr Pitt's promises of peace and prosperity rang false. The letters marched like a thousand tiny black men: an army. He closed his eyes. War and the possibility of war were all that people talked of, paying scant attention to Mr Pitt's protestations.

It was odd that there had not been trouble over the Beaubigny affair since it seemed that only a pretext was wanted, a spark to fire the dry tinder of international relations. And it was not just the Jacobins who were eager for war. He had had dinner with Appleby and Richard White two nights earlier. White was already a lieutenant with five year's seniority and the air of a post-captain. His standing was high enough to command an appointment as second lieutenant on Sir Sydney* Smith's crack frigate *Diamond*. He had drunk to the prospects of 'glorious war' with a still boyish enthusiasm which had made Appleby curl his lip.

The dinner had been only a qualified success. Revived friendships had a quality of regret about them. White had become an

*Nelson's spelling

27

urbane young man, possessed of disproportionate self-confidence so that Drinkwater had difficulty in recognising the frightened boy who had once sobbed in the blackness of *Cyclops*'s cockpit. Appleby too, had changed. The years had not been kind to him. The once portly surgeon had the loose flesh of penury, something of the old buoyancy was missing, eroded by years of loneliness and hard living, but beneath the ravages of time there were glimpses of the old Appleby, pedagoguish, prolix but astute as ever.

'Bound to be war,' he had said in answer to Drinkwater's worried questioning, while White eagerly agreed. 'And it will be a collision of mighty forces which England will be hard put to defeat. Oh, you can scoff, Mr White, but you siblings that thirst for glory chase moonbeams.'

'He's still a boy,' Appleby had muttered when the lieutenant had gone to relieve himself. 'But God help his men when he's made post, which will not be long if this war comes soon. I hope their lordships give him a tolerant, experienced and understanding first lieutenant.'

'He's certainly changed,' agreed Drinkwater, 'it seems he's been spoiled.'

'Promotion too rapid, cully. It works for a few, but not all.'

No, the dinner had not been a success.

Yet it was not entirely the bickering of his old friends that had failed to make it so. It was the approach of war that stirred unease in Nathaniel. The faint, inescapable thrill of coming excitement mixed with the fear he had already felt on the beach at Beaubigny caused his pulse to race, even now.

If war came was this tiny cutter the place to be? What chance had he of promotion? He must not think of competing with White, that was impossible. In any case *Kestrel* was a fine little ship. Providence had brought him here and he must submit to his fate. It had not been entirely unkind to him so far. He contemplated the shelf of books, his own journals and the notebooks left him by Mr Blackmore, late sailing master of *Cyclops*. He had been touched by that bequest. The mahogany box containing his quadrant was lashed in a corner and his Dollond glass nestled in the pocket of his coat, hung on the door peg with the French sword. A collection of purchases, gifts and loot; the sum total of his possessions. Not much after thirty years of existence. Then his eye fell on the watercolour of the *Algonquin* off St Mawes, painted for him by his wife.

A knock at the door recalled him to the present. 'What is it?'

'Boat, zur.'

He threw his legs over the rim of the cot. 'Lieutenant Griffiths?'

'Aye zur.'

'Very well, I'll be up directly.' He slipped into his shoes and drew on the plain blue coat. Opening the door he jammed his hat on his head and leapt for the ladder, clearing the companionway with a bound and sucking gratefully at the raw, frosty air.

Griffiths brought orders from the port admiral. That afternoon *Kestrel* took the tide into the Barn Pool and warped alongside the mast hulk *Chichester*. The following morning the dockyard officials came aboard and consulted Griffiths. By the time the hands were piped to dinner *Kestrel*'s standing rigging had been sent down and by nightfall her lower mast had been drawn out of her by the hulk's sheers. Next day the carpenters were busy altering her carlings to take the new mast.

'We're to fit a longer topmast,' Griffiths explained, 'to set a square t'gallant above the topsail, see.' He swallowed the madeira and looked at Drinkwater. 'I don't think we'll be playing cat and mouse again, *bach*, not after that episode at Beaubigny. We're going to look a regular man o'war cutter when the artificers have finished, and become a bloody nursemaid to the fleet. Now, to other matters. The clerk of the cheque will see the men are paid before Christmas. But they're to have only half of their due until after, see. Give 'em the lot and they'll be leaving their brains in the gutters along with their guts and we'll have to beg the foot patrols for help. I want a crew aboard this cutter after Christmas.'

Drinkwater acknowledged the sense of Griffiths's draconian measures. His commander had somewhat anticipated the festive season, if his high colouring and desire to talk were anything to go by.

'And let the pawn shops know the people are being paid. That way their women might get to hear of it and it may not all go down the drain.' He paused to drink, then reached into his tail pocket. 'Here, this was given me at the port admiral's office.' He pulled out a crumpled letter and held it out. The superscription was in a familiar hand.

'Thank you, sir.' Drinkwater took the letter and turned it over,

29

impatient for the privacy of his own cabin. Griffiths hoisted himself on to his settee and closed his eyes. Drinkwater made to leave.

'Oh, Mr Drinkwater,' an eye opened. 'The importunate ninny with an undeserved cockade who gave me that letter told me I ought to give you leave over Christmas.' Drinkwater paused, looking from the letter to Griffiths. 'I do not hold with such impertinence.' There was a long silence during which they eye slowly closed. Drinkwater stepped puzzled into the lobby.

'You can take leave when that t'gallant yard is crossed, Mr Drinkwater, and not a moment sooner.'

Half smiling Drinkwater closed the door and slipped into his own cubbyhole. He hastily slit the wafer and began to read.

My Darling Nathaniel,

I write in haste, Richd. White called on me today on his way to see Sir S. Smith's prize agent at Portsmouth and promised to collect a letter for you on his return this evening. He is expectant of seeing you in Plymouth I understand. Thank you for yours of 29th. The news that you are likely to be idle at Plymouth combines with my great anxiety and apprehension I feel over the news of France and I worry greatly. Should it be true that war is likely as Richd. is convinced, I cannot miss an opportunity to see my dearest. Please meet the London mail Christmas Eve. Until then, my love,

> *I remain, Ever your Devoted Wife,*
> *Elizabeth*

Drinkwater grinned to himself in anticipation. Perhaps his judgement of White had been a trifle premature. Only a friend would have thought of that. Warmed by his friend's solicitude and happy that he was soon to see Elizabeth he threw himself into the refitting of the cutter with enthusiasm. And for a time the shadow of war receded from his mind.

The topgallant yard was crossed, braced and the new sail sent up and bent on by the 23rd December. By the morning of Christmas Eve the rigging was set up. Drinkwater notified the clerk of the cheque and he sent a shrivelled little man with a bound chest, a marine guard and a book as big as a hatch-board to pay the cutter's people. By noon the harbour watch had been set and *Kestrel* was almost deserted, many of her crew of volunteers being residents of Plymouth. Free of duty, Drinkwater

30

hurried below to shift his coat, ship his hanger and then made his way ashore. He was met by Tregembo who knuckled his forehead, ablaze in all the festive finery of a tar, despite the chill, with a beribboned hat and blue monkey jacket spangled with brass buttons, a black kerchief at his muscular neck, and feet shoved awkwardly into cheap pumps.

'I booked your room, zur, at Wilson's like you axed, zur, an' beggin' your pardon, zur, but the London mail's delayed.'

'Damn!' Drinkwater fished in his pocket for a coin, aware of Tregembo looking nervously over his shoulder. Behind him stood a girl of about twenty, square built and sturdy, slightly truculent in the presence of the officer, as though embarrassed for the station of her man. The red ribbon in her hair was carelessly worn, as though new purchased and tied with more ardour than art. 'Here,' he began to fish for another coin. Tregembo flushed.

'No, zur. It ain't that, er, zur, I was wondering if I could . . .' He hung his head.

'I expect you aboard by dawn on the 26th or I'll have every foot patrol in Plymouth out for a deserter.' Drinkwater saw the look of relief cross Tregembo's face.

'Thank 'ee, zur, and a merry Christmas to you an' Mrs Drinkwater.'

Elizabeth arrived at last, wearied by her journey and worried over the possibility of war. They greeted each other shyly and there was a reticence about them, as if their previous intimacies were not to be repeated until released from their present preoccupations. But the wine warmed them and their own company insulated them at last against the world outside, so that it was breakfast of Christmas morning before Elizabeth first spoke of what troubled her.

'Do you think war is likely, Nathaniel?'

Drinkwater regarded the face before him, the frown on the broad sweep of the brow, the swimmingly beautiful brown eyes and the lower lip of her wide mouth caught apprehensively in her teeth. He was melted with pity for her, aware that for him war might have its terrible compensations and grim opportunities, whereas for her it offered the corrosion of waiting. Perhaps for the remainder of her life. He wanted to lie to her, to tell her everything would be all right, to soothe her fears with platitudes.

But that would be contemptible. Leaving her with a false half-hope would be worse than the truth.

He nodded. 'Everyone is of the opinion that if the French invade Holland it is most likely. For my own part, Bess, I promise you this, I shall be circumspect and take no unnecessary risks. Here,' he reached out for the coffee pot, 'let us drink a toast to ourselves and to our future. I shall try for my commission and at the present rate of progress, retire a half-pay commander, superannuated through old age to bore you with tales of my exploits . . .' He saw her lips twist. Elizabeth, bless her, was gently mocking him.

He grinned back. 'I shall not be foolhardy, Bess, I promise.'

'No, of course not,' she said taking the coffee cup from him. And as he withdrew his hand the mark of the splinter was still visible on his palm.

'*Hannibal*, sir, Captain Colpoys, just in from a cruise. Missed Christmas, poor devils.' Both men regarded the battleship anchoring across the Sound.

Griffiths nodded. 'The big boy-o's have all shaken the cobwebs from their topsails and are back to ground on their own chicken bones again. It's time we put to sea again Mr Drinkwater. This is a time for little birds with keen eyes; the elephants can wait a while longer. D'you have my gig ready in ten minutes.'

Waiting for Griffiths to return from the port admiral's, Drinkwater paced the deck. The hands were making preparation to sail, skylarking until sent below by a fine drizzle, while he was oblivious of the grey pall that rolled up the Hamoaze.

Farewells, he concluded, were damnable.

Tregembo came aft and stood uncertainly next to him.

'What is it Tregembo?'

The seaman looked unhappily at his feet. 'I was wondering, zur . . .'

'Don't tell me you want leave of absence to see your doxy?'

Tregembo hung his head in assent.

'Damn it Tregembo, you'll get her with child or catch pox. I'm damned if I'll physic you!' Drinkwater instantly regretted the unkindness caused by his own misery.

'She ain't like that, zur . . . and I only want a quarter hour, zur.'

Drinkwater thought of Elizabeth. 'Damn it Tregembo, not a moment more then.'

'Thank 'ee, zur, thank 'ee.' Drinkwater watched him hurry off.

Idly he wondered what the future held. The shots at Beaubigny might have formed a pretext for war, for *Kestrel*'s broadside had been an aggressive act. It was odd that the French had not made more of it, at least one of their men had been killed. But the advantages of peace were being protested by Pitt and such an insignificant cruiser as *Kestrel* could not be allowed to provide a *casus belli*. That, at least, had been the British position, and she had been kept refitting at Plymouth until the air cleared. All the same it was deuced odd that the French had failed to capitalise on the violation of their littoral.

He dismissed the thought. Now the cutter was ordered to join the growing number of brigs and sloops of war keeping the French coast under observation. Since Lord Hood had cruised with home-based frigates and guardships in the summer, the dockyard had been busy. Thanks to the Spanish and Russian crises of the preceding three years the fleet was in a reasonable state of preparedness. Across the Channel the Paris mob had massacred the Swiss guard and in September the French had invaded Savoy. It was known that Rear-Admiral Truguet had been ordered to sea with nine sail of the line. In November the Austrian Netherlands were overrun and the French seized control of the Scheldt. This made the whereabouts of all French naval squadrons crucial to the defence of Great Britain. There were thirty-nine battleships at Brest, ten at Lorient and thirteen at Rochefort. As 1793 approached the Admiralty was taking a close look at them.

The grey overcast of Saturday 29th December 1792 seemed leaden, but the wind had backed into the north-west, the showers had ceased and the cloud was beginning to disperse. Griffiths and Drinkwater stood watching a brig-sloop running down the Sound for the open sea.

'*Childers*, Commander Robert Barlow,' muttered Drinkwater half to himself.

Griffiths nodded. 'Off to reconnoitre Brest Road,' he added confidentially.

On the last day of the old year, the wind veered northerly and blew from a clear sky. At noon a guard boat brought Griffiths the orders he had been expecting. By sunset *Kestrel* had left Smeaton's Eddystone lighthouse astern and was scudding south to the support of *Childers*.

During the night the wind freshened to a severe gale and *Kestrel* was hove to, her bowsprit reefed, her topmast and yards sent down and double breechings securing her guns. At first light a sail was seen to the westward and an exchange of signals revealed her as *Childers*. Taking the helm himself Griffiths steered *Kestrel* under the brig's lee and luffed. In his tarpaulin Barlow bellowed at them: 'Fired on by French batteries at St Matthew . . . honour of the flag, return to port . . . making for Fowey . . .' His words were ripped away by the gale.

'Probably of the opinion he's the first to be fired on, eh, Mr Drinkwater?' growled Griffiths, regarding his junior from beneath a wet and bushy white eyebrow.

'Aye, sir, and hastening home to make a noise of it if I'm not mistaken.'

Griffiths chuckled. Barlow's indignation was clear, even across the strip of white and foaming water. 'He'll be in a post-chaise before that brig's fetched an anchor, I'll warrant,' said Griffiths, heaving on the tiller and calling two men to relieve him.

The two little ships parted, plunging to windward with the spray shooting over them, the sea streaked pale by parallel lines of spume that tore downwind. Here and there a fulmar banked and swooped on rigid, sabre-shaped wings, breaking the desolation of the view.

Three weeks later Louis XVI was guillotined and on the first day of February the French Naval Convention declared war on the Dutch Stadtholder and His Majesty King George III.

Chapter Four   March–September 1793
A Hunter Hunted

'Cap'n's compliments, sir, an' he'd be obliged if you'd attend him in the cabin.' Odd that a little cutter could produce a servant as diplomatic as Merrick. Drinkwater turned the deck over to Jessup and went below, crabbing down the companionway against the heel.

'Nothing in sight, sir,' he said removing his hat 'apart from *Flora*, that is.'

Griffiths nodded without looking up from his orders just received from the frigate. 'Sit down, Mr Drinkwater.'

Drinkwater eased himself on to the settee and stretched. Griffiths pushed a decanter across the table without a word, flicking a glance in Drinkwater's direction only to see that the latter had hold of it before he let go. Claret from their last capture, an unhandy little *bugalet* bound to the Seine from Bordeaux. Good wine too, and a tidy sum made from the sale. Drinkwater sipped appreciatively and watched his commander.

In the months since *Kestrel* had become a lookout cruiser and commerce raider, a gatherer of intelligence and a dealer of swift demoralising blows, Drinkwater and Griffiths had developed a close working relationship. The acting lieutenant had quickly realised that he shared with his commander a rare zeal for efficiency and a common love of driving their little ship for its own sake.

Griffiths folded the papers and looked up, reaching for the claret. 'Our orders, Mr Drinkwater, our orders. Another glass, is it . . .?' Drinkwater waited patiently.

Referring to the frigate's captain Griffiths said, 'Sir John Warren has sent a note to say that he's applied for us to join his flying squadron when it is formed.'

Drinkwater considered the news. Operating with frigates might be to his advantage. It all depended on how many young lieutenants were clamouring for patronage. Captains commanding Channel cruisers could have the pick of the list. So perhaps his chances were not very good. 'When will that be, sir?'

Griffiths shrugged. 'Who knows, *bach*. The mills of Admiralty grind as slow as those of God.'

Clearly Griffiths did not relish the loss of independence, but he looked up and added, 'In the meantime we have a little job to do. Rather like our old work. There's a mutual friend of ours who wishes to leave France.'

'Mutual friend, sir?'

'You know, Mr Drinkwater, fellow we landed at Criel. He goes under the name of Major Brown. His commission's in the Life Guards, though I doubt he's sat a horse on the King's Service. Made a reputation with the Iroquois in the last war, I remember. Been employed on "special service" ever since,' Griffiths said with heavy emphasis.

Drinkwater remembered the fat, jolly man they had landed on his first operation nearly a year ago. He did not appear typical of the officers of His Majesty's Life Guards.

Griffiths sensed his puzzlement. 'The Duke of York, Mr Drinkwater, reserves a few commissions for meritorious officers,' he smiled wryly. 'They have to *earn* the privilege and almost never see a stirrup iron.'

'I see, sir. Where do we pick him up? And when? Have we any choice?'

'Get the chart folio, *bach*, and we'll have a look.'

'God damn this weather to hell!' For the thousandth time during the forenoon Griffiths stared to the west, but the hoped-for lightening on the horizon failed to appear.

'We'll have to take another reef, sir, and shift the jib . . .' Drinkwater left the sentence unfinished as a sheet of spray whipped aft from the wave rolling inboard amidships, spilling over the rail and threatening to rend the two gigs from their chocks.

'But it's August, Mr Drinkwater, August,' his despairing appeal to the elements ended in a nod of assent, Drinkwater turned away.

'Mr Jessup! All hands! Rouse along the spitfire jib there! Larbowlines forward and shift the jib. Starbowlines another reef in the mains'l!' Drinkwater watched with satisfaction as the men ran to their stations, up to their knees in water at the base of the mast.

'Ready, forrard!' came Jessup's hail.

Drinkwater noted Griffiths's nod and watched the sea. 'Down helm!'

As the cutter luffed further orders were superfluous. *Kestrel* was no lumbering battleship, her crew worked with the sure-footed confidence of practice. With canvas shivering and slatting in a trembling that reached to her keel, the cutter's crew worked furiously. The peak and throat halliards were slackened and the mainsheet hove in to control the boom whilst the leech cringle was hauled down. By the mast the luff cringle was secured and the men spread along the length of the boom, bunching the hard, wet canvas and tying the reef points.

Forward men pulled in the traveller inhaul while Jessup eased the outhaul. By the mast the jib halliard was started and waist deep in water on the lee bow the flogging jib was pulled inboard. Within a minute the spitfire was shackled to the halliard, its tack hooked to the traveller and the outhaul manned. Even as the big iron ring jerked out along the spar the halliard tightened. The sail thundered, its luff curving away to leeward as *Kestrel* fell into the trough of the sea, then straightened as men tallied on and sweated it tight. 'Belay! Belay there!'

'Ready forrard!'

Drinkwater heard Jessup's hail, saw him standing in the eyes, his square-cut figure solid against the pitch of the horizon and the tarpaulin whipping about his legs, for all the world a scarecrow in a gale. Drinkwater resisted a boyish impulse to laugh. 'Aye, aye, Mr Jessup!'

He turned to the helmsman, 'Steady her now,' and a nod to Poll on the mainsheet. *Kestrel* gathered way across the wind, her mainsail peak jerking up again to its jaunty angle and filling with wind.

'Down helm!' She began to turn up into the wind again, spurred by that sudden impetus; again that juddering tremble as her flapping sails transmitted their frustrated energy to the fabric of the hull. 'Heads'l sheets!'

'Full an' bye, starboard tack.'

'Full an' bye, sir,' answered the forward of the two men leaning on the tiller.

'Is she easier now?'

'Aye sir, much,' he said shifting his quid neatly over his tongue in some odd sympathy with the ship.

Kestrel drove forward again, her motion easier, her speed undiminished.

'Shortened sail, sir,' Drinkwater reported.

'*Da iawn*, Mr Drinkwater.'

The wind eased a little as the sun set behind castellated banks of cloud whose summits remained rose coloured until late into the evening. In the last of the daylight Drinkwater had studied the southern horizon, noted the three nicks in its regularity and informed Griffiths.

'One might be an armed lugger, sir, it's difficult to be certain but he's standing west. Out of our way, sir.'

Griffiths rubbed his chin reflectively. 'Mmm. The damned beach'll be very dangerous, Mr Drinkwater, very dangerous indeed. The surf'll be high for a day or two.' He fell silent and Drinkwater was able to follow his train of thought. He knew most of Griffiths's secrets now and that *Flora*'s order had hinged on the word 'imperative'.

'It means,' explained Griffiths, that Brown has sent word to London that he is no longer able to stay in France or has something very important to acquaint HMG with,' he shrugged. 'It depends . . .'

Drinkwater remembered the pigeons.

'And if the weather is too bad to recover him, sir?'

Griffiths looked up. 'It mustn't be, see.' He paused. 'No, one develops a "nose" for such things. Brown has been there a long time on his own. In my opinion he's anxious to get out tonight.'

Drinkwater expelled his breath slowly, thinking about the state of the sea on the landing. He stared to the westward. The wind was still strong and under the windsea a westerly swell rolled up the Channel. He was abruptly recalled from his observations by the lieutenant. Griffiths was halfway out of the companionway.

'Come below, Mr Drinkwater, I've an idea to discuss with you.'

'Let go.' The order passed quietly forward from man to man and the cat stopper was cast off. *Kestrel*'s anchor dropped to the sandy bottom of the little bay as her head fell off to leeward and the seamen secured the sails, loosing the reefs in the mainsail and bending on the big jib. *Kestrel* had stood slowly in for the rendezvous immediately after dark. Now she bucked in the heavy swell as it gathered up in the shelving bay to fling itself into a white fury on the crescent of sand dimly perceptible below the cliffs that almost enclosed them.

'Hold on.' The cable slowed its thrumming rumble through the hawse as the single compressor nipped it against the bitts. The cutter jerked her head round into sea and swell as the anchor brought up. 'Brought to it,' came the word back from forward.

'Are you ready, Mr Drinkwater?' The acting lieutenant looked about him. His two volunteers grunted assent and Drinkwater found the sound of Tregembo's voice reassuring. The other man, Poll, was a pugnacious red-bearded fellow who enjoyed an aggressive reputation aboard *Kestrel*. 'Aye, sir, we're ready . . . Come lads.'

The three men moved aft where Jessup, judging his moment nicely, had dropped the little jolly boat into the sea as *Kestrel*'s bow rose. As her bottom smacked into the water the davit falls were let fly and unrove. The boat drifted astern until restrained by its painter, then it was pulled carefully alongside and Drinkwater, Tregembo and Poll jumped into it.

Forward Tregembo received the eye of four-inch hemp from the deck and secured it round the forward thwart. Amidships Poll secured the shaded lantern and loosed the oar lashings while Drinkwater saw that the coil of line aft was clear to run, as was the second of small rope attached to the grapnel. They would have to watch their feet in those two coils.

'Ready lads?' Tregembo and Poll answered in the affirmative and Drinkwater hailed the deck in a low voice, 'Let go the painter and veer away the four-inch.'

'Aye, aye, sir.' Drinkwater could see heads bobbing at the rail as Jessup eased the little boat downwind. 'Good luck, Mr Drinkwater,' came Griffiths's low voice.

Bucking astern Drinkwater raised his arm in acknowledgement and turned his attention to the beach. Tregembo touched his shoulder.

'Lantern's ready, zur.'

'Very well.' They were bobbing up and down now, the seas shoving the craft shorewards, the hemp rope restraining it, jerking it head to sea then veering away again as they rolled into ever steepening seas. The moment he saw the waves begin to curl, gathering themselves before tumbling ashore as breakers, Drinkwater ordered the shaded lantern shown seaward. Almost immediately the boat came head to sea and remained there. Tregembo came aft.

'They're holding, zur.'

'Very well.' Drinkwater slipped off his shoes. He was already stripped to his shirt. As he stood up to fasten the light line about himself Tregembo said: 'I'll go zur, it ain't your place, zur, beggin' your pardon.'

Drinkwater grinned in the darkness. 'It *is* my place, Tregembo, do you tend the lines, on that I rely absolutely . . . now Poll, pass me the grapnel and I'll secure the stern.'

Thanking providence that it *was* August, Drinkwater slipped over the transom and kicked out shorewards, the small grapnel over his shoulder, shaking the lines free.

He felt himself caught in the turbulence of a breaking wave, then thrust forward, the thunder of the surf in his ears, his legs continually fouling the ropes. Desperately he turned on his side and kicked frantically with his free leg, thrashing with his unencumbered arm. The undertow dragged him back and he felt his hand drive into sand. Another wave thundered about him, forcing the breath out and turning him over so that the ropes caught. Again his hand encountered sand and he scrabbled at it, panic welling in his winded guts.

Then he was ashore, a raffle of rope and limbs, stretched out in the final surge of a few inches of water, grasping and frightened.

Another wave washed around him as he lay in the shallows, then another as he struggled to his feet. Recovering his breath by degrees he sorted out the tangle of ropes, knowing Tregembo and Poll had each an end over opposite quarters. The need to concentrate steadied him. He drove the grapnel into the sand and jerked the line hard. He felt it tighten and saw it rise dripping and straight. Wading out he could just see the grey shape of the boat bobbing above the white line of the breakers. He untied the line from his waist and belayed it slackly around one of the exposed grapnel flukes. Moored head and stern the boat seemed safe and Drinkwater settled down to wait. Presently, despite the season, he was shivering.

An hour later he was beginning to regret his insistence on making the landing. He was thoroughly cold and thought he detected the wind freshening again. He watched where *Kestrel* lay, watched for the lantern at the masthead that would signal his recall. But he knew Griffiths would wait until the last moment. Even now he guessed Jessup and the hands would be toiling to get a spring on the cable so that, when the time came, the cutter could be cast away from the wind and sail off her anchor. She was too close inshore to do anything else. He preoccupied himself as best he could and was oblivious of the first shots. When he did realise something was wrong he could already see the flashes of small arms on the cliff top and just below it, where a path dropped down to the beach. From his shelter he leapt out and raced for the grapnel, looking along the sand expectantly.

He saw the man break away from the shadow around the base of the cliff. Saw him stumble and recover, saw the spurts of sand where musket balls struck.

'Over here!' he yelled, reaching the grapnel.

He uncoiled the loop of light line and passed it around his waist in a bowline with a three fathom tail. The man blundered up grasping.

'Major Brown?'

'The same, the same . . .' The man heaved his breath in as Drinkwater passed the end of the line round his waist.

'A kestrel . . .'

'. . .for a knave .' Brown finished the countersign as Drinkwater grasped his arm and dragged him towards the sea. Already infantrymen were running down on to the beach. Resolutely Drinkwater turned seawards and shouted: 'Heave in!'

He saw Tregembo wave and felt the line jerk about his waist. The breath was driven out of him as he was hauled bodily through a tumbling wavecrest. He lost his grip on the spy. Bobbing to the surface he glimpsed the night sky arched impassively above his supine body as he relinquished it to Tregembo's hauling. He desperately gasped for breath as the next wave rolled over him. Then he was under the transom of the boat, feeling for the stirrup of rope Poll should have rigged. His right leg found it and he half turned for Major Brown who seemed waterlogged in his coat.

'Get him in first, Tregembo,' Drinkwater gasped, 'he's near collapse.'

Somehow they pulled him up to the transom and Drinkwater helped turn him round with his back to the boat. 'Get clear Mr Drinkwater!' It was Tregembo's voice and Drinkwater was vaguely aware of the two seamen, their hands on the shoulders of the Major, lifting him, lifting him, then suddenly plunging him down hard, down so that he disappeared then thrust to the surface where they waited to grab him and drag him ungainly into the boat. Drinkwater felt the tug on the line as Brown went inboard. He wearily replaced his foot in the stirrup and tried to heave himself over the transom but his chilled muscles cramped. Tregembo grabbed him and in a second he was in the bottom of the boat, on top of Brown and it no longer mattered about the coils of rope.

'Beg pardon, zur,' Tregembo heaved him aside with one hand and then his axe bit into the quarter knee cutting the grapnel line. Forward Poll showed the lantern and on board *Kestrel* all hands walked away with the hemp rope. Musket shot whistled round them and two or three struck splinters from the gunwales.

Wearily Drinkwater raised his head, eager to see the familiar loom of *Kestrel* over him. Ten yards to go, then safety. To seaward he thought he saw something else. It looked very like the angled peaks of a lugger's sails.

Even as he digested this they were alongside and arms were reaching down to help him out of the boat on to the deck. Roughly compassionate, Griffiths himself threw a boat cloak around Drinkwater while the latter stuttered out what he had seen.

'Lugger is it? Aye, *bach*, I've seen it already . . . are you all right?'

'Well enough,' stammered Drinkwater through chattering teeth.

'Get sail on her then. Mr Jessup! Larboard broadside, make ready . . .' Griffiths had given him the easy, mechanical job, Jessup's job, while he recovered himself. He felt a wave of gratitude for the old man's consideration and stumbled forward, gathering the men round the halliards at the fiferail. Staysail and throat halliards went away together, then the jib and peak halliards. The great gaff rose into the night and the sails slatted and cracked, the mast trembled and *Kestrel* fretted to be off.

There was a flash from seaward and the whine of a ball to starboard, surprising the men who had not yet realised the danger from the sea but who assumed they were to fire a defiant parting broadside at the beach.

The halliards were belayed and Drinkwater went aft to Griffiths.

'*Da iawn*, sheet all home to starboard then stand by to cut that cable.'

'Aye, aye, sir.' Drinkwater felt better. From somewhere inside, fresh reserves of strength flowed through him. The exercise at the halliards had invigorated him. He called the carpenter to stand handy with his axe and found Johnson already at his station. The sails thundered less freely now the sheets were secured.

'Larbowlines, man your guns, stand by to fire at the lugger!' Griffiths's words were drowned as the lugger's gunfire rent the air. A row of spouts rose close to starboard. 'Short by heaven,' muttered Drinkwater to himself.

'Cut!'

The axe struck twice at the cable. It stranded, spinning out the fibres as the strain built up, then it parted. *Kestrel*'s bow fell off the wind.

'Meet her.' The stern was held by the spring, led from aft forward and frapped to the end of the severed cable. *Kestrel* spun, heeled to the wind and drove forward.

'Cut!'

At the after gunport Jessup sawed against the cavil and the spring parted. Leaving her jolly boat, two anchors and a hundred fathoms of assorted rope, *Kestrel* stood seaward on the larboard tack.

Drinkwater turned to look for the lugger and was suddenly aware of her, huge and menacing ahead of them. He could see her three oddly raked masts with their vast spread of high peaked sails athwart their hawse and he was staring into the muzzles of her larboard broadside.

'Oh my God! She'll rake, sir, she'll rake!' he screamed aft, panic obscuring the knowledge that they had to stand on to clear the bay.

'Lie down!' Griffiths's rich voice cut through the fear and the men dropped obediently to the deck. Drinkwater threw himself behind the windlass, aware that of all the cutter's people he was the most forward. When the broadside came it was ragged and badly aimed. The lugger was luffing and unsteady but her guns took their toll. The wind from a passing ball felt like a punch in the chest but Drinkwater rose quickly from his prone position, adrenalin pouring into his bloodstream, aware that the worst had passed. Other shots had struck home. Amidships a man was down. The lee runner and two stays were shot through and the mainsail was peppered with holes made by canister and two ball. Daylight would reveal another ball in the hull and the topsides cut up by more canister.

Griffiths had the helm himself now, holding his course, the bowsprit stabbing at the overhanging stern of the lugger as she drew out on the beam at point blank range. Drinkwater saw the captain of number 2 gun lower his match and his eyes lifted to watch the result of the discharge. As they crossed the stern of the lugger the priming spurted and the four-pounder roared. Not twenty feet away from him Drinkwater stared into the eyes of a tall Frenchman who stood one foot on the rail, grasping the mizen shrouds. Even in the darkness Drinkwater detected the commanding presence of the man who did not flinch as the ball tore past him. The two little ships were tossing in the rough sea and most of *Kestrel*'s shot passed harmlessly over the lugger, but the flashes and roar of their cannon, firing as they bore, were gratifying to the cutter's crew.

Kestrel cleared the lugger's stern and Drinkwater walked slowly aft as Griffiths bore away. 'Get a couple of pairs of dead-eyes and lanyards into that lee rigging Mr Jessup,' he said passing the bosun who was securing the guns. He said it absently, his mind full of the sight of that immobile Frenchman.

'Do you think she'll chase, sir,' he wearily asked Griffiths.

He was relieved to hear Griffiths's reply took notice of reality.

'Bound to, boy-o, and we must run. Now slip below and shift that wet gear. Major Brown is opening my cognac. Help yourself and then we'll trice up a little more canvas and see what she'll do.'

She did very well. She was still being chased at daylight by which time they had rigged preventer backstays, had the squaresails drawing and stunsails set to leeward. At eight bells in the morning watch Drinkwater logged eleven knots as the cutter staggered, her bow wave a mass of foam driving ahead of her. Aft, by the weather running backstay, Griffiths hummed a tune, never once looking astern. By mid afternoon they could see the white cliffs of Dover and the lugger had abandoned them. Leaving the deck to Jessup they dined with Major Brown.

'That *chasse marée* was the *Citoyenne Janine*, French National Lugger,' said Brown, hungrily devouring a slice of ham. 'She's at the disposal of an audacious bastard called Santhonax . . . By heaven Madoc, I thought they had me that time; Santhonax had clearly got wind of my departure and intended to cut you off.' He munched steadily and swallowed, gulping half a glass of brandy. 'They were after me within an hour of my leaving Paris . . . but for the skill and enterprise of your young friend here they would have succeeded.'

Drinkwater muttered something and helped himself to the ham, suddenly very hungry.

'Mr Drinkwater has done well, Major. You may assume he has my full confidence.'

Brown nodded. 'Damned well ought to have. Shameful trick you played on him that night last November.' They all grinned at the release from tension and the bottle went round, jealously guarded from *Kestrel*'s urgent, hurrying list.

'Excuse me, sir,' said Drinkwater, 'But how did you know the identity of the lugger? Did you see her commander?'

'Santhonax? Yes. That fellow standing at her stern. He don't command the vessel, it runs at his convenience. The French Ministry of Marine have given him a roving commission, not unlike my own,' he paused and tossed off his glass. 'I'll lay even money on his being as familiar with the lanes of Kent as any damned hop picker.' He shrugged, 'But I've no proof. Yet. You could tell the lugger was the *Citoyenne Janine*. Even in the dark you could see the black swallowtail flag. For some reason Santhonax likes to fly it, some bit of damned Celtic nonsense. Sorry Madoc, no offence.'

Drinkwater had not seen the flag but he wondered at the recondite nature of Brown's knowledge. He did not yet appreciate the major's capacity for apparently trifling details.

'It's going to be a bloody long war, Madoc,' continued the Major. 'I can tell you this, the god-damned Yankees are involved. We'll fight them again yet, you see. They've promised the Frogs vast quantities of grain. Place would starve without their help, and the revolutionaries'll make trouble in Ireland . . . that'll be no secret in a month or two.' He paused frowning, gathering words suitable to convey the enormity of his news and Drinkwater was reminded of Appleby. 'They're going to carry their bloody flag right through Europe, mark my words . . .' He helped himself to another slice of ham. Drinkwater knew now why the man had appeared so jovial all those months ago. He himself felt the desire to chatter like Brown, as a reaction to the events of the night before. How much worse for Brown after that terrible isolation. Once ashore he would have to be circumspect but here, aboard *Kestrel*, he occupied neutral ground, was among friends. He emptied his glass for the fourth time and Griffiths refilled it.

'Did you get Barrallier out?' Brown asked settling back and addressing Drinkwater.

'Yes, sir, we picked him up at Beaubigny.'

'Beaubigny?' Brown looked startled and frowned. 'Where the devil's that? I arranged for Criel.' He looked at Griffiths who explained the location.

'I protested, Major, but two aristos had Dungarth's ear, see.'

Brown nodded, his eyes cold slits that in such a rubicund face seemed quite ugly.

'And one was a, er, misanthrope, eh?'

Griffiths and Drinkwater both nodded. 'And was De Tocqueville with Barrallier?'

'Yes,' said Griffiths, 'with a deal of specie too.' Brown nodded and relapsed into thought during which Drinkwater heard him say musingly 'Beaubigny . . .'

At last he looked up, a slightly puzzled expression on his face as though the answer was important. 'Was there a girl with them?' he asked, 'a girl with auburn hair?'

'That's correct, sir,' put in Drinkwater, 'with her brother, Etienne.'

Brown's eyebrows rose. 'So you know their names?'

'Aye, sir, they were called Montholon.' It seemed odd that Brown, a master of secrets should evince surprise at what was common gossip on Plymouth hard. 'Barrallier told us, sir,' continued Drinkwater, 'it did not seem a matter for secrecy.'

'Ha!' Brown threw back his head and laughed, a short, barking laugh like a fox. 'Good for Barrallier,' he said half for himself. 'No, 'tis no secret' but I am surprised at the girl leaving . . .' A silence fell over the three of them.

Brown ruminated upon the pieces of a puzzle that were beginning to fit. He had not known that it had been *Kestrel* that had caused the furore off Carteret, but he had been fortuitously close to the row that had erupted in Paris and well knew how close as a cause of war the incident had become. *Childers*'s comparatively innocent act had been just what the war hawks needed, having stayed their hands a month or so earlier.

The major closed his eyes, recalling some fascinating details. Capitaine de frégate Edouard Santhonax had been instrumental in checking the Convention's belligerence. And apart from the previous night, the last time Brown had seen Santhonax, the handsome captain had had Hortense Montholon gracing his arm. She had not seemed like a woman fleeing from revolution.

Lieutenant Griffiths watched his passenger, aware of mystery in the air and hunting back over the conversation to find its cause, while Drinkwater was disturbed by a vision of auburn hair and fine grey eyes.

Chapter Five

Incident off Ushant

In the weeks that followed Drinkwater almost forgot about the incident at Beaubigny, the rescue of Major Brown and the subsequent encounter with the *chasse marée*. Occasionally, on dark nights when the main cabin was lit by the swinging lantern, there appeared a ghost of disquieting beauty and auburn hair. And that half drowned sensation, as Tregembo hauled him through the breakers with the dead weight of the major threatening to drag them both to the bottom, emerged periodically to haunt half-awake hours trying to sleep. But they were mere shades, thrown off with full consciousness together with recollections of the swamps of Carolina and memories of Morris, the sodomite tyrant of *Cyclops*'s cockpit.

The spectre of the fugitives of Beaubigny appeared once in more positive form, revived by Griffiths. It was only a brief item in an already yellowing newspaper concerned with the death of a French nobleman in the gutters of St James's. Footpads were suspected as the gentleman's purse was missing and he was known to have been lucky at the tables that evening. But the man's name was De Tocqueville and Griffiths's raised eyebrow over the lowered paper communicated to Drinkwater a suspicion of assassination.

Such speculations were swept aside by duty. Already the Channel was full of French corsairs, from luggers to frigates, which commenced that war on trade at which they excelled. Into this mêlée of French commerce-raiders and British merchantmen, solitary British frigates dashed, noisily inadequate. Then on June 18th Pellew in *La Nymphe* took *Cleopâtre* off the Start and his knighthood sent a quiver of ambition down many an aspiring naval spine.

Kestrel, meanwhile, attended to more mundane matters, carrying despatches, fresh vegetables, mail and gossip to and from the detached cruisers, a maid of all work that fled from strong opposition and struck at weaker foes. Pellew took some men from her to supplement his crew of Cornish tin miners, despite Griffiths's protest, but they suffered only twice from this abuse. *Kestrel*'s people, mostly volunteers, were a superlative crew, worthy of a flagship under the most punctilious admiral.

'Better'n than aught the Cumberland Fleet can offer,' Jessup claimed with pride, alluding to the Thames yachts that made a fetish of such niceties as sail drill. Griffiths too reserved an approbatory twinkle in his eye for a smart manoeuvre executed under the envious glare of a frigate captain still struggling with a crew of landsmen. He could imagine the remarks on a score of quarterdecks about the 'damned insolence of unrated buggers'.

Amid this activity Drinkwater was aware that he was part of a happy ship, that Griffiths rarely flogged, nor had need to, and that these were halcyon days.

Whatever his misgivings about his future they were hidden from the taut deck of the cutter and reserved for the solitude of his cabin. The demands of watch and watch, the tension of chase or flight and the modest profits on prizes were in part compensation for the lack of prospects on his own, personal horizon.

December found them off the low island of Ushant cruising in search of Warren with the news that the commodore's squadron, after many delays and dockyard prevarications, would assemble under his command at Falmouth in the New Year.

It was a day of easterly wind which washed the air clear of the damp westerlies that had dogged them through the fall. Depression had followed depression across the Atlantic, eight weeks in which *Kestrel* had sought her principals under the greatest difficulties, her people wet and miserable, her canvas sodden and hard, her galley stove mostly extinguished.

The bright sunlight lay like a benefice upon the little ship so that she seemed reborn, changing men's moods, the skylarking crew a different company. Damp clothing appeared in the weather rigging giving her a gipsy air.

The low island that marked the western extremity of France lay astern on the larboard quarter and from time to time Drinkwater took a bearing of the lighthouse on the rising ground of Cape Stiff. He was interrupted in one such operation by a hail from the masthead: 'Deck there! Sail to windward!'

'Pass the word for the captain.'

'Aye, aye, sir.'

Griffiths hurried on deck, took a look at the island and the masthead pendant streaming over the starboard quarter in the easterly wind. 'Up you go Mr Drinkwater.'

Agilely Drinkwater ascended the mast, throwing a leg over the top-gallant yard. He needed but a single glance to tell him it was not *Flora* and to confirm a suspicion he knew he shared with Griffiths consequent upon the easterly breeze. The great naval arsenal of Brest lay ahead of them. The sail he was looking at had slipped down the Goulet that morning. Beyond he could see another.

'Two frigates, sir,' he said reaching the deck, 'bearing down on us and making sail.'

Griffiths nodded. 'Mr Jessup!' He cast about for the boatswain who was hurrying on deck, struggling into his coat. 'Sir?'

'We'll put her before the wind, I want preventer backstays and every stitch she'll carry. Mr Drinkwater, a course clear of the Pierres Vertes to open the Fromveur Passage . . .' He issued more orders as the hands tumbled up but Drinkwater was already scrambling below to consult the chart.

The Île d'Ouessant, or Ushant to countless generations of British seamen, lies some thirteen miles west of the Brittany coast. Between the island and Point St Matthew a confused litter of rocks, islets and reefs existed, delineated within a pecked line on the cutter's chart as: 'numerous dangerous shoals, rocks, and Co wherein are unpredictable tide rips and overfalls.' Even in the mildest of weather the area is subject to Atlantic swells and the ceaseless run of the tide which at springs reaches a rate of seven and a half knots. When the wind and tide are in opposition they generate a high, vicious and dangerous sea. At best the tide rips and overfalls rendered the area impossible to navigation. So great were the dangers in the locality as a whole that a special treaty had been drawn up between England and France that provided for the latter country to maintain a lighthouse on Point Stiff 'in war as in peace, for the general benefit of humanity'. This tower had been erected a century earlier to a design by Vauban on the highest point of the island.

Two passages run through the rocks between Ushant and the mainland. The Chenal du Four, a tortuous gut between St Matthew and Le Four rocks, while the Fromveur lies along the landward side of Ushant itself. It was the latter that Drinkwater now studied.

As he poured over the chart Drinkwater felt the sudden increase of speed that followed the clatter, shudder and heel of the gybe. *Kestrel* thrust through the water responsive to the urgency felt by her commander. Bracing himself he slipped into his own cabin and took from the bookshelf a stained notebook. It had once belonged to Mr Blackmore, sailing master of the frigate *Cyclops*. He riffled through the pages, finding what he was looking for, his brow frowning in concentration. He looked again at the chart, a copy of an early French survey. The litter of dangers worried him, yet the Fromveur itself looked straight and deep. He cursed the lack of Admiralty enterprise that relied on commanders purchasing their own charts. Even *Kestrel*, employed as she had been on special service, received no more than an allowance so that Griffiths could have only what he could purchase.

Drinkwater went on deck. Ushant was on the starboard bow now and a glance astern showed the nearer frigate closing them fast. The sooner they got into the Fromveur and out-performed her the better. Drinkwater recalled Barrallier's superior air, his confidence in the sailing qualities of French frigates and his astonishment at finding Griffiths navigating the French coast on obsolete charts: the old government of France had established a chart office more than seventy years earlier, he had said.

A feeling of urgency surged through him as he bent over the compass, rushing below to lay off the bearings. Already the Channel flood had swept them too far to the north, pushing them relentlessly towards the rocks and reefs to starboard. He hurried back on deck and was about to request Griffiths turn south when another hail reached the deck.

'Breakers on the starboard bow!'

Jessup started for the mainsheet. 'Stand by to gybe!' he shouted. By gybing again *Kestrel* could stem the tide and clear the rocks by making southing. The men were already at their stations, looking expectantly aft, awaiting the order from Griffiths.

'Belay that, Mr Jessup . . . Are they the Pierres Vertes, Mr Drinkwater?'

'Yes, sir.' Griffiths could see the surge of white water with an occasional glimpse of black, revealing the presence of the outcrops. To gain southing would allow the frigate to close.

'Steer nor' west . . . harden your sheets a trifle, Mr Jessup . . . Mr Drinkwater, I'm going inside . . .' His voice was calm, reassuring, as though there was no imminent decision to be taken. Drinkwater was diverted by the appearance of a shot hole in the topgallant, a ball smacked into the taffrail, sending splinters singing across the deck. A seaman was hit, a long sliver of pitch pine raising a terrible lancing wound. They had no surgeon to attend him.

To clear the reef the French frigate had altered to larboard, her course slightly diverging from that of the cutter so that a bow gun would bear. The smoke of her fire hung under her bow, driven by the following wind.

'Steer small, damn your eyes,' Griffiths growled at the helmsman. Drinkwater joined him in mental exercises in triangulation. They knew they must hold *Kestrel* close to the Pierres Vertes to avoid the tide setting them too far to the north on to the Roche du Loup, the Roche du Reynard and the reefs between; to avoid the temptation of running into clear water where the dangers were just submerged.

The Pierres Vertes were close now, under the bow. The surge and undertow of the sea could be felt as the tide eddied round them. *Kestrel* staggered in her onward progress then, suddenly, the rocks lay astern. A ragged cheer came from the men on deck who were aware that their ship had just survived a crisis.

The relief was short lived.

'Deck there! Sail to starboard, six points on the bow!' Drinkwater could see her clearly from the deck. A small frigate or corvette reaching down the Passage Du Fromveur, unnoticed in their preoccupation with the rocks but barring their escape.

'Take that lookout's name, Mr Drinkwater, I'll have the hide off him for negligence . . .'

Another hole aloft and several splashes alongside. One ball richochetted off the side of a wave and thumped, half spent, into the hull. They were neatly trapped.

Drinkwater looked at Griffiths. The elderly Welshman bore a countenance of almost stoic resignation in which Drinkwater perceived defeat. True, *Kestrel* might manoeuvre but it would only be out of form, out of respect for the flag. It was unlikely she would escape. Griffiths was an old man, he had run out of resolution; exhausted his share of good fortune. He seemed to know this as a beaten animal slinks away to die. To surrender a twelve-gun cutter to superior force would be no dishonour.

As if to emphasise their predicament the new jolly boat, stowed in the stern davits, disintegrated in an explosion of splinters, the transom boards of the cutter split inwards and a ball bounced off the breech of No 11 gun, dismounting it with an eerie clang and whined off distorted over the starboard rail.

'Starboard broadside make ready!' Griffiths braced himself. 'Mr Drinkwater, strike the colours after we've fired. Mr Jessup we'll luff up and d'you clew up the square sails . . .'

A mood of sullen resignation swept the deck like a blast of canister, visible in its impact. It irritated Drinkwater into a sudden fury. A long war Appleby had said, a long war pent up in a French hulk dreaming of Elizabeth. The thought was violently abhorrent to him. Griffiths might be exchanged under cartel but who was going to give a two-penny drum for an unknown master's mate? They would luff, fire to defend the honour of the flag and then strike to the big frigate foaming up astern.

Ironic that they would come on the wind to do so. Reaching the only point of sailing on which they might escape their pursuers. If, that is, the rocks were not there barring their way.

Then an idea struck him. So simple, yet so dangerous that he realised it had been bubbling just beneath conscious acceptance since he looked at the notebook of old Blackmore's. It was better than abject surrender.

'Mr Griffiths!' Griffiths turned.

'I told you to stand by the ensign halliards . . .'

'Mr Griffiths I believe we could escape through the rocks, sir. There's a passage between the two islands . . .' He pointed to the two islets on the starboard beam; the Îles de Bannec and de Balanec. Griffiths looked at them, uncertainty in his eyes. He glanced astern. Drinkwater pressed his advantage. 'The chart's old, sir. I've a more recent survey in a manuscript book . . .'

'Get it!' snapped Griffiths, suddenly shedding his mood with his age. Drinkwater needed no second bidding and rushed below, stumbling in his haste. He snatched up Blackmore's old, stained journal and clambered back on deck where a pale, tense hope was alive on the faces of the men, Jessup had the hands aloft and the squaresails were coming in. A party of men was busily lashing the dismounted four pounder. Griffiths, now indifferent to the two ships closing ahead and astern like the jaws of pincers, was examining the gap between the two islands.

'Here sir . . .' Drinkwater spread the book on the companion-way top and for a minute he and Griffiths bent over it, Drinkwater's finger tracing a narrow gutway through the reefs. A muttering of Welsh escaped the old man and then Drinkwater made out: 'Men ar Reste . . . Carrec ar Morlean . . .' He pronounced it 'carreg' in the Welsh rather than the Breton, as he stared at the outlying rocks that strewed the passage Drinkwater was suggesting, like fangs waiting for the eager keel of *Kestrel*.

'Can you get her through?' he asked shortly.

'I'll try, sir. With bearings and a lookout at the cross trees.'

Griffiths made up his mind. 'Put her on the chart.' He called one of the seamen over to hold the book open and stand by it. Drinkwater bent over the compass, his heart pounding with excitement. Behind him a transformed Griffiths rapped out orders.

'Mr Jessup! I'm going through the rocks. D'you attend to the set of the sails to get the best out of her . . .'

'Aye, aye, sir.' Jessup bustled off and his action seemed to electrify the upper deck. Men jumped eagerly to belaying pins, stood expectantly beside sheets and runners, while the helmsmen watched their commander, ready at a word to fling their weight on the great curved ash tiller.

There was a crash amidships and the pump trunking flew apart, the wrought arm bending impossibly. Yet another ball thumped into the hull and a glance astern showed the frigate huge and menacing. No more than two miles ahead of them the corvette, her main topsail to the mast, lay in their track. Drinkwater straighten from his extempore chart table.

'East, nor'east, sir, upon the instant . . .'

Griffiths nodded. 'Down helm! Full and bye! Heads'l sheets there! You there!' he pointed at Number 12 gun's crew, ' . . .a knife to that preventer backstay.' *Kestrel* came on to the wind, spray bursting over the weather bow. Drinkwater looked into the compass bowl and nodded, then he ran forward. 'Tregembo! Aloft there and watch for rocks, tide rips and guns . . .' and then, remembering the man's smuggling past from a gleam of exhilaration in his eye, 'The tide's in our favour, under us . . . I need to know bloody fast . . .'

'Aye, aye, zur!' The windward shrouds were bar taut and Drinkwater followed half way up. Though fresh, the wind had little fetch here and they ought to see tidal runs on the rocks. He bit his lip with anxiety. It was well after low water now and *Kestrel* was rushing north eastwards on a young flood.

'Run, zur, fine to starboard . . .' Tregembo pointed. 'And another to larboard . . .' Drinkwater gained the deck and rushed aft to bend over the chart. Four and a half fathoms over the Basse Blanche to starboard and less than one over the Melbian to larboard.

'Can you lay her a little closer, sir?' Griffiths nodded, his mouth a tight line. Drinkwater went forward again and began to climb the rigging. As he hoisted himself alongside Tregembo, his legs dangling, a terrific roar filled the air. The glass, the Dollond glass which he had just taken from his pocket, was wrenched from his hand and his whole body was buffetted as it had been in the breakers the night they picked up Major Brown. He saw the glass twinkle once as the sunlight glanced off it, then he too pitched forward, helpless as a rag doll. He felt a strong hand clutch his upper arm. Tregembo hauled him back on the yard while below them both the little telescope bounced on a deadeye and disappeared into the white water sluicing past *Kestrel*'s trembling side.

Drinkwater drew breath. Looking aft he saw the big frigate turning south away from them, cheated of her prey, the smoke from her starboard broadside drifting away. Across her stern he could see the letters of her name: *Sirène*. She would give them the other before standing away to the south south eastward on the larboard tack.

Drinkwater turned to Tregembo. 'Thank you for your assistance,' he muttered, annoyed at the loss of his precious glass. He stared ahead, ignoring the corvette obscured by the peak of the straining mainsail and unaware of the final broadside from *Sirène*.

White water was all around them now, the two green-grey islets of Bannec and Balanec, rapidly opening on either bow. The surge and suck of the tide revealed rocks everywhere, the water foaming white around the reefs. Ahead of them he could see no gap, no passage.

Hard on the wind *Kestrel* plunged onwards, driven inexorably by the tide which was running swiftly now. Suddenly ahead he could see the hummock of a black rock: the Ar Veoe lay dead in their path. Patiently he forced himself to line it up with the forestay. If the rock drew left of the stay it would pass clear to larboard, if to the right they would clear it to starboard but run themselves into danger beyond. If it remained in transit they would strike it.

The dark bulk of the Men ar Reste drew abeam and passed astern.

Ar Veoe remained in transit and on either hand the reefs surrounding the two islets closed in, relative motion lending them a locomotion of their own.

Twisting round Drinkwater hailed the deck: 'She's not weathering the Ar Veoe, sir!' He watched as Griffiths looked at the book. They *had* to pass to the east of that granite stump. They could not run to leeward or they would be cast on the the Île de Bannec and irrevocably lost.

The gap was lessening and the bearing remained unaltered. They would have to tack. Reaching for a backstay Drinkwater slid to the deck. Ignoring the smarting of his hands he accosted Griffiths.

'She's getting to loo'ard. We *must* tack, sir, immediately . . . there is no option.' Griffiths did not acknowledge his subordinate but raised his head and bawled.

'Stand by to go about! Look lively there!'

The men, tuned now to the high pitch of their officers, obeyed with flattering alacrity. '*Myndiawl*, I hope you know what you're doing,' he growled at Drinkwater. 'Get back aloft and when we've sufficient offing wave your right arm . . .' His voice was mellow with controlled tension, all trace of defeat absent, replaced with a taut confidence in Drinkwater. Briefly their eyes met and each acknowledged in the other the rarefied excitement of their predicament, a balance of expertise and terror.

By the time Drinkwater reached the crosstrees what had been the weather rigging was slack. *Kestrel* had tacked smartly and now her bowsprit stabbed south-east as she crabbed across the channel, the tide still carrying her north-east. Drinkwater had hardly marshalled his senses when instinct screamed at him to wave his right arm. Obediently the helm went down and beneath him the yard trembled with the mast as the cutter passed through the wind again.

Kestrel had barely steadied on the starboard tack as the hummocked, fissured slab of the Ar Veoe rushed past. The white swirl of the tide tugged the weed at its base and a dozen cormorants, hitherto sunning their wings, flapped away low over the sea. On either side danger was clearly visible. The Carrec ar Morlean lay on the starboard quarter, the outcrops of the Île de Bannec to larboard. *Kestrel* rushed at the gap, her bowsprit plunging aggressively forward. The rocks drew abeam and Drinkwater slid to the deck to lay another position on the makeshift chart. Griffiths peered over his shoulder. They were almost through, a final gap had to be negotiated as the Gourgant Rocks opened up to starboard. Cannon shot had long since ceased and the hostile ships astern were forgotten as the beginnings of relief showed in their eyes. The Gourgants drew astern and merged with the seemingly impenetrable barrier of black rock and white water through which they had just passed.

'Deck there!' It was Tregembo, still aloft at his post. 'Rock dead ahead and close zur!' Griffiths's reaction was instinctive: 'Up helm!'

Drinkwater was half way up the starboard shrouds when he saw it. *Kestrel* had eased off the wind a point but was far too close. Although her bowsprit swung away from the rock the run of the tide pushed her stern round so that a brief vision of rending timber and a rudderless hulk flashed across Drinkwater's imagination. He faced aft and screamed 'Down helm!'

For a split second he thought Griffiths was going to ignore him; that his insubordination was too great. Then, shaking with relief he saw the lieutenant lunge across the deck, pushing the tiller to larboard.

Kestrel began to turn as the half-submerged rock rushed at her. It was too late. Drinkwater was trembling uncontrollably now, a fly in a web of rigging. He watched fascinated, aware that in ten, fifteen seconds perhaps, the shrouds to which he clung would hang in slack festoons as the cutter's starboard side was stove, the mast snapped like celery and she rolled over, a broken wreck. Below him men rushed to the side to watch: then the tide took her. *Kestrel* trembled, her quarter lifting on the wave made against the up-tide side of the rock, then swooped into the down-tide trough as the sea cast her aside like a piece of driftwood. They could see bladder wrack and smell bird droppings and then they were past, spewed out to the northward. A few moments later the Basse Pengloch, northern post of the Île de Bannec, was behind them.

Shaking still, Drinkwater regained the deck. 'We're through sir.' Relief translated itself into a grin made foolish by blood trickling from a hard-bitten lip.

'Aye, Mr Drinkwater we're through, and I desire you to pass word to issue grog to all hands.'

'Deck there!' For a second they froze, apprehension on their faces, fearing another outcrop ahead of them; but Tregembo was pointing astern.

When he descended again to return the borrowed telescope to Griffiths, Drinkwater said, 'The two frigates and the corvette are still hull up, sir, but beyond them are a number of tops'ls. It looks as if we have just escaped from a fleet.'

Griffiths raised a white eyebrow. 'Indeed . . . in that case let us forget *Flora*, Mr Drinkwater, and take our intelligence home. Lay me a course for Plymouth.'

'Aye, aye, sir,' Drinkwater turned away. Already the excitement of the past two hours was fading, giving way to a peevish vexation at the loss of his Dollond glass.

Chapter Six

A Night Attack

What neither Griffiths nor Drinkwater knew was that the frigates from which they had escaped off Ushant had been part of Admiral Vanstabel's fleet. The admiral was on passage to America to reinforce the French squadron sent thither to escort the grain convoy safely back to France. The importance of this convoy to the ruined economy of the Republic and the continued existence of its government had been brought to British notice by Major Brown.

Vanstabel eluded pursuit but as spring of 1794 approached the British Admiralty sent out the long awaited flying squadrons. That to which *Kestrel* was attached was under the command of Sir John Borlase Warren whose broad pendant flew in the 42-gun frigate *Flora*. Warren's frigates hunted in the approaches to the Channel, sometimes in a pack, sometimes detached. *Kestrel*'s duties were unimaginatively recorded in her log as 'vessel variously employed'. She might run orders from *Flora* to another frigate, returning with intelligence. She might be sent home to Falmouth with dispatches, rejoining the squadron with mail, orders, a new officer, her boats full of cabbages and bags of potatoes, sacks of onions stowed between her guns.

It was a busy time for her company. Their constant visits to Falmouth reminded Drinkwater of Elizabeth whom he had first met there in 1780 and the view from Carrick Road was redolent of nostalgia. But he enjoyed no respite for the chills of January precipitated Griffiths's malaria and while his commander lay uncomplaining in his cot, sweating and half-delirious, Drinkwater, by express instruction, managed the cutter without informing his superiors.

Griffiths's recovery was slow, interspersed with relapses. Drinkwater assumed the virtual command of the cutter unopposed. Jessup, like all her hands, had been impressed by the acting lieutenant's resource in the escape from Vanstabel's frigates. 'He'll do all right, will Mr Drinkwater,' was his report to Johnson, the carpenter. And Tregembo further enhanced Drinkwater's reputation with the story of the retaking of the *Algonquin* in the American war. The Cornishman's loyalty was as touching as it was infectious.

Unbeknown to Warren, Drinkwater had commanded *Kestrel* during the action of St George's Day. Fifteen miles west of the Roches Douvres Warren's squadron had engaged a similar French force under Commodore Desgareaux. At the time Warren had with him the yacht-like *Arethusa* commanded by Sir Edward Pellew, *Concorde* and *Melampus*, with the unspritely *Nymphe* in the offing and unable to come up in time.

During the battle *Kestrel* acted as Warren's repeating vessel, a duty requiring strict attention both to the handling of the cutter and the accuracy of her signals. That Drinkwater accomplished it shorthanded was not known to Warren. Indeed no mention was even made of *Kestrel*'s presence in the account published in the *Gazette*. But Warren did not diminish his own triumph. Commodore Desgareaux's *Engageante* had been taken, shattered beyond redemption, while the corvette *Babet* and the beautiful frigate *Pomone* were both purchased into the Royal Navy. Only the *Resolue* had escaped into Morlaix, outsailing a pursuit in which *Kestrel* had played a small part.

'No mention of us sir,' said Drinkwater dejectedly as he finished reading Warren's dispatch from the *Gazette*.

'No way to earn a commission is it, eh?' Griffiths commiserated, reading Drinkwater's mind as they shared a bottle over the newspaper. He looked ruefully at his subordinate's set face.

'Never mind Mr Drinkwater. Your moment will yet come. I met Sir Sydney Smith in the dockyard. He at least had heard we tried to cut off the *Resolue*.' Griffiths sipped from his glass and added conversationally, '*Diamond* is at last joining the squadron, so we will have an eccentric brain to set beside the commodore's square one. What d'you think of that then?'

Drinkwater shrugged, miserable with the knowledge that Elizabeth was not far from their mooring at Haslar creek and that the addition of *Diamond* to the squadron opened opportunities for Richard White. 'I don't know, sir. What do you predict?'

'Stratagems,' said Griffiths in a richly imitated English that made Drinkwater smile, cracking the preoccupation with his own misfortune, 'stratagems, Sir Sydney is the very devil for audacity . . .'

'Well gentlemen?' Warren's strong features, thrown into bold relief by the lamplight, looked up from the chart. He was flanked by Pellew, Nagle of the *Artois* and the irrepressibly dominating Smith whose bright eyes darted restlessly over the lesser officers: *Flora*'s first lieutenant and sailing master, her lieutenant of marines and his own second lieutenant who was winking at a slightly older man, a man in the shadows, among his superiors on sufferance.

'Any questions?' Warren pursued the forms relentlessly. The three post captains shook their heads.

'Very well. Sir Ed'd, then, leads the attack . . . Captain Nagle joins me offshore: the only problem is *Kestrel* . . .' They all looked at the man in the shadows. He was not so young, thought Sir Sydney, the face was experienced. He felt an arm on his sleeve and bent his ear. Lieutenant Richard White whispered something and Sir Sydney again scrutinised the acting lieutenant in the plain blue coat. Warren went on: 'I think one of my own lieutenants should relieve Griffiths . . .' Smith watched the mouth of the man clamp in a hard line. He was reminded of a live shell.

'Come, come, Sir John, I am sure Mr Drinkwater is capable of executing his orders to perfection. I am informed he did very well in your action in April. Let's give him a chance, eh?' He missed the look of gratitude from the grey eyes. Warren swivelled sideways. 'What d'you think Ed'd?'

Pellew was well-known for promoting able men almost as much as practising shameless nepotism when it suited him. 'Oh give him some rope, John, then he can hang himself or fashion a pretty bowline for us all to admire.' Pellew turned to Drinkwater. 'How is the worthy Griffiths these days, mister?'

'Recovering, Sir Edward. Sir John was kind enough to have his surgeon repair his stock of quinine.'

Warren was not mollified by this piece of tact and continued to look at Drinkwater with a jaundiced eye. He was well aware that both Smith and Pellew had protégés of their own and suspected their support of a neutral was to block the advancement of his own candidate. At last he sighed. 'Very well.'

Sir John Warren's Western Squadron had been in almost continual action during that summer while Admiral Howe's desultory blockade conducted from the comfort of an anchorage at Spithead or Torbay found many critics. Nevertheless the advocates of the strategic advantages of close blockade could not fail to be impressed by the dash and spirit of the frigates, albeit with little effect on the progress of the war. There had been a fleet action too: the culmination of days of manoeuvring had come on the 'Glorious First of June' when, in mid-Atlantic, Earl Howe had beaten Villaret Joyeuse and carried away several prizes from the French line of battle. Despite this apparently dazzling success no naval officer aware of the facts could fail to acknowledge that the victory was a strategic defeat. The grain convoy that Villaret Joyeuse protected and that Vanstabel had succoured, arrived unmolested in France.

Alongside that the tactical successes in the Channel were of little importance, though they read well in the periodicals, full of flamboyant dash and enterprise. Corrosive twinges of envy settled round Drinkwater's heart as he read of his own squadron's activities. Lieutenant White had been mentioned twice, through the patronage of Smith, for Warren was notoriously parsimonious with praise. It was becoming increasingly clear to Drinkwater that, without similar patronage, his promotion to lieutenant, when it came, would be too late; that he would end up the superannuated relic he had jestingly suggested to Elizabeth.

Yet he was eager to take part in the operation proposed that evening aboard *Flora*, eager to seize any opportunity to distinguish himself and guiltily grateful to White whose prompting of Smith's intervention had clearly diverted Warren's purpose.

Six months after his defeat Villaret Joyeuse was known to be preparing to slip out of Brest once more. Cruising westward from St Malo *Diamond* had discovered a convoy of two storeships being escorted by a brig-corvette and a *chasse marée*, an armed lugger. Aware of the presence of Warren's squadron in the offing they made passage at night, sheltering under batteries at anchor during daylight.

The weather had been quiet, though the night of the attack was heavily overcast, the clouds seeming to clear the mastheads with difficulty like a waterlogged ceiling, bulging and imminent in their descent. The south-westerly wind was light but had a steadiness that foreshadowed a blow, while the slight sea rippled over a low, ominous swell that indicated a disturbance far to the west.

With Griffiths sick, Drinkwater and Jessup felt the want of more officers but for the descent on the convoy they had only to keep station on *Diamond*, Sir Sydney having left a single lantern burning in his cabin for the purpose. Just visible to the westward was the dark bulk of *Arethusa*.

Drinkwater went below. The air in the cabin was stale, smelling sweetly of heavy perspiration. Griffiths lay in his cot, propped up, one eye regarding Nathaniel as he bent over the chart. The acting lieutenant was scratching his scar, lost in thought. After a while their eyes met.

'Ah, sir, you are awake . . . a glass of water . . .' He poured a tumbleful and noted Griffiths's hands barely shook as he lifted it to his lips. 'Well Mr Drinkwater?'

'Well, sir, we're closing on a small convoy to attack a brig-corvette, two transports and a lugger . . . we're in company with *Arethusa* and *Diamond*.'

'And the plan?'

'Well sir, *Arethusa* is to engage the brig, *Diamond* will take the two transports – she has most of *Arethusa*'s marines for the purpose – and we will take the lugger.'

'Is she an armed lugger, a *chasse marée*?'

'I believe so sir, my friend Lieutenant White was of the opinion that she was. *Diamond* reconnoitred the enemy . . .'. He tailed off, aware that Griffiths's opinion of White was distorted by understandable prejudice.

'The only opinion that young man had which was of the slightest value might more properly be attended by fashion-conscious young women . . .' Drinkwater smiled, disinclined to argue the point. Still, it was odd that a man of Griffiths's considerable wisdom could so misjudge. White was typical of his type, professionally competent, gauche and arrogant upon occasion but ruthless and brave.

Griffiths recalled him to the present. 'She'll be stuffed full of men, Nathaniel, you be damned careful, the French overman to the extent we sail short-handed . . . What have you in mind to attempt?' Griffiths struggled on to one elbow. 'It had better convince me, otherwise I'll not allow you to carry it out.'

Drinkwater swallowed. This was a damned inconvenient moment for a return of the old man's faculties. 'Well sir, Sir John has approved . . .'

'Damn Sir John, Nathaniel. Don't prevaricate. The question is do *I* approve it?'

*   *   *

63

Six paces forward, six paces aft. Up and down, up and down, *Diamond*'s bell chiming the half hours until it was several minutes overdue. 'Light's out in *Diamond*'s cabin, sir.' It was Nicholls, the poor lookout, sent aft to interrupt Drinkwater's train of thought.

Smith was to signal which side of *Diamond* the *Kestrel* was to pass as soon as his officers, from the loftier height of her fore-mast, made out the enemy dispositions. 'Call all hands, there, all hands to general quarters!'

Minutes passed, then: 'Two lights, sir!'

So it was to larboard, to the eastward that they were to go. He gave his orders. Course was altered and the sheets trimmed. They began to diverge and pass the frigate, shaking out the reef that had held them back while *Diamond* shortened sail. Giving the men a few moments to make their preparations Drinkwater slipped below.

'Enemy's in sight, sir . . .' Griffiths opened his eyes. His features were sunk, yellow in the lamplight, like old parchment. But the voice that came from him was still resonant. 'Be careful, boy-o,' he said with almost paternal affection, raising a wasted hand over the rim of the cot. Drinkwater shook it in an awkward, delicate way. 'Take my pistols there, on the settee . . .' Drinkwater checked the pans. 'They're all ready, Nathaniel, primed and ready,' the old man said behind him. He stuck them in his belt and left the cabin. On deck he buckled on his sword and went round the hands. The men were attentive, drawing aside as he approached, muttering 'good lucks' amongst themselves and assuring him they knew what to do. As he walked aft again a new mood swept over him. He no longer envied White. He was in a goodly company, knew these men well now, had been accepted by them as their leader. A tremendous feeling of exhilaration coursed through him so strongly that for a moment he remained staring aft, picking out the pale streak of their wake while he recovered himself. Then he thought of Elizabeth, her kiss and parting remark: 'Be careful, my love . . .' So like Griffiths's and tonight so enormously relevant. He was on the verge of breaking that old promise of circumspection and giving way to reckless-ness. Then, unhidden, a fragment of long past conversation rose like flotsam on the whirlpool of his brain. 'I have heard it said,' Appleby had averred, 'that a man who fails to feel fear when going into action is usually wounded . . . as though some nervous

64

defence is destroyed by reckless passion which in itself presages misfortune . . .'

Drinkwater swallowed hard and walked forward. Mindful of his sword and the loaded pistols in his belt, he began to slowly ascend the rigging, staring ahead for a sight of the enemy.

'Make ready! Make ready there!' The word was passed in sibilantly urgent whispers. 'Aft there, steer two points to larboard! Larboard guns train as far forrard as you can!'

And then the need for silence was gone as, a mile west of them a ragged line of fire erupted into the night where one of the frigates loosed off her broadside. The rolling thunder of her discharge came downwind to them.

Drinkwater could see the lugger clearly now. He stood on the rail, one hand round the huge running backstay. She was beating up to cover a barque, presumably one of the storeships. He ordered the course altered a little more and noted where the sheets were trimmed.

At three hundred yards the lugger opened fire, revealing herself as a well-served *chasse marée* of about ten guns. Drinkwater held his fire.

'When your guns bear, open fire.' Men tensed in the darkness as he said: 'Luff her!'

Kestrel's sails shivered as she turned into the wind. The crash and recoiling rumble of the guns exploded down her larboard side. Forward a bosun's mate had the jib backed, forcing the cutter on to her former tack. As she closed the *chasse marée* Drinkwater studied his opponent for damage, wondering if the specially prepared broadside had done anything.

It was impossible to say for certain but he heard shouts and screams and already his own gun captains were reporting themselves ready. He waited for Jessup commanding the battery. 'All ready Mr Drinkwater!'

'Luff her!'

A hundred yards range now and a flash and crash, a scream and a flurry of bodies where the Frenchman's broadside struck, then *Kestrel* fired back and steadied for the final assault on the enemy. As the last few yards were eaten up Drinkwater was aware of a furious exchange of fire where *Arethusa* and the brig-corvette engaged; then he snapped: 'Boarders!'

The cutter was gathering way, heading straight for the lugger. The French commander was no sluggard and sought to rake her.

A storm of shot swept *Kestrel*'s deck. Grape and langridge forced Drinkwater's eyes tight shut as the whine and wind of its passing whistled about him. Thumps, shouts and screams forced his eyes open again. Soon they must run on board of the lugger . . . would the distance never lessen?

He could hear shouts of alarm coming from the Frenchman then he felt the deck tremble under his feet as *Kestrel*'s bowsprit went over the lugger's rail with a twanging of the bobstay. Then the deck heeled as a rending crash told where her stem bit into the enemy's chains and *Kestrel* slewed round. The guns fired again as they bore and the two hulls jarred together.

'Boarders away!'

The noise that came from forward was of a different tenor now as the Kestrels left their guns and swept over the rail. Forward and aft lashings were caught round the lugger's rufftree rail and the two ships ground together in the swell.

Drinkwater leapt across the gap, stepped on the lugger's rail and landed on the deck. He was confronted by two men whose features were pale blurs. He remembered his own orders and screamed through clenched teeth. Behind him the two helmsmen came aboard, their faces blackened, like his own, by soot from the galley funnel.

Drinkwater fired his pistol at the nearer Frenchman and jabbed his hanger at the other. They vanished and a man in front thrust at him with a boarding pike. He parried awkwardly, sliding on the deck, taking the thrust through his coat sleeve and driving the muzzle of the discharged pistol into the man's exposed stomach. His victim doubled over and Drinkwater savagely struck at the nape of his neck with the pommel of his sword. Something gave beneath the ferocity of the blow and like a discarded doll the man dropped into the anonymous darkness of the bloody deck.

He moved on and three, then four men were in front of him. He slashed with the hanger, hurled the pistol at another then whipped the second from his belt. Pulling the trigger the priming flashed but it misfired and with a triumphant yell the man leapt forward. Drinkwater was through the red-rimmed barrier of fighting madness now. His brain worked with cool rapidity, emotionless. He began to crouch instinctively, to turn his head away in a foetal position, but his passive submission was deceptive; made terrible by the sword. Bringing the hilt down into his belly, the blade ran vertically upwards between his right ear and shoulder. He sensed the man slash at where he had been, felt him stumble on to the exposed sword-blade in the confusion. Drinkwater thrust with his legs, driving upwards with a cracking of back muscles. Supported by fists, belly and shoulder the disembowelling blade thrust deep into the man's guts, through his diaphragm and into his lungs. Half crouched with the dying Frenchman collapsed about his shoulder he felt the sword nick his own ear. The weight of the body sliding down his back dragged the hanger over his shoulder and he tore it clear with both hands as another man pointed a pistol at his exposed left flank. The blade came clear as the priming flashed. In a terrible swipe the steel scythed round as the pistol discharged.

Drinkwater never knew where the ball went. Maybe in the confusion the fellow had forgotten to load it or it had been badly wadded and rolled out. Nevertheless his face bore tiny blue spots where the grains of spent powder entered his flesh. His left eye was bruised from the shock wave and blinded by yellow light but he went on hacking at the man, desperately beating him to the deck.

Drinkwater reeled from the discharge of the pistol, his head spinning. The other men had disappeared, melted away. The faces round him were vaguely familiar and he no longer had the strength to raise his arm and strike at them. It had fallen silent. Oddly silent. Then Jessup appeared and Drinkwater was falling. Arms caught him and he heard the words 'Congratulations, sir, congratulations . . .' But it was all a long way off and oddly irrelevant and Elizabeth was giving him such an odd, quizzical look.

When he awoke he was aware that he was in the cabin of *Kestrel* and that pale daylight showed through the skylight. He was bruised in a score of places, stiff and with a raging headache. A pale shape fluttered round other men, prone like himself. One, on the cabin table all bloody and trembling, the pale form, ghostly in a dress of white bent over him. Drinkwater saw the body arch, heard a thin, high whimper which tailed to a gurgle and the body relaxed. For a second he expected Hortense Montholon to round on him, a grey-eyed Medusa, barbering in hell and he groaned in primaeval fear, but it was only Griffiths probing a wound who looked round, the front of his nightshirt stiff with blood. Drinkwater realised he could only see through one eye, that a crust of dried blood filled his right ear. He tried to sit up, feeling his head spin.

'Ah, Mr Drinkwater, you are with us again . . .' Drinkwater got himself into a sitting position. Griffiths nodded to the biscuit barrel on the locker. 'Take some biscuits and a little cognac . . . you will mend in an hour or so.' Drinkwater complied, avoiding too protracted a look at the several wounded lying gasping about the cabin.

'A big butcher's bill, Mr Drinkwater, *Diamond*'s surgeon is coming over . . . Eight killed and fifteen wounded badly . . .' A hint of reproach lay in Griffiths's eyes.

'But the lugger, sir?' Drinkwater found his voice a croak and remembered himself screaming like a male banshee.

'Rest easy, you took the lugger.' Griffiths finished bandaging a leg and signalled the messman to drag the inert body clear of the table. 'When you've recovered yourself I want you to take charge of her, Jessup's fitting things up at the moment. I've my own reasons for not wanting a frigate's mate sent over.'

On deck Drinkwater looked about him. It was quite light now and the wind was freshening. The squadron was hove to, the coast of France blue grey to the south of them. *Arethusa* and *Diamond* lay-to apparently unscathed, as were the two transports. But the French corvette, her tricolour fluttering beneath the British ensign, had lost a topmast, was festooned in loose rigging with a line of gunports opened into one enormous gash. Her bulwarks were cut up and she had about her an air of forlorn hopelessness.

Kestrel's own deck showed signs of enemy fire. A row of stiffened hammocks lay amidships, eight of them. Her bulwarks were jagged with splinters while aloft her topmast was wounded and her topsail yard hung down in two pieces which banged against the mast as she rolled. A party of men were lowering the spar to the deck.

Tregembo rolled up, a grin on his face. 'We did for 'em proper 'andsome, zur.' He nodded cheerfully to starboard where eighty yards distant the lugger lay a shambles. Her rails were almost entirely shot away. That first, double-shotted broadside had been well laid. With her rails had gone the chains and she had rolled her topmasts over the side. Tendrils of blood could still be seen running down her brown sides.

'Oh, my God,' whispered Drinkwater to himself.

'Ay, there'll be some widders in St Malo tonight I'm thinking, zur . . .'

'How many were killed aboard her, Tregembo, d'you know?' Drinkwater asked, knowing the mutual comprehension of the Cornish and Bretons.

'I heard she had ninety-four zouls on board, zur, an' we counted four dozen still on their legs. Mr Jezzup's got his mate Short over there along of him, keeping order.' Tregembo smiled again. Short was the more ruthless of *Kestrel*'s two bosun's mates and on a bigger ship would have become a brutal bully. 'Until you'm ready to take over, zur.' Tregembo concluded with relish. Mr Drinkwater had been a veritable fury in last night's fight. He had been just the same in the last war, Tregembo had told his cronies, a terrible man once he got his dander up.

The boat bearing *Diamond*'s surgeon arrived and Appleby climbed wearily aboard. He stared at Drinkwater unblinking, shaking his head in detached disapproval as he looked about the bloody deck.

'Devil's work, Nathaniel, damned devil's work,' was all he said by way of greeting and Drinkwater was too tired to answer as Appleby had his bag passed up. He took passage in *Diamond*'s boat across to the lugger.

The shambles apparent from *Kestrel*'s deck was ten times worse upon that of the lugger. In an exhausted state Drinkwater stumbled round securing loose gear, assessing the damage and putting the *chasse marée* in a fit state to make sail. He avoided the sullen eyes of her captive crew and found himself staring at a small bundle of bunting. It was made fast to the main flag halyards and stirred something in his brain but he was interrupted by a boat from *Flora*. *Kestrel* was to escort the prizes to Portsmouth, among them the lugger. At noon the British frigates stood westward, the prizes north-north-east.

It was late afternoon before Drinkwater emerged from the brief but deep sleep of utter exhaustion. He was slumped in a chair and woke to surroundings unfamiliar enough to jar his brain into rapid recollection. As he emerged into full consciousness he was aware of a fact that needed urgent clarification. He rushed on deck, ignoring the startled look of the two helmsmen. He found what he was looking for amidships and pulled the black flag from where it had been shoved on lowering. He held it out and the wind caught it, fluttering the soft woollen material

69

and arousing the attention of three of the Bretons exercising forward.

It was a black swallowtail flag.

'Mr Short!'

'Sir?' Short hurried up.

'What's the name of the lugger?'

Short scratched his head. 'Er *Cityee-en Jean*, I think sir.'

'*Citoyenne Janine*?'

'Yeah, that's it, sir.' The man nodded his curly head.

'Where's her commander? Who was in charge when we took her? Is Tregembo in the prize crew?'

Short recoiled at the rapid questioning. 'Well, sir, that blackguard there, sir,' He pointed at a man standing by the forward gun. 'As to Tregembo, sir, he ain't in the crew, sir . . .'

'Damn. Bring that man aft here . . .' Drinkwater unhitched the black flag as Short shoved the man aft. He wore a plain blue coat and while not very senior, was clearly an officer of sorts.

'*Òu est vôitre capitaine*?', He asked in his barbarous French. The Frenchman frowned in incomprehension and shrugged.

'*Vôtre capitaine*?' Drinkwater almost shouted.

Understanding woke in the man, and also perhaps a little cunning, Drinkwater thought. '*Mon capitaine*?' he said with some dignity. '*M'sieur, je suis le capitaine*.'

Drinkwater held the flag under his nose. '*Qu'est-ce que c'est*?' He met the Frenchman's eyes and they looked at each other long enough for Drinkwater to know he was right. Even as the Frenchman shrugged again Drinkwater had turned aft.

He noticed the aftermost guns turned inboard, each with a seaman stationed with a lighted match ready to sweep the waist. Drinkwater did not remember turning any guns inboard but Short seemed in total control and relishing it. The presence of *Kestrel* on the weather beam was reassuring and Drinkwater called 'Carry on Mr Short,' over his shoulder as he slid down the companionway, leaving the startled Short gaping after him while the Frenchman turned forward, a worried frown on his face.

Below, Drinkwater began to ransack the cabin. It had two cots one of which was in use. He flung open a locker door and found some justification for his curiosity. Why did the skipper of a small lugger have a bullion-laden naval uniform, along with several other coats cut with the fashionable high collar?

With a sense of growing conviction Drinkwater pulled out

drawers and ripped the mattress off the cot. His heart was beating with excitement and it was no surprise when he found the strong box, carefully hidden under canvas and spunyarn beneath the stern settee. Without hesitation he drew a pistol and shot off the lock. Before he could open it Short was in the doorway, panting and eager for a fight.

To Drinkwater he looked ridiculous but his presence was reassuring.

'Obliged to you Mr Short but there's nothing amiss. I'm just blowing locks off this fellow's cash box,' Short grinned. 'If there's anything in it, Mr Short, you'll get your just deserts.'

'Aye, aye, sir.' Short closed the door and Drinkwater expelled his breath. At least with such a maniac on board there was little chance of being surprised by the enemy attempting to retake their ship. He dismissed the memory of similar circumstances aboard *Algonquin*. When one sailed close to the wind the occasional luff was easily dismissed. Provided one avoided a dismasting.

He opened the box. There was money in it. English money. Sovereigns, guineas and coins of small denominations. There were also a number of charts rolled up and bound with tape. They were charts of the English coast, hand-done on linen-backed paper with the carefully inscribed legend of the French Ministry of Marine. A small signal book with a handwritten code was tied up with a bundle of letters. These Drinkwater gave only a cursory glance, for something else had caught his eye, something which he might almost have imagined himself to have been looking for had not the notion been so improbable.

It was a single letter, written in a female hand on rice paper and bound with a thin plait of hair. Human hair.

And the hair was an unmistakable auburn.

Chapter Seven   December 1794–August 1795

An Insignificant Cruiser

Villaret Joyeuse escaped from Brest at Christmas dogged by
Warren and his frigates. In Portsmouth *Kestrel* lay in Haslar
Creek alongside the *Citoyenne Janine* while they awaited the
adjudication of the prize court. No decision was expected until
the New Year and as the officers of the dockyard seemed little
inclined to refit the cutter until then, *Kestrel*'s people were
removed into the receiving guardship, the *Royal William*.
Drinkwater took leave and spent Christmas with Elizabeth.
They were visited by Madoc Griffiths. The old man's obvious
discomfiture ashore was as amusing as it was sad, but by the
evening he was quite at ease with Elizabeth.

At the end of the first week in January the prize court decided
the two transports be sold off, the corvette purchased into the
service and the lugger also brought into the navy. Griffiths was
triumphant.

'Trumped their ace, by damn, Mr Drinkwater. Hoist 'em with
their own petards . . .' He read the judgement from a Portsmouth newspaper then grinned across the table, over the
remnants of a plum duff, tapping the wine-stained newsprint.

'I'm sorry, sir, I don't see how . . .'

'How I hoist 'em? Well the frigate captains had an agreement
to pool all prize money so that they shared an equal benefit from
any one individual on detached duty. I, being a mere lieutenant,
and *Kestrel* being a mere cutter, was neither consulted nor
included. As a consequence, apart from the commodore's share,
we will have exclusive rights to the condemned value of the
Citoyenne Janine. You should do quite handsomely, indeed you
should.'

'Hence the insistence I took the prize over . . .?'

'Exactly so.' Griffiths looked at his subordinate. He found
little of his own satisfaction mirrored there, riled that this rather
isolated moment of triumph should be blemished. In his
annoyance he ascribed Drinkwater's lack of enthusiasm to base
motives.

'By damn, Mr Drinkwater, surely you're not suggesting that as
I was sick you should receive the lion's share?' Griffiths's tone

was angry and his face flushed. Drinkwater, preoccupied, was suddenly aware that he had unintentionally offended.

'What's that, sir? Good God, no! Upon my honour sir . . .' Drinkwater came out of his reverie. 'No sir, I was wondering what became of those papers and charts I brought off her.'

Griffiths frowned. 'I had them despatched to Lord Dungarth. Under the circumstances I ignored Warren. Why d'ye ask?'

Drinkwater sighed. 'Well, sir, at first it was only a suspicion. The evidence is very circumstantial . . .' he faltered, confused.

'Come on, *bach*, if there's something troubling you, you had better unburden yourself.'

'Well among the papers was a private letter. I didn't pass it to you, I know I should have done, sir, and I don't know why I didn't but there was something about it that made me suspicious . . .'

'In what way?' asked Griffiths in a quietly insistent voice.

'I found it with a lock of hair, sir, auburn hair, I, er . . .' He began to feel foolish, suddenly the whole thing seemed ridiculously far fetched. 'Damn it, sir, I happen to think that the man who used the lugger, the man we're convinced is some kind of a French agent, is also connected with the red-haired woman we took off at Beaubigny.'

'That Hortense Montholon is in some kind of league with this Santhonax?'

Drinkwater nodded.

'And the letter?'

Drinkwater coughed embarrassed. 'I have the letter here, sir. I took it home, my wife translated it. It was very much against her will, sir, but I insisted.'

'And did it tell you anything, this letter?'

'Only that the writer and this Santhonax are lovers.' Drinkwater swallowed as Griffiths raised an interrogative eyebrow. 'And that the letter had been written to inform the recipient that a certain mutual obstacle had died in London. The writer seemed anxious that the full implications of this were conveyed in the letter and that it, in some way, made a deal of difference . . .'

'Who is the writer?' Griffiths asked quietly.

Drinkwater scratched his scar. 'Just an initial, sir, "H.",' he concluded lamely.

'Did you say *are* lovers?'

Drinkwater frowned. 'Yes sir. The letter was dated quite

recently, though not addressed.'

'So that if you are right and they were from this woman who is now resident in England she and Santhonax are maintaining a correspondence at the very least?'

'The letters suggested a closer relationship, sir.'

Griffiths suppressed a smile. Having met Elizabeth he could imagine her explaining the contents of the letter in such terms. 'I see,' he said thoughtfully. After a pause he asked, 'What makes you so sure that this Miss "H" is the young woman we took off at Beaubigny and what is the significance of this "mutual obstacle"?'

It was the question Drinkwater had been dreading but he was too far in now to retreat and he took encouragement from Griffiths's interest. 'I'm not sure, sir. It is a feeling I have had for some time . . . I mean, well as you know my French is poor, sir, limited to a few stock phrases, but at the back of my mind is the impression that she didn't want to come with us that night . . . that she was there on sufferance. I remember her standing up in the boat as we came off the beach and the French opened fire. She shouted something, something like "don't shoot, I'm your friend, I'm your friend!"' He tried to recall the events of the night. 'It ain't much to go on, sir, we were all very tired after Beaubigny.' He paused, searching Griffiths's face for some sign of contemptuous disbelief. The old man seemed sunk in reflection. 'As for the "obstacle",' Drinkwater plunged on, 'I just had this conviction that it was De Tocqueville . . .' He cleared his throat and in a firmer voice said, 'To be honest, sir, it's all very circumstantial and I apologise about the letter.' Drinkwater found his palms were damp but he felt the relief of the confessional.

Griffiths held his hand up. 'Don't apologise, *bach*, there may be something in what you say. When we mentioned the Montholons and Beaubigny to Major Brown something significant occurred to him. I don't know what it was but I am aware that this Captain Santhonax is not only an audacious officer but is highly placed enough to exert influence on French politics.' He paused. 'And I have often wondered why no action was ever taken after our broadside at Beaubigny. One can only assume that the matter was hushed up.' Griffiths lifted an eyebrow. 'Yet the French were damned touchy with Barlow and *Childers* a few weeks later . . .'

'That thought had occurred to me, sir.'

'Then we are of one mind, Mr Drinkwater,' said Griffiths closing the subject with a smile. Drinkwater relaxed, remembering Dungarth's words all those months ago. He began to see why Griffiths was regarded as a remarkable man. He doubted he could have told anyone else but the Welshman. The old lieutenant sat for a moment in silence, staring at the wine rings on the table cloth. Then he looked up. 'Do you return the letter to me, Mr Drinkwater. I'll inform his lordship of this. It may bear investigation.'

Relieved, Drinkwater rose and went to his cabin, returning to pass the letter to Griffiths.

'Thank you,' said the lieutenant, looking curiously at the thin plait of auburn hair. 'Well, Mr Drinkwater, out of your prize money I think you should purchase a new coat, your starboard shoulder tingle is well enough for sea service but won't do otherwise,' Griffiths indicated the repair he had effected to his coat. Elizabeth had already chid him for it. 'Take yourself to Morgan's, opposite the Fountain at number 85. You'll get yourself anything there, even another Dollond glass to replace that precious bauble you lost off Ushant . . .' They both laughed and Griffiths shouted at the messman, Meyrick, to come and clear the table.

Lieutenant Griffith's expectations of stratagems from Sir Sydney's fertile brain were to have a drastic effect upon the fortunes of *Kestrel* though not in the manner the old man had had in mind. Sir Sydney had conceived the idea that a French-built lugger attached to the squadron would prove a great asset in deceiving the enemy, plundering coastal trade and gathering intelligence. Her commander would be his own nomination in the person of Lieutenant Richard White, and *Kestrel*, with her unmistakably English rig, would be free for other duties.

Auguste Barrallier, now employed in the Royal Dockyard, arrived to authenticate the lugger's repairs and was affable to Drinkwater, watching progress from the adjacent cutter. Nathaniel did his best to disguise his pique when White arrived from Falmouth with a crew of volunteers from Warren's frigates. White, to his credit, made no attempts to lord over his old friend. He brought letters from Appleby and an air of breezy confidence that only a frigate cruising under an enterprising officer could engender. Appleby, it appeared, did not see eye to eye with this captain and White dismissed the surgeon with something like contempt. But Drinkwater was pleased when the lugger dropped out of sight behind Fort Blockhouse.

Her replacement as Warren's despatch vessel left *Kestrel* languishing between the greenheart piles in Haslar Creek through the still, chill grey days of January when news came of war with the Dutch. February passed and then, almost immediately it seemed, the windy equinoctials of March were over. A start had been made on removing the scars of her late action. But it was half-hearted, desultory work, badly done and Griffiths despaired, falling sick and passing to the naval hospital. Jessup took to the bottle and even Drinkwater felt listless and dispirited, sympathising with the bosun and affecting to ignore his frequent lapses.

Drinkwater's lassitude was due in part to a spiritual exhaustion after the action off the Île Vierge which combined with a helplessness consequent upon his conviction that a link existed between the mysterious Santhonax and Hortense Montholon. In sharing this suspicion with Griffiths, Drinkwater had sought to unravel it, imaging the old sea-officer might have some alchemical formula for divining such things. But this had proved foolish, and now, with Griffiths sick ashore and the authorities lacking interest in the cutter, Drinkwater felt oppressed by his helplessness, aground in a backwater of naval affairs that seemed to have no incoming tide to refloat his enthusiasm.

To some extent Elizabeth was to blame. Their proximity to Drinkwater's home meant that he took what leave he could. With Griffiths ashore his presence aboard *Kestrel* two or three times a week was sufficient. And the seduction of almost uninterrupted domestic life were sweet indeed. To pay for this lack of vigilance *Kestrel* lost six men to desertion and Drinkwater longed for orders, torn between Elizabeth and the call of duty.

Then, one sharp, bright April morning when the sun cracked over the roofs of Portsea with an expectant brilliance, a post captain came aboard, clambering over the rail from a dockyard boat unannounced, anonymous in plain clothes. He had with him a fashionably dressed and eccentric looking man who seemed familiar with the cutter.

It was Tregembo who warned Drinkwater and he had only learned from the grinning crew of the dockyard skiff that the gentlemen were of some importance. Some considerable importance in fact. Suddenly guilty, and thanking providence that this morning he had happened to be on board, Drinkwater hurried on deck, but the strangers were nowhere to be seen. Then a seaman popped out of the hold.

'Hey, sir, some bleeders down 'ere are poking about the bottom of the ship. One of 'em's a bleeding Frog unless I'm a Sumatran strumpet, sir . . .'

Bursting with apologies Drinkwater flung himself below to make his introductions. The intruders were dimly visible peering into *Kestrel*'s bilge having prised up a section of the ceiling.

'Good morning, gentlemen, please accept my . . . good lord! M'sieur Barralier is it not?'

'Ah! My young friend, 'ullo. I have not come to build you your frigate, alas, but this is Captain Schank, and we have come to, how you say – modify – your fine cutter.'

Drinkwater turned to the gentleman rising from his knees and brushing his breeches. Captain Schank waved aside his apologetic protestations and in five minutes repaired his morale and reinspired him.

Later that day in Haslar Hospital Drinkwater explained to Griffiths.

'What he does is this, sir. He reinforces the keel with cheeks, then he cuts slots like long mortices through which he drops these plates, centre plates he calls 'em. The idea's been used in America for some time, on a small scale, d'you see. Captain Schank saw them when he was master's mate but,' Drinkwater smiled ruefully, 'master's mates don't carry much weight in these matters.'

Griffith's brow wrinkled in concentration. 'Sort of midships leeboards, is it?'

'Aye, sir, that's it exactly,' replied Drinkwater nodding enthusiastically. 'Apparently you point up better to windward, haul your wind closer and reduce leeway significantly.'

'Wait,' interrupted Griffiths pondering, 'I recollect the name now. He built *Trial* like that in ninety or ninety-one. She and *Kestrel* were on the same lines. Yes, that's the man. *Trial*'s fitted with three of these, er, centre plates . . .' They began discussing the advantages it would give *Kestrel* and then Griffiths asked 'If they are doing all this have you got wind of any likely orders for us?'

Drinkwater grinned. 'Well, sir, nothing official, sir, but scuttlebutt has it that we're for the North Sea station, Admiral MacBride's squadron.'

It seemed to Nathaniel as he left the hospital that the news might restore Griffiths's health more rapidly than the doctors' physic.

The drawings spread over the cabin table slid to the deck from where the master shipwright recovered them, an expression of pained forbearance on his face. Captain Schank he knew and could tolerate, his post-rank was sufficiently awe-inspiring, but this younker who was no more than a master's mate: God preserve patient and professional craftsmen from the meddling of half-baked theorists.

'But if, as you say, it is the depth that's effective, sir, and the cutter's to work in shallow water, then a vertically supported plate might be very dangerous.' Drinkwater's imagination was coping with a vision of *Kestrel*'s extended keel digging into a sandbank, oversetting her and possibly splitting her keel. 'But if you had a bolt forward here,' he pointed to the plan, 'then it would hinge and could rise up into the casing without endangering the cutter.' He looked at the captain.

'What d'you think Mr Atwood?' The master shipwright looked over the pencil marks, an expression of scepticism on his face.

Drinkwater sighed with exasperation. Dockyard officers were beginning to rile him. 'Barrallier could do it, sir,' he said in a low voice. He thought he detected a half smile twitch Schank's face. Atwood's back stiffened. After a second or two of real attention to the plan he straightened up. 'It could be done, sir,' he ignored Drinkwater, 'but I don't want that Froggie whoremonger with his dancing master ways messing about with it . . .'

A day later they were warped alongside the sheer hulk and the mast was removed. Then they were hauled out. The work went well and a week later Griffiths reappeared with a cheerful countenance and a lightness of step that betrayed neither his age nor his recent indisposition.

He advised Drinkwater to air his best uniform coat, the new acquisition from Mr Morgan's 'We are invited to dine with Lord Dungarth, Mr Drinkwater, at the George . . . hey Merrick! God I'm getting old, why do the damned artificers always leave a job half finished, dismantling the companionways and leaving rickety ladders? Ah, Merrick, pass along my best uniform coat and air Mr Drinkwater's. Polish his best shoes and get some shark-skin for that damned murderous French skewer he calls a sword,' he turned to Drinkwater, all traces of fever absent from his face. 'I've a feeling there's more to tonight's meal than mere manners . . .' Drinkwater nodded, aware that Griffiths's instinct was usually uncannily accurate and glad to have the old man on board again.

The George Inn at Portsmouth was traditionally the rendezvous of captains and admirals. Lieutenants like Griffiths patronised the Fountain, while master's mates and midshipmen made a bear pit of the Blue Posts, situated next to the coach office. There were, therefore, a number of raised eyes when, amidst an unseasonal swirl of rain and wind, Griffiths and Drinkwater entered the inn and the removal of their cloaks revealed them as an elderly lieutenant and what appeared to be a passed over mate.

Their presence was explained by the appearance of Lord Dungarth who greeted them cordially. 'Ah, there you are gentlemen, pray be seated. Flip or stingo on such a wretched night? Well Madoc, what is it like wiping the arses of frigate captains after your independence, eh?'

Griffiths smiled ruefully. 'Well enough, my lord,' he said diplomatically. An elderly captain at the next table turned a deep puce with more than a hint of approaching apoplexy in it and muttered that the service was 'Going to the dogs.'

Dungarth went on heedlessly, an old, familiar twinkle in his eye. 'And you Nathaniel, I heard you took that lugger single-handed. An exaggeration I suppose?'

'Aye my lord, a considerable one I'm afraid.'

Dungarth went on, 'I suppose the dockyard are prevaricating with your refit in the customary fashion, eh?'

Griffiths nodded. 'Yes, my lord. I believe they consider us too insignificant a cruiser to take note of,' he said, a bright gleam in his eye and noting Dungarth cast significant glances at other officers in the room, several of whom Drinkwater recognised as dockyard superintendents.

'Insignificant!' exclaimed his lordship. 'Indeed. Damned crowd of peculating jobbers, rotten to the core. The greatest treason is to be found in His Majesty's dockyards, from time to time they hang an arsonist to assure their lordships of their loyalty . . .' Dungarth distributed the glasses. 'Your health gentlemen. Yes, you remark me well, one day they will receive their just deserts. You remember the *Royal George*, Nathaniel, aye and you've good cause to . . . Well gentlemen if you feel recovered from this damnable weather I've a fine jugged hare and a saddle of mutton awaiting you.' They emptied their glasses and followed Dungarth to a private room. Drinkwater was aware that their exit appeared most welcome.

Conversation remained light. Dungarth had dismissed his servants and they attended to themselves. As they finished the hare he announced 'I am expecting another guest before the night is out, but let the business of the evening wait upon his arrival, it is a long time since I set a t'gallant stuns'l even over a meal . . .'

They were attacking the mutton when a knock at the door occurred.

'Ah Brown, come and sit down, you know the company.'

Major Brown, smoothing his hair and muttering that the night was foul and diabolical for early June, nodded to the two naval officers. 'Your servant, my lord, gentlemen.

'Sit down, some of this excellent mutton? Madoc would you assist the major? Good . . .' Dungarth passed a plate. Drinkwater was aware that Griffiths's theory about the reason for their summons to dinner might be right. Major Brown had brought more than a waft of wet air into the room. Dungarth shed his familiar air and became crisply efficient. 'Well? D'ye find anything?'

Brown fixed Dungarth with a stare. 'Nothing of real significance. And you my lord?'

'No.' Dungarth looked at Griffiths and Drinkwater objectively, apparently forgetful that the last hour had been spent in genial conversation. He asked Nathaniel to pass another bottle from the sideboard then said: 'The information you forwarded, Madoc, that Nathaniel here found aboard the *chasse marée* confirms what we have for some time suspected, that Capitaine Santhonax is an agent of the French government with considerable contacts in this country. The later information that you submitted about Nathaniel's supposed link between him and the Montholon woman seems not to be so . . .' Drinkwater swallowed awkwardly.

'Hmm, the evidence was somewhat circumstantial my lord, I thought it my duty . . .'

'You did quite rightly. Do not reproach yourself. We took it seriously enough to send Brown here to ferret out the whereabouts of Miss Montholon since there had been other indications that your theory might not be as wild as it might first appear.' He paused and Drinkwater found his heart-beat had quickened. He waited patiently while Dungarth sipped his wine and dabbed his lips with a napkin.

'When De Tocqueville died in London it was given out that he had been robbed by footpads. He had been robbed all right, a considerable sum was found to be missing from his lodgings, not his person. They had also been ransacked. The count had been run through by a sword. Murdered; and in the subsequent search of his rooms, papers were discovered that indicated he had not only contracted a marriage with Miss Montholon but arranged for its solemnisation. The woman was therefore located living with the count's mother in Tunbridge Wells. Although there was an outpouring of grief it came, I believe, mainly from the mother . . . Major . . .'

Brown swallowed hastily and took up the tale. 'As I mentioned to you some time ago Santhonax was known to me as a *capitaine de frégate*, yet he has never held an independent command, always being on detached duty like myself. We know he is the head of naval intelligence for the Channel area and extensively employs *chasses marées*, like the one you captured, to make contact with his agents in this country. He is also bold enough to land, even, perhaps to spend some time in England . . .'

Brown chewed then swallowed a final mouthful and washed it down in complete silence. He continued: 'We believe him responsible for the death of De Tocqueville and your suggestion that there might be a connection with Mlle Montholon was most interesting.' He shrugged with that peculiar Gallic gesture that seemed so out of place. 'Though the letter you captured might confirm a suspicion it does not prove a fact, and to date surveillance has failed to indicate anything other than that Mlle Montholon is the unfortunate affianced of the late count who, in her present extremity, is a companion to her late lover's mother, herself widowed by the guillotine. I am told that their mutual grief is touching . . .' Brown's ironic tone led Drinkwater to assume that his own suspicions were not yet satisfied.

'But is Santhonax likely to continue his activities after losing his papers?' asked Griffiths.

'I do not think a man of his calibre and resource will lightly be deterred,' answered Dungarth. 'Besides, it depends how incriminating he regards what he lost. We are all hostages to fortune in this business but the odds against someone finding and identifying the letter and its writer must be very long. After all I doubt the lugger was the only one in the Channel that night with charts of our coasts, nor money. The gentlemen devoted to free trade might conceivably be similarly equipped . . .'

'But the uniform, my lord,' put in Drinkwater. Dungarth shrugged. 'I'll warrant Santhonax will not abandon his little projects over that, though doubtless whoever ordered his lugger to assist that convoy is now regretting his action. No, we'll back Nathaniel's hunch a little longer with surveillance on the De Tocqueville *ménage*. As for you fellows,' the earl leaned forward and fished in his tail pocket, drawing out a sealed packet, 'here are your orders to cruise in the Channel — in theory, against the enemy's trade. In fact I want you to stop every lugger, punt, smack and galley 'twixt the North Foreland and the Owers and search 'em. Perhaps we'll apprehend this devil Santhonax before more mischief occurs . . . Now Nat pass that bottle or, here, Madoc you are partial to sercial, those damned slaving days, I suppose.' The atmosphere changed, lightened a little as a sense of self-satisfaction embraced them.

'My lord,' said Griffiths at last, 'I should like to solicit your interest in favour of a commission for Mr Drinkwater here. Is there no way you might induce their lordships to reward a deserving officer?'

Drinkwater thrust aside a haze that was not entirely due to the tobacco smoke out of which he had been conjuring images of the beautiful Hortense.

Dungarth was shaking his head, his speech slurring slightly. 'My dear Madoc I would like nothing better than to oblige by confirming Nathaniel's commission but, by an irony, I am out of favour with the present Board having criticised Earl Howe's failure to stop that deuced grain fleet. Brown's intelligence was laid before the Board and they had plenty of warning that it should be stopped at all costs. We might have destroyed France at a blow.' Dungarth was leaning forward, his voice sharp and a cold fire in his hazel eyes. Then he sat back, slumping into his chair and brushing a weary hand across his forehead. 'But the pack of poxed fools ignored me and Brown's sojourn at the peril of his life was wasted . . .'

Later, splashing through puddles as the rain gurgled in drain-pipes and their white hose were spattered black; leaning together like sheer-legs, Griffiths and Drinkwater staggered back from the George. They had dined and drunk to excess and Griffiths kept muttering apologies that Dungarth had failed him in the matter of the commission while Nathaniel assured him with equal insistence that it did not matter. Drinkwater felt fortified against disappointment. The evening had brought him a kind of victory and in his drunken state his belief in providence was absolute. Providence had brought him to *Kestrel* and providence had had a hand in his presence at Beaubigny. Providence would see he had a lieutenant's cockade when it was due. And the ringing in his ears said the time was not yet.

It was only when they passed the momentary shelter of the dockyard gate and Griffiths roared the countersign at the sentry that it occurred to Nathaniel how foolish they must seem. And suddenly he wished he were in bed beside Elizabeth instead of lurching along in the wet and windy darkness supporting his increasingly heavy commander.

Chapter Eight   September–December 1795

The Black Pendant

The *Royal William*, receiving ship, was one of the oldest vessels in the British Navy. She had brought Wolfe's body home from Quebec and now played host to the bodies of unfortunate men waiting to be sent to ships. Like all such hulks she smelt, not the familiar living odour of a ship in commission but a stale, damp, rotting smell that spoke of stagnation, of neglect, idleness and despair. At the time of Drinkwater's visit she had nearly three hundred wretched men on board, from which *Kestrel* must replace her deserters. There were pressed men, Lord Mayor's men and quota men. There were even, God help them, volunteers, an isolated minority of social misfits with no other bolt hole to run to. There were disenchanted merchant sailors, home after long voyages and taken by the press or the patrolling frigates in The Soundings and sent into Portsmouth in the despatch boats. There were the pressed men, the pariahs, the drunks and the careless who had been caught by the officers of the Impress Service and brought by the tenders to be incarcerated on the *Royal William* until sent to ships. Here they were joined by village half-wits and petty thieves generously supplied by patriotic parish fathers as part of their quota. From London the debtors, felons, reprieved criminals and all the inadequate and pathetic flotsam of eighteenth-century society came fortnightly by the Tower tender. As a consequence the old ship groaned with misery, dirt, indiscipline and every form of vermin parasitic upon unwashed humanity. *Royal William* was little distinguishable from the prison hulks further up the harbour with her guard boats, gratings and sentries.

The regulating captain in charge of the Impress Service regarded Drinkwater with a jaundiced eye. For a moment or two Drinkwater could not understand the man's obvious hostility, then he recognised the apoplectic captain from the George the night they had dined with Dungarth.

'Six men! Six! Now where in the world d'you think I can find six men, God rot ye? And for what? A third rate? A frigate? No! But for some poxy little cutter whose officers spend their time ashore in ill-mannered abuse of their betters. No sir! You may think that because I have a deck full of hammocks I've men to spare. I don't doubt that suspicion had crossed your mind, but six men for an unrated cutter . . .' Drinkwater stood silently waiting for the man to finish blustering and cursing until, at last, he turned up a ledger, ran his finger down a column, shook his head and slammed the book shut.

'Scratch!' He shouted.

An obsequiously cowed clerk entered, dragging a misshapen foot behind him. 'Sir?'

'Present complement and dispositions please.'

'Ah, yes sir, er,' the man thought for a moment then rattled off, 'two hundred and ninety-one men on board sir. Sixty-two prime seamen, eighty-five with previous service, ninety-one mayor's men and fifty-three from the parishes. Er, three tailors among 'em, four blacksmiths, a locksmith, four cobblers, one apothecary under sentence for incest . . .' The man's eyes gleamed and Drinkwater was reminded of some carrion eater that subsisted on the dying bodies of ruined men.

'Yes, yes,' said the regulating captain testily, obviously considering his clerk was ruining his own case, 'now the dispositions.'

'Ah, yes, sir, well, most for Captain Troubridge on the *Culloden*, thrity-eight to go to Plymouth for *Engadine*, two dozen for *Pomone*, six to be discharged as unfit and the balance replacements for the Channel Fleet, sir, leaving a few odds and ends . . .'

'They will do us, sir,' suggested Drinkwater in an ill-timed remark that robbed the regulating captain of his triumph.

'Hold your damned tongue!' He snapped, nodding his thanks to the clerk. 'Now my young shaver, you perceive I do *not* have men to spare for your cutter. Tell your commander he can do his own recruiting. As far as I'm concerned the thing's impossible, quite impossible. My lieutenants are out scouring the country for the fleet, your damned cutter can go to the devil!' The regulating captain's face was belligerently red. He dismissed Drinkwater with a wave and the latter followed the sallow, misshapen little clerk in brown drab out of the cabin.

Furious Drinkwater made eagerly for the side, anxious to escape the stink of the ship when he felt a hand on his arm. 'Do not act so intemperately, young man, pray stay a moment.' The clerk's tone was all wheedling. 'For a consideration, sir,' he whined, 'I might be able to oblige a young gentleman . . .'

Drinkwater turned back, contempt rising in him like bile in the throat. Then he recalled the state of the cutter and the pressing need for those few extra men. He swallowed his dislike. Finding he had a couple of sovereigns on him he held one out to the clerk who took it in the palm of his hand and stared at it.

Drinkwater sighed and gave him the second coin. Like a gin-trap the man's hand closed on the gold and he spoke insolently. 'Now, young man we can perhaps do a little business . . . your name?' The clerk opened his book on an upright desk and ran a finger down a column of names, muttering to himself. He drew up a list and handed it to Drinkwater. 'There, Mr Drinkwater, six men for your cutter . . .' he chuckled wickedly, 'you might find the apothecary useful . . .'

'Send a boat for 'em in the morning,' said Griffiths, removing his hat and sitting heavily. Meyrick brought in a pot of coffee and a letter. Griffiths opened it and snorted. 'Huh! and about time too. It seems we are at last to be manned on the proper establishment,' his face dropped, 'oh . . .'

'What is it, sir?'

'You . . . you are to sail as master, your acting commission will be revoked. As we are no longer on special service only one commissioned officer is required.' Griffiths lowered the letter. 'I am very sorry.'

'But we are operating under Dungarth's orders,' said Drinkwater bitterly.

Griffiths shook his head, 'Nominally we're part of MacBride's squadron now, clerks, Mr Drinkwater, the bloody world is run by clerks.'

Drinkwater felt a terrible sense of disappointment. Just when *Kestrel*'s fortunes seemed to offer some promise after the long sojourn in the dockyard this news came.

'No matter, sir. What is to be our complement?' he asked hurriedly, eager for distraction.

'Er, myself, you as sailing master, two mates, Jessup, Johnson the carpenter, a warrant gunner named Traveller, a purser named Thompson and a surgeon named Appleby.'

'Appleby?'

'God, man, we're going to be damned cramped.'

The six men sent from the *Royal William* were a pathetic group.

They were not, by any stretch of the imagination, seamen. Even after three days on board Short's starter and Jessup's rattan had failed to persuade them that they were in the navy. Above his head Drinkwater could hear the poor devils being roundly abused as he discussed the final stowing of the cutter's stores and powder with Jessup. Already he forsaw the course events would take. They would be bullied until one of them would be provoked into a breach of discipline. The flogging that would inevitably follow would brutalise them all. Drinkwater sighed, aware that these things had to be.

'Well, Mr Jessup, we'll have to conclude these arrangements in the gunner's absence. I just hope he's graced us with his presence by the time we're ready to sail.'

'Aye sir, he'll be here. I seen him last evening Gosport side, but Jemmy Traveller is like to be last to join. His wife runs a pie shop near the ordnance yard. Jemmy's always busy counting shillings and making guineas.'

'So you know him?'

Jessup nodded. 'Aye with him in the *Edgar*. With Lord Rodney when we thrashed the Dons in eighty.'

'The Moonlight Action?'

'Aye, the same.'

'I remember ...' But Drinkwater's reminiscences were abruptly curtailed by a shout on deck.

'Hey, sirrah! What in God's name d'you think you're about! Instruct the man, thrashing him is of no use.'

'What the devil?' Drinkwater leapt up and made for the companionway. He reached the deck as a portly man climbed awkwardly down from the rail. The familiar figure of Appleby stood scowling at Short.

'Ah, Nathaniel, I'm appointed surgeon to this, this,' he gestured extravagantly round him and gave up. Then he shot a black look at Short. 'Who's this damned lubber?'

The bosun's mate was furious at the intrusion. Veins stood out on his forehead as he contained his rage, the starter dangling from his wrist vibrated slightly from the effort it was costing Short.

'This is Short, Mr Appleby, bosun's mate and a first-class seaman.' Drinkwater took in the situation at a glance, aware that his reaction was crucial both to discipline and to those petty factions that always cankered in an over-crowded man o'war.

'Very well, Mr Short, if they cannot yet splice you must remember it takes time to make a real seaman of a landlubber.' He smiled at Short, who slowly perceived the compliment, and turned to the new hands who were beginning to realise Appleby might prove an ally. Drinkwater spoke sharply but not unkindly. 'You men had better realise your duty is plain and you're obliged to attend to it or take the consequences. These can be a deal more painful than Mr Short's starter or Mr Jessup's cane . . .' He left the sentence in mid air, hoping they would take heed of it. Comprehension began to spread across the face of one of them and Drinkwater grasped Appleby's elbow and propelled him aft. He felt the surgeon resist then succumb. Reaching the companionway Drinkwater called forward, 'Mr Short! Have those men get the surgeon's traps aboard, lively now!'

Appleby was slightly mollified by this piece of solicitude and his natural sociability gave way to Drinkwater's distracting barrage of questions.

'So what happened to *Diamond*? How's the squadron managing without us? How much prize money has Richard White made? What on earth are you doing here? I wondered if it was to be you when Griffiths mentioned the name, but I couldn't see you exchanging out of a frigate for our little ship.' Appleby felt himself shoved into a tiny box of a cabin and heard his young friend bawl for coffee. Drinkwater laughed as he saw the expression the surgeon's face. Appleby was taking in his surroundings.

'I manage to fit,' grinned Drinkwater, 'but a gentleman of your ample build may find it something of a squeeze. This is my cabin, yours is across the lobby.' Drinkwater indicated the doorway through which the landsmen were just then lugging Appleby's gear. Appleby nodded, his chins doing a little rippling dance eloquent of disappointment. 'Better than that claustrophobic, blasted frigate,' he said rather unconvincingly. 'All that glitters is not, etcetera, etcetera,' he joked feebly.

Drinkwater raised his eyebrows. 'You surprise me. I thought Sir Sydney a most enterprising officer.'

'A damned eccentric crank, Nathaniel. The frigate was fine, but Sir William festering Sydney had a lot of damned fool ideas about medicine. Thought he could physic the sick better than I . . . used to call me a barber, confounded insolence, and me a warrant surgeon before he was a midshipmite. Ouch! This coffee's damned hot.'

Drinkwater laughed again. 'Ah, I recollect you don't like intruders, no more than we do here, Harry,' he said pointedly. For a minute Appleby looked darkly at his friend, stung by the implied rebuke. Then Drinkwater went on and he forgot his wounded pride. 'By the way, d'you remember that fellow we brought ashore wounded at Plymouth?'

Appleby frowned, 'Er, no . . . yes, a Frenchman wasn't he? You brought a whole gang of 'em out, including a woman if I recollect correctly.'

'That's right,' Drinkwater paused, but Appleby brushed aside the memory of Hortense.

'I take it from your self-conceit the patient survived?'

'Eh? Oh, yes, but he succumbed to assault in the streets of London.'

'Tch, tch, now you will appreciate my own despair when I exhaust myself patching you firebrands up, only to have you repeatedly skewering yourselves.'

They sipped their coffee companionably but it was not difficult to see that poor Appleby had become a most prickly shipmate.

'And what is our commander like?' growled Appleby.

'Excellent, Harry, truly excellent. I hope you like him.' Appleby grunted and Drinkwater went on wrily, 'It is only fair to warn you that he is quite capable of probing for a splinter or a ball.'

Appleby gave a sigh of resignation then wisely changed the subject.

'And you, I mean we, no longer poach virgins off the French coast, I assume? That seemed to be the opinion current in the squadron when this cutter cropped up in conversation.'

Drinkwater laughed again. 'Lord no! It'll be all routine stuff now. We're fleet tender to Admiral MacBride's North Sea Fleet. It'll be convoys and cabbages, messages, tittle-tattle and perhaps, if we're very lucky, a look into Boulogne or somewhere. All damned boring I shouldn't wonder.'

Appleby did not need to know about Dungarth's special instructions. After all he had only just joined. He was not yet one of the Kestrels.

'Your standing at Trinity House must be high, Mr Drinkwater,' said Griffiths, 'they have approved the issue of a warrant without recourse to further examination. The Navy Board have acted with uncommon speed too,' he added with a significant glance at Drinkwater implying *Kestrel* should not suffer further delay. 'Now Mr Appleby?'

'These new men are infested, sir,' complained the surgeon, referring to the draft received from the *Royal William*. Griffiths looked wearily back at the man.

'Aye, Mr Appleby and that won't be all they've got. What d'you suggest we do, send 'em back, is it?'

'No sir, we'll douse them in salt water, ditch their clothing and issue slops . . .' He trailed off.

'Now Mr Appleby, do you attend to your business and I'll attend to mine. Your sense of outrage does your conscience credit but is a disservice to your professional reputation.'

Drinkwater watched Appleby sag like a pricked balloon. No, he thought, he is not yet one of us.

The keen clean Channel breeze came over the bow as they stood down past the guardship at the Warner and on through the anchored warships at St Helen's, their ensign dipping in salute and the spray playing over the weather rail and hissing merrily off to leeward. Apart from an ache in his heart at leaving Elizabeth, Drinkwater was glad to have left Portsmouth, very glad.

'Very well, Mr Drinkwater . . .' It was Jeremiah Traveller, a mirror image of Jessup, who, as gunner took a deck watch releasing Nathaniel from the repressive regime of four hours on deck and four below which he and Jessup had hitherto endured. They called the hands aft as eight bells struck and then, the watch changed, he slid below.

In his cabin he took out his journal, turning the pages of notes and sketches made in Portsmouth, a myriad of dockyard details, all carefully noted for future reference. He stared at his drawing of the centre plates. Beating out of Portsmouth they had already felt the benefit of those. Opening his inkwell he picked up the new steel pen that he had bought at Morgan's. *Kestrel* was already a different ship. With a cabin full of officers at meal times the old intimacy was gone. And Appleby had driven a wedge between Drinkwater and Griffiths, not intentionally, but his very presence seemed to turn Griffiths in upon himself and the greater number of officers increased the isolation of the commander.

Drinkwater sighed. The halcyon days were over and he regretted their passing.

Autumn gave way to the fogs of November and the first frosts, these periods of still weather were linked by a dreary succession of westerly gales that scudded up Channel to force them to reef hard and run for cover.

They had no luck with Dungarth's commission though they stopped and searched many coastal craft and chased others. Drinkwater began to doubt his earlier convictions as ridiculous imaginings. The wily Santhonax had disappeared, or so it seemed. From time to time Griffiths went ashore and although he shared fewer confidences with Nathaniel now, he did not omit to convey the news. A brief shake of the head was all that Drinkwater needed to know the quarry had gone to earth.

Then, during the tail of a blow from south-west, as the wind veered into the north-west and the sky cleared to patchy sunshine, as Drinkwater dozed the afternoon watch away in his cot, the cabin door flew open.

'Zur!' It was Tregembo.

'Eh? What is it?' he sat up blinking.

'Zur, cap'n compliments, an' we've a lugger in sight, zur. She's a big 'un an' Lieutenant Griffiths says to tell 'ee that if your interested, zur, she's got a black swallowtail pendant at her masthead . . .'

'The devil she has,' said Drinkwater throwing his legs over the cot and feeling for his shoes. Sleep left him instantly and he was aware of Tregembo grinning broadly.

Chapter Nine December 1795

The Star of the Devil

Drinkwater rushed on deck. Griffiths was standing by the starboard rail, white hair streaming in the wind, his face a hawk-like mask of concentration on the chase, the personification of the cutter's name. Bracing himself against the scend of the vessel Drinkwater levelled his glass to starboard.

Both lugger and cutter were running free with *Kestrel* cracking on sail in hot pursuit. Drinkwater watched the altering aspect of the lugger, saw her grow just perceptibly larger as *Kestrel* slowly ate up the yards that separated them. Almost without conscious thought his brain was resolving a succession of vectors while his feet, planted wide on the planking, felt *Kestrel*'s response to the straining canvas aloft.

Drinkwater could see a bustle on the stern of the lugger and was trying to make it out when Griffiths spoke from the corner of his mouth.

'D'you still have that black pendant on board?'

'Yes sir, it's in the flag locker.'

'Then hoist it . . .'

Drinkwater did as he was bid, mystified as to the significance of his actions and the importance of Brown's bit of 'Celtic nonsense'. But to Griffiths the black flag of the Breton held a challenge to his heart, it was he or Santhonax and he acknowledged the encounter in single combat.

There was a sound like tearing calico. A well-pointed ball passed close down the starboard side and Drinkwater could see the reason for the bustle aft. The lugger's people had a stern chaser pointing astern. Through his glass he could see her gun crew reloading and a tall man in a blue coat staring at them through a telescope. As he lowered the glass to address an officer next to him Drinkwater saw the face in profile. The dark, handsome features and the streaming curls, even at a distance, were unmistakably those of Santhonax.

Beside him Griffiths breathed a sigh of confirmation.

'Now Mr Traveller,' he said to the gunner, 'let us see whether having you on board improves our gunnery.'

Jeremiah Traveller rolled forward, his eyes agleam. The

Kestrels had been at General Quarters since they sighted the lugger and every man was at taut as a weather backstay. Although her ports were closed to prevent water entering the muzzles, the gun crews were ready, their slow matches smouldering in the linstocks and the breeches charged with their lethal mixture of fine milled powder and the most perfect balls the gun captains could find in the racks. Now they watched Traveller elbow aside the captain of Number 1 gun and lower himself to sight along the barrel.

Drinkwater cast his eyes aloft. The huge mainsail was freed off to larboard, the square top and topgallant sails bowed their yards, widened by stunsails, and the weather clew of the running course was set. *Kestrel*, with a clean bottom, had rarely sailed better, tramping the waves underfoot and scending down their breaking crests.

A movement forward caught his attention and he watched Traveller straighten up, the linstock in his hand, waiting for the moment to fire. Swiftly Drinkwater clapped his glass to his eye. The stern of the lugger swung across the lens, her name gold on blue scrollwork: *Étouile du Diable*.

The report of the bow chaser rolled aft and Drinkwater saw a hole appear in the chase's mizen. Then her stern chaser fired and through his feet he felt the impact strike the hull.

'*Myndiawl!*' growled Griffiths beside him.

'We're overhauling him fast, sir,' said Drinkwater by way of reassurance. He felt a sense of unease emanating from the commander and began to divine the reason. Santhonax could haul his wind in a moment. *Kestrel*, with her squaresails set, would take much longer.

Traveller fired again and a cheer from forward told of success. The mizen yard sagged in two pieces, the sail collapsing and flogging. The triumph was illusory and Griffiths swore again. That loss of sail would the sooner compel Santhonax to turn to windward.

'Get the course and kites in Mr Drinkwater,' snapped Griffiths.

'In t'gallant stuns'ls . . .' Drinkwater began bawling orders. Men left each gun and swarmed aloft to handle the sails and rig in the booms. Short chivvied them up. A cluster gathered round the mast, tallying on to the ropes under Jessup's direction, a group on the downhauls and sheets, a couple to ease the tacks and halliards. Drinkwater saw Jessup's nod.

'Shorten sail!' Forward Traveller fired again but Drinkwater was watching the stunsails belly forward, lifting their booms.

'Steady there,' said Griffiths quietly to the helmsman. A broach now would be disastrous. The men on deck tramped away with the downhauls and sheets and the stunsails came down, flapping on to the deck like wounded gulls.

Vaguely aware of a second thump into the hull and a patch of blue sky through the topsail Drinkwater ordered in the topgallant.

'There she goes,' shouted Griffiths as *Étoile du Diable* swung to starboard, briefly exposing her stern. 'Fire as you bear!' he called to the gun captains, left by their charges as their crews shortened sail.

But as he turned Santhonax's stern chaser roared, double shotted. The ball skipped once on a wave top, smashed through *Kestrel*'s starboard rail and clove both helmsmen in two.

Griffiths leapt to the tiller and leant his weight against it.

'Leggo weather braces! Haul taut the lee! Man the sheets there!' He pushed down on the big tiller and brought *Kestrel* round in the wake of the lugger.

It was as well he did so for as he passed Santhonax fired his starboard broadside. Most of the shot plunged into the smooth, green with the upwellings from her rudder, that trailed astern of *Kestrel*'s turning hull. But two balls struck the cutter, one demolishing four feet of cap and ruff tree rail, the other opened the muzzle of Number 11 gun like a grotesque iron flower.

Drinkwater had the topgallant in its buntlines and until he doused the topsail *Kestrel* would not point as close to the wind as the lugger. Already the alteration of course had increased the apparent wind speed over the deck. Spray was coming aboard now as *Kestrel* began to drop back from the chase, the angle between them widening.

It seemed an age before the squaresails were secured. Forward Traveller and the headmost gun captains were ganging away. Johnson, the carpenter, was hovering at Griffiths's elbow. 'He's hulled us, sir, I'll get a man on the pump . . .' Griffiths nodded.

'Sail shortened, sir.'

'Harden right in, Mr Drinkwater, and lower those bloody centre plates.'

'Aye, aye, sir!'

Kestrel hauled her wind as close as possible, narrowing the angle with the lugger. The chase ran on for an hour in a westerly direction and pointing their pieces carefully the gunners of both ships continued their duel. The Kestrels cheered several times as splinters were struck from the rail of the lugger but their hearts were no longer in the fight.

Drinkwater had a sight of the deck of the *Étoile du Diable* as she heeled over to larboard, exposing the view. Even with all the quoins out they were having trouble pointing their guns while the Kestrels had all theirs rammed in to level their own cannon and the labour of hauling their carriages uphill against the list. Three men had gone below to Appleby nursing splinter wounds when a shot from the *Étoile du Diable*, fired below the horizontal, ricochetted off the face of a wave and hit *Kestrel*'s starboard chain-whale from below. The *lignum vitae* deadeye of the after mainmast stay was shattered and the lanyard parted. A second ball carried away the topmast stay and a sudden crack from aloft showed the topmast tottering slowly to larboard.

'Goddamn . . . cut that away!' But Drinkwater was already rushing forward, leaping into the weather rigging with an axe. The passage of a final ball winded him and left him clinging trembling to the lower shrouds, gasping for breath like a fly in a web. He felt the shrouds shudder as the topmast tore down the lee side, shaking the mast and carrying the yards with it. A stunsail boom end caught the mainsail and opened a small split which slowly enlarged itself. The wreckage fell half in the water, half on the larboard waist. *Kestrel* lost way.

She was beaten.

On the starboard bow *Étoile du Diable* drew ahead. Upon her quarter stood Santhonax with his plumed hat in his hand.

He waved it over his head. Then he jumped down amongst the gunners who had served the still smoking stern chaser.

'*Cythral*,' muttered Griffiths, his eyes glittering after the enemy. 'Let fly the sheets!' he shouted.

Drinkwater climbed down to the deck.

'Mr Drinkwater!'

'Sir?'

'Secure what you can of that gear overside.' Their eyes met in disappointment.

' "Pride cometh before a fall", Mr Drinkwater. See what you can do.'

'Aye, aye, sir.'

Drinkwater went forward again. Leaning over the side he surveyed the raffle of spars, canvas and cordage, of blocks and ironwork. And something else.

At the trailing masthead, one end of its halliard broken and dragging along the cutter's side, was the black swallowtail pendant, mocking them.

PART TWO

The North Sea

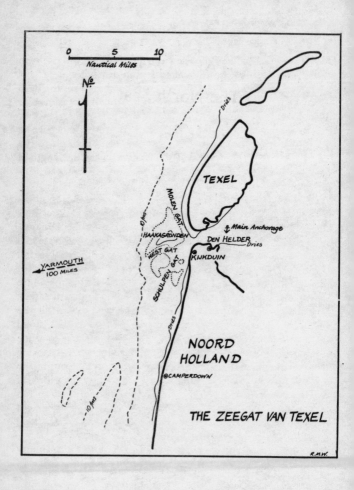

THE ZEEGAT VAN TEXEL

Chapter Ten December 1795–November 1796

The Apothecary

Short drew back his well-muscled arm then brought the cat down on the man's back. 'Seven!' called Jessup dispassionately.

The red weals that lay like angry cross hatching over the flesh were suppurating and blood began to ooze from the broken skin.

'Eight!'

Drinkwater could see the man's face in profile from where he stood by the starboard runner. Although he bit hard on the leather pad the victim's eyes glared forward, along the length of the gig across the transom of which he was spreadeagled.

'Nine!'

The inevitable had happened. The offender was the apothecary embarked from the *Royal William* and named Bolton. Bolton seemed unwilling or unable to make the best of his circumstances. He appeared to be a man penned up within a private hell that left him no rest. Appleby called him 'an human pustule, full of corrupt fluid and ripe for lancing'. He went about heedless of his surroundings to the point of apathy, tough enough to endure Short's abuse and starting without a word or apparent effect. What seemed to Short to be intransigence attracted all the bosun's mate's bullying fury. Short was unused to such stolid indifference and when violence failed he had recourse to crude innuendo. He found his barbs reached their mark. Ransacking every corner of his mind for human failings, he scoured the depths of every depravity, insensitive to the changing look of increasing desperation in Bolton's eyes. Pursued, Bolton ran until at last, flushed from cover, he turned at bay. Short had got there in the end over some clumsiness at gun drill, some trivial thing for which he had been waiting.

'Bolton! You crap-brained child-fucker . . .' And the rammer had swung round, driven into Short's guts with a screech of mortification from Bolton.

'Twelve!' Short was panting now, the bruise in his midriff paining him. Harris, the second bosun's mate, relieved him, taking the cat and running the tails through his left hand, squeezing out the blood and plasma. Harris spread his legs and drew back his arm.

'Thirteen!'

They were all on deck. Griffiths, Drinkwater and Traveller with their swords, the hands ranged in the waist, their faces dull, expressionless.

'Fourteen!'

Kestrel lay hove-to, her staysail aback. There had been no waiting for the punishment. They had only just secured the guns at which they had been exercising. In a cutter there were no bilboes and Griffiths ordered the flogging immediately.

'Fifteen!'

The sentence had been three dozen lashes. Already the man's back was a red and bloody mess. He was whimpering now. Broken. Drinkwater felt sickened. Although Griffiths was no tyrant and Nathaniel recognised the need to keep order, no amount of flogging would make a seaman out of Bolton. God alone knew what ailed the man, though Drinkwater had heard from the misshapen clerk on the receiving ship he had been sentenced for incest. But whatever madness or torment hounded him he had taken enough now. The punishment should be suspended and Drinkwater found himself staring at Griffiths, willing him to stop it.

'Sixteen!' A low, animal howl came from Bolton which Drinkwater knew would rise to a scream before the man lost consciousness. Whatever guilt lay on the man's soul he expiated it now, slowly succumbing to the rising pain of his opened back.

'Seventeen!'

'Belay there!' Griffiths's voice whipped out. A ripple of relief ran through the assembled people. 'That'll do, cut him down, pipe the watch below, Mr Jessup!'

Drinkwater saw Bolton stiffen as a bucket of sea water was thrown over his back. Then he fainted. Appleby came forward to attend him. Drinkwater turned away.

'Leggo weather staysail sheet, haul taut the lee!'

Was there a perceptible resentment in the way the order was obeyed? 'Lively now! 'Vast and belay!' He walked aft. Or was he too damned sensitive?

'Steer north by east.'

'Nor' by east it is, sir.'

Kestrel steadied on her course and made after the convoy.

She had not been a happy ship since she had left Portsmouth. Her officers were a discordant mixture of abrasive characters.

Appleby's pompous superiority which suited the bantering atmosphere of a crack frigate's gunroom was out of place here. Even Drinkwater found him difficult at times, for age and bachelorhood had not moderated his tendency to moralise. Griffiths had withdrawn as Drinkwater had known he would and their former intimacy was in abeyance. Jessup and Traveller, old acquaintances of long standing and great experience, employed their combined talents to prick Appleby's self-esteem, while the two master's mates, Hill and Bulman, both promoted quartermasters, survived by laughing or scowling as occasion seemed to demand.

Drinkwater felt a sense of personal isolation and took refuge in his books and journal, maintaining a friendship with Appleby when the latter was amenable but quietly relieved that his tiny cabin allowed him an oasis of privacy. This disunity of the officers spilled forward to combine with a growing resentment among the men over lack of pay and for whom the small, wet cutter was a form of purgatory.

They had weathered the great gale of mid-November shortly after their arrival in the Downs and barely a fortnight later learned of the mutiny on the *Culloden*. There had been an exchange of knowing looks round *Kestrel*'s cabin when Appleby had read the newspaper report, but the unreported facts sent a shiver of resentment through the crew.

The news that the authorities had agreed to favour the mutineers' petition without punishment had been followed by information that the law had exacted its terrible penalty. Imagination conjured a picture of the jerking bodies, run aloft by their own shipmates in all the awful guilt-sharing ceremonial of a naval execution while the marine drummers played the *rafale* and the picket trained their levelled muskets on the seaman. In the atmosphere prevalent aboard the cutter it was an image that lingered unbidden.

Griffiths looked aft over the transom and jolly boat in its stern davits. Above his head the ensign drooped like a rag but the morning, though chill, was fresh. A mood of mild enthusiasm infused Madoc Griffiths and he wondered if it was the effect of the man beside him. Drinkwater spoke with an old lilt in his voice, a tone that had been absent for some time now.

'I've given the matter a deal of thought, sir, and I reckon that it ain't unreasonable to bring Bolton aft as an additional messman. The mess is damned crowded, Merrick could do with some assistance and Short is still plotting against Bolton . . . pending your approval, of course, sir . . .'

Griffiths nodded. 'Very well, Mr Drinkwater, see to it. Glad I am that you are mindful of the hands. It is not always possible for a commander since he has other things to concern him, but it should be the prime consideration of his second. 'Tis a pity more do not follow your example.'

Drinkwater coughed with embarrassment. He was simply determined to do whatever lay in his power to ameliorate the condition of Bolton, the most abused and useless of *Kestrel*'s company. Here the man might be induced to assist Appleby medicinally and give his mind something to work on beyond its own self-consuming preoccupation. And perhaps thereby Drinkwater might stem the rot that he instinctively felt was destroying the cohesion of them all.

'See to that at once, Mr Drinkwater, and when you have done so sway out both gigs, run the larboard broadside out and the starboard in as far as the breechings will permit. It's a grand day for scraping the weed from the waterline and there'll be no wind before nightfall.'

If the mood of his sailing master had lightened his heart Lieutenant Griffiths did not find that of his surgeon so enjoyable. He looked up at Appleby an hour later from a table split by sunny squares let in through the skylight while from overside the rasp of bass brushes attacked the weed.

'He's not yet fit to return to duty,' said Appleby cautiously.

'Who is not fit, Mr Appleby? Bolton is it?'

'Yes sir,' said Appleby, aware that Griffiths was being deliberately obtuse.

'The man I had flogged?'

'Yes sir. He took it badly. At least three of Short's stripes were low, one seems to have damaged the left kidney.' Griffiths's face was expressionless. 'There has been some internal haemorrhaging, passing out with the man's urine, he's weak and the fever persists.'

'So cosset him, doctor, until he's fit again.'

'Yes sir.' Appleby stood his ground.

'Is there something else?'

'Sir, I . . .' Perspiration stood like pearls on Appleby's forehead as he balanced himself against the increasing list induced by the gun trucks squealing overhead as they prepared to scrape the other side. 'I was sorry that you found it necessary to flog Bolton, sir, his state of mind concerns me. I had thought you a most humane officer . . .'

'Until now?' asked Griffiths sharply, his eyebrows knitting together in a ferocious expression made more terrifying by the colour mounting to his cheeks. Appleby's courage was tested and, though his chins quivered gently, he lowered his head in silent assent.

With an effort Griffiths mastered himself and rose slowly to his feet, expelling breath in a long, low whistle. He leaned forward resting himself on his hands.

'Mr Appleby, indiscipline is a most serious crime in a man of war, especially when striking a superior is concerned . . .' He held up a hand to stop Appleby's protest. 'Provocation is no mitigation. That too is in the nature of things. We live in a far from perfect world, Mr Appleby, a fact that you should by now have come to terms with. As commander I am not permitted the luxury of sympathising with the individual.' Griffiths looked significantly at Appleby. 'Even the well-intentioned may sometimes be misguided, Mr Appleby.' He paused, allowing the implication to sink in. The surgeon's mouth opened and then closed again, Griffiths went on.

'There is some deep unhappiness in Bolton. Ah, you are surprised I noticed, eh? Nevertheless I did,' Griffiths smiled wryly. 'And Short tripped the spring of some rare device in his brain. Well Short has a sore belly as a consequence, see, so some justice had been done. I appreciate your concern but, if Bolton is a rotten apple you must see *Kestrel* as little more than a barrel full of ripe ones.' Griffiths paused and, just as Appleby opened his mouth to speak, added 'I offer this explanation not to justify myself but out of respect for your intelligence.'

Appleby grunted. He knew Bolton's insubordination could not go unpunished but he felt the case justified a court-martial at a later date. Griffiths's summary justice had clashed with his professional opinion. By way of rebuke Griffiths added 'Mr Drinkwater has suggested that Bolton comes aft as an additional messman. I am sorry that the suggestion did not come from you.'

Griffiths watched Appleby leave the cabin. It was strange how two men could take alarm from the same cause and react so differently as a result. Or was it his own reactions that were so disparate? Prejudice and partiality played such a large part in the affairs of men it was impossible to say.

Christmas and the arrival of 1796 passed almost unnoticed by the crew of *Kestrel*. They had not been long left independent and a peremptory order to join Admiral MacBride in the Downs had put paid to their chasing in the Channel after the mauling they had received from the *Étoile du Diable*. Although they did not know it at the time the failure of Dungarth's department to locate the mysterious Capitaine Santhonax had brought him into worse odour with their Lordships than his remonstrances over Howe's failure to turn Brown's intelligence reports to good account in 1794. As a consequence *Kestrel* found herself employed on pedestrian duties. In company with the ship-sloop *Atropos* the cutter was assigned to convoy work. From the Thames to the Tyne and back again with two score or so of colliers, brigs and barques, all commanded by hard case Geordie masters with independent views was, as Nathaniel had predicted, boring work. It could be humiliating too. When *Kestrel* was ordered up to Leith Road to escort the crack passenger and mail smack to London with a cargo of gold, the packet master treated the occasion as a race. With a prime crew protected by press exemption and a reputation for smart passages, the smack proved a formidable opponent. She had a fuller hull than her escort and properly should have been beaten by the man o' war cutter. But *Kestrel* carried her mainsail away off Flamborough Head while the smack drove on and left her hull down astern of the packet. Had not the wind hauled to the south-east and *Kestrel* not been able to point harder by virtue of her new centre plates, they might never have seen their charge again. As it was they caught her by the Cockle Gatt and stormed through Yarmouth Roads neck and neck with the flood tide under them.

During the summer they had idled round the dispersed herring fleet in the North Sea on fishery protection. Sickened by a diet of herrings, all chance of action seemed to elude them. Only twice did they have to chase off marauders, both Dutch and neither very eager. The expected depredations of French corsairs never materialised and it was confidently asserted that a nation that subsisted on snails and frogs was unlikely to have the sense to favour herrings. In reality French privateers found richer pickings in the Channel.

The war was going badly for Britain. In January Admiral Christian's West Indies expedition was severely mauled by bad weather and dispersed. In February a Dutch squadron got out of the Texel and then, in late summer Spain went over to the French camp in an uneasy alliance.

At the conclusion of the fishing season *Kestrel* was ordered to refit before the onset of winter, the weatherly cutters being better ships to keep the sea than larger, more vulnerable units of the fleet. Along with these orders came news that Sir Sydney Smith had been taken prisoner on a boat expedition.

It brought a measure of personal satisfaction to Harry Appleby.

Leaning on the rail Drinkwater stared across the muddy waters of the Medway, over the flat extreme of the Isle of Grain to the Nore lightvessel, a half smile on his face

'What the deuce are you grinning at, Nat?' Drinkwater's reverie was abruptly shattered by the portly bulk of Appleby.

'Nothing Harry, nothing.' He crackled the letter in his pocket.

'Thinking of Elizabeth no doubt.' Appleby looked sideways. 'Ah you are surprised our worthy commander is not the only person capable of divining others' thoughts,' he added with a trace of bitterness, 'and the symptoms of love have long been known. Oh, I know you think I'm good only for sawing off limbs and setting broken bones, but there's little enough of that to occupy me so that I am reduced to observing my fellows.'

'And what have you observed of late then?'

'Why, that you have received a letter from Elizabeth and will be looking for some furlough before we sail.' 'Is that all?' replied Drinkwater with mock disappointment. 'No my friend, I doubt there'll be time for leave, Griffiths is eager to be gone. Ah, but it's a beautiful morning ain't it?' he added, sniffing to windward.

'Nat.' Appleby was suddenly serious.

'Uh?' Drinkwater turned abstractedly, 'what is it?'

'I have also been observing Bolton. What d'ye make of him?'

'Bolton?' Drinkwater frowned. 'He seems well enough content since we brought him aft. Surely you're in a better position to answer your own question since he's been pounding pestle and mortar in your service.'

Appleby shook his head. 'No. I mean the inner man. What d'ye make of the inner man?'

Drinkwater's pleasant introspection following the arrival of

Elizabeth's letter was gone beyond recall. He sighed, slightly resentfully.

'For heaven's sake, Harry, come to the point.'

'Do you know what passed between Bolton and Short the afternoon they had their altercation?'

Drinkwater hesitated. He had not mentioned Bolton's crime aboard *Kestrel*. The relish with which the twisted clerk had mentioned it had sickened Nathaniel. He had had no desire to promulgate such gossip. He shook his head. 'No. Do you?'

Appleby's chins quivered in negation. 'I gather it was some sort of an unpleasant accusation. The point is Nat, and recollect that I spend a great deal of time between decks and am party to much of the rumour that runs about any vessel, the point is that I'd say he was eating himself up.'

'What d'you mean?'

'His mind is close to the precipice of insanity. I've seen it before. He lives in his skull, Nat, a man with a bad conscience.'

Drinkwater considered what Appleby had said. A ship was no place for a man with something on his mind. 'You reckon he's winding himself up, eh?'

Appleby nodded. 'Like a clock spring, Nat . . .'

Drinkwater stood on the Gun Wharf at Sheerness and shivered, watching the boats coming and going, searching for *Kestrel*'s gig among them. Beside him James Thompson, the purser, stood with the last of his stores. Merrick and Bolton were with him. Drinkwater was anxious to get back on board. The winter afternoon was well advanced and the westerly wind showed every sign of reaching gale force before too long.

Their refit was completed and they were under orders to join Vice-Admiral Duncan at Yarmouth.

'Here's the gig now,' said Thompson and turned to the two messmen, 'get that lot into the boat smartly now, you two.' Drinkwater watched the boat pull in, Mr Hill at the tiller. As soon as it was secure he passed a bundle of charts, the letters and newspapers to the master's mate. Then he stood back while a brace of partridges, some cheeses, cabbages, an exchanged cask of pork and some other odds and ends were lowered into the boat.

'Bulman completed watering this afternoon, Mr Drinkwater,' volunteered Hill.

Drinkwater nodded. Thompson looked at Drinkwater. 'That's it, then.'

'Very well, James, let's get on board before this lot breaks,' he nodded to the chaos of cloud speedily eclipsing the pale daylight to the west, behind the broken outlines of the old three-deckers that formed the dockyard workers' tenements.

'Come on you two, into the boat . . .' Merrick descended the steps. 'Come on Bolton!' The man hesitated at the top, then turned on his heel.

'Hey!'

Drinkwater looked at Thompson. 'He's running, James!'

'The devil he is!'

'Mr Hill, take charge! Come on James!'

At the top of the steps Drinkwater saw Bolton running towards the old battleships.

'Hey!'

The wind was sweeping the wharf clear and Bolton pushed between two lieutenants who spun, a swirl of boat cloaks and displaced tricornes. Drinkwater began to run, passing the astonished officers. Already Bolton had reached the shadows in the lane leading to what was called the Old Ships, traversing the dockyard wall and away from the fort at Garrison Point. He knew that Bolton could not pass the sentries at the gates or cross the ditches that surrounded the place. He was making for the Old Ships and a possible way to Blue Town, the growing collection of inns, tradesmen's dwellings and brick built houses that was accumulating outside the limits of the dockyard.

Abruptly he reached a ditch, James Thompson puffing up beside him. At the top of the low rampart a short glacis sloped down to the water. It was slightly overgrown now, elderberry bushes darker patches against the grey-green grass. The pale sky in the west silhouetted a movement: Bolton. Drinkwater began running again. Thompson came after him then tripped and fell, yelling obscenities as he discovered a patch of nettles.

Drinkwater ran on, disturbing a rabbit which bobbed, grey-tailed, ahead of him before turning aside into a burrow. Then he approached the first of the hulks, vaguely aware that behind him shouts indicated where someone had turned out a foot patrol.

The old battleship rose huge above him, its lines made jagged with additions: chimneys, privvies and steps. The rusting chains from her hawse pipes disappeared into the mud and men were trudging aboard, looking at him curiously as he panted past them. The smell of smoke and cooking assailed his dilating nostrils and he drew breath.

A shadow moved out from the far hulk, a running man stooped along the tideline and Drinkwater wished he had a pistol. Bolton was making for a ramshackle wooden bridge that lay over the fosse, an unofficial short cut from the Old Ships to Blue Town. It was getting quite dark now. He clattered across the black planking over mud and a silver thread of water. The violent tug of the rising wind at his cloak slowed him and the breath was rasping in his throat at the unaccustomed exercise. To his right the flat expanse of salt marsh gave way to the Medway, palely bending away to Blackstakes and Chatham. To the left the huddle that was Blue Town.

It was almost dark when he entered the first narrow street. He passed an inn and halted. Bolton had evaded him. He must draw breath and wait for that foot patrol to come up, then they must conduct a house-to-house search.

'Shit!' Exasperation exploded within him. They had been at Sheerness for weeks. Why had Bolton chosen now to desert? He turned to the inn to make a start in the search. In the violence of his temper he flung open the door and was utterly unprepared for the disturbingly familiar face that confronted him.

The two men gaped in mutual astonishment, each trying to identify the other. For Edouard Santhonax recognition and capture were instinctively things to avoid. His reaction was swift the instant he saw doubt cloud Drinkwater's eyes. For Nathaniel, breathless in pursuit of Bolton, the appearance of Santhonax was perplexing and unreal. As his brain reacted to the change of quarry Santhonax turned to escape through a rear exit.

He attempted to shout 'Stop! In the King's name', but the ineffective croak that he emitted was drowned in the buzz of conversation from the artisans and seamen in the taproom. He pushed past several men who seemed to want to delay him. Eventually he struggled outside where he ran into the foot patrol. A sergeant helped him up.

'This way,' wheezed Drinkwater, and they pounded down an alleyway, no one noticing Bolton crouched beneath a hand cart in the inn yard, his heart bursting with effort, the scarred and knotted muscles of his back paining him from the need to draw deep gulps of air into his heaving lungs.

The sergeant spread his men out and they began to search the surrounding buildings. Drinkwater paused to collect his thoughts, realising they were now hunting two men, though the soldiers did not yet know it. He thought Santhonax might have doubled on him. It was quite dark and Drinkwater was alone. He could hear the sergeant and his men calling to each other further down the lane. Then the rasp of a sword being drawn sounded behind him.

He spun round.

Santhonax stood in the alleyway, a grey shadowy figure with a faint gleam of steel barring the passage. Drinkwater hauled out his hanger.

They shuffled cautiously forward and Drinkwater felt the blades engage. He could hear a voice in his head urging him not to delay, to attack simply and immediately; that Santhonax was quite probably a most proficient swordsman. Now!

Barely beating the blade and lunging low, Drinkwater extended. But Santhonax was too quick and leapt back, riposting swiftly though off balance. Drinkwater's parry was clumsy but effective.

They re-engaged. Drinkwater was blown after his run. Already his hanger felt heavy on his arm. He felt Santhonax seize the initiative as his blade was beaten, then, with an infinite slowness, the rasp of steel on steel, he quailed before the extension. He clumsily fell back, half turning and losing his balance and falling against the wall. He felt the sharp prick of the point in his shoulder but the turn had saved him, he was aware of Santhonax's breath hot in his face, instinctively knew the man's belly was unguarded and turned his point.

'*Merde!*' spat the Frenchman leaping back and retracting his sword. Drinkwater's feeble counter attack expended his remaining energy on thin air. Then he was aware of the swish of the *molinello*, the downward scything of the slashing blade. He felt the white fire in his right shoulder and arm and knew he was beaten.

He had been precipitate. He had broken his promise of circumspection to Elizabeth. As he awkwardly sought to parry his death thrust, the hanger weighing a ton in his hand, he felt Santhonax hesitate; was aware of running feet pounding up the alleyway from his rear, of something warm and sticky trickling over his wrist. Then he was falling, falling while running, shouting men were passing over him and above them the wind howled in the alleyway and made a terrible rushing noise in his ears.

He could run no more.

Chapter Eleven   December 1796–April 1797

A Time of Trial

'Hold still!'

'Damn it Harry . . .' Drinkwater bit his lip as *Kestrel* slammed into a wave that sent a shudder through her fabric.

'There!' Appleby completed the dressing.

'Well?'

'Well what?'

'What effect is it going to have? My arm's damned stiff. Will I fence again?'

Appleby shrugged. 'The bicep was severely lacerated and will be stiff for some time, only constant exercise will prevent the fibres from knotting. The wound is healing well, though you will have a scar to add to your collection.' He indicated the thin line of pale tissue that ran down Nathaniel's cheek.

'And?'

'Oh, mayhap an ache or two from time to time,' he paused, 'but I'd say you will be butchering again soon.'

Drinkwater's relief turned to invective as *Kestrel* butted into another sea and sent him sprawling across Appleby's tiny cabin, one arm in and one arm out of his coat. In the lobby he struggled into his tarpaulin while Appleby heaved himself on to his cot, extended one leg to brace himself against the door jamb, and reached for his book. Drinkwater went on deck.

Eight bells struck as he cleared the companionway. The wind howled a high-pitched whine in the rigging, a cold, hard northerly wind that kicked up huge seas, grey monsters with curling crests which broke in rolling avalanches of white water that thundered down their advancing breasts with a noise like murder, flattening and dissipating in streaks of spindrift.

Spume filled the air and it was necessary to turn away from the wind to speak. As he relieved Jessup a monstrous wave towered over the cutter, its crest roaring over, marbled green and white, rolling down on them as *Kestrel* mounted the advancing sea.

'Hold hard there! Meet her!' Men grabbed hold-fasts and the relieving tackles on the tiller were bar taut. Drinkwater tugged the companionway cover over as the roar of water displaced the howl of wind and he winced with the pain of his arm as he clung on.

Kestrel staggered under the tremendous blow and then the sea was all about them, tearing at them, sucking at their legs and waists, driving in through wrist bands, down necks and up legs, striving to pluck them like autumn leaves from their stations. A man went past Drinkwater on his back, fetching up against number ten gun with a crunch of ribs. Water poured off the cutter as she rode sluggishly over the next wave, her stout, buoyant hull straining at every strap and scarph. Men were securing coils of rope torn from belaying pins and relashing the gigs amidships. Shaking the water from his hair Drinkwater realised, with a pang of anger that fed on the ache in his bicep, that he would be cold and wet for the next four hours. And the pain in his arm was abominable.

The winter weather seemed to match some savage feeling in Drinkwater's guts. The encounter with Capitaine Santhonax had left a conviction that their fates were inextricably entwined. The ache of this wound added a personal motive to this feeling that lodged like an oyster's irritant somewhere in his soul. What had been a vague product of imagination following the affair off Beaubigny had coalesced into certainty after the encounter at Sheerness.

I cannot escape, Nathaniel wrote in his journal, *a growing sense of apprehension which is both irrational and defies the precepts of reason, but it is in accord with some basic instincts that are, I suppose, primaeval*. He laid his goosequill down. No one but himself had realised his assailant was not Bolton for they had found the wretch in the inn yard, cramped in the stable straw and he had been taken defending himself with a knife. The sergeant had drawn his own conclusions. Lugged unconscious aboard *Kestrel*, Drinkwater had been powerless to prevent the foot-patrol from beating up Bolton before throwing him into a cell. In the confusion Santhonax had vanished.

Drinkwater sighed. Poor Bolton had been found hanged in his cell the next morning and Drinkwater regretted he had never cleared the man of his own wounding. But *Kestrel* was at sea when he recovered his senses and even then it was some time before the dreams of his delirium separated from the recollection of events.

Drinkwater kept the news of the presence of Santhonax to himself with the growing conviction that they would meet again.

Santhonax's presence at Sheerness seemed part of some diabolical design made more sinister by the occurrence of an old dream which had confused the restless sleep of his recovery. The clanking nightmare of drowning beneath a white clad lady had been leant especial terror by the medusa head that stared down at his supine body. Her face had the malevolent joy of a jubilant Hortense Montholon, the auburn hair writhed to entangle him and his ears were assailed by the cursing voice of Edouard Santhonax. But now, when he awoke from the dream, there was no comforting clanking from *Cyclops*'s pumps to chide him for foolish imaginings. Instead he was left with the sense of foreboding.

His wound healed well, though the need to keep active caused many a spasm of pain as the weather continued bad. In a perverse way the prevailing gales were good for *Kestrel*, preventing any grievances becoming too great, submerging individual hatreds in the common misery of unremitting labour. The cold, wet and exhaustion that became part of their lives seemed to blur the edges of perception so that the common experience drove men together and all struggled for the survival of the ship. *Kestrel* was now on blockade duty, that stern and rigorous test of men and ships. Duncan's cutters were his eyes, stationed as close to the Texel as they dared, watching the dutch naval arsenal of Den Helder just beyond the gap between Noord Holland to the south and the island of Texel to the north.

The channel that lay between the two land masses split into three as it opened into the North Sea, like a trident pointing west. To the north, exit from the haven was by the Molen Gat, due west by the West Gat and southwards, hugging the Holland shore past the fishing village, signal station and battery of Kijkduin, lay the Schulpen Gat.

These three channels pierced the immense danger of the Haak Sand, the Haakagronden that surfaced at low water and upon whose windward edges a terrible surf beat in bad weather. Fierce tides surged through the gattways and, when wind opposed tide, a steep, vicious breaking sea ran in them.

Duncan's cutters lay off the Haakagronden in bad weather, working up the channels when it eased and occasionally entering the shaft of the trident, the Zeegat van Texel, to reconnoitre the enemy. Drinkwater's eyebrows were rimed with salt as he took cross bearings of the mills and church towers that lined the low, grass-fringed dunes of Noord Holland and Texel, a coastline that sometimes seemed to smoke as it seethed behind the spume of the breakers beating upon the pale yellow beach. It was a dreary, dismal coast, possessed of shallows and sandbanks, channels and false leads. The charts were useless and they came to rely on their own experience. Once again Drinkwater became immersed in his profession and, as a result of their situation, the old intimacy with Griffiths revived. Even the ship's company, still restless over their lack of pay, seemed more settled and Griffiths seemed justified in his suggestion that Bolton might have been a corrupting influence.

Even Appleby had ceased to be so abrasive and was more the jolly, easily pricked surgeon of former times. He and Nathaniel resumed their former relationship and if Griffiths still occasionally appeared remote in the worries of his command and harassed by senior officers safe at anchor in their line-of-battleships, the surgeon was more able to make allowances.

Drinkwater was surprised that in the foul weather and the staleness of the accommodation Griffiths did not succumb to his fever but the continuous demands made upon him did not affect his health.

'It is often the way,' pronounced Appleby when Drinkwater mentioned it. 'While the body is under stress it seems able to stand innumerable shocks, as witness men's behaviour in action. But when that stimulus is withdrawn, perhaps I should say eased, the tension in the system, being elastic and at its greatest extension, retracts, drawing in its wake the noxious humours and germs of disease.'

'You may be right, Harry,' said Drinkwater, amused at the pompous expression on the surgeon's face.

'May, sirrah? Of course I am right! I was right about Bolton, was I not? I questioned his mental stability and, poof! Suddenly he's off and then, when he's taken he becomes a suicide.' Appleby flicked his fingers.

Drinkwater nodded. 'Aye Harry, but even you doubted your own prognosis when he did not run earlier. He did leave it to the last minute, even you must admit that.'

'Nat, my boy,' gloated Appleby the gleam of intellectual triumph in his eyes, 'one always has to leave suicide until the last minute!'

'You're just good at guess-work, you damned rogue,' he said, wondering what Appleby would make of his own suspicions and convictions.

'Oh ho! Is that so?' said Appleby rolling his eyes in mock outrage, his chins quivering. 'Well my strutting bantam cock, listen to old Harry, there's more that I can tell you . . .' He was suddenly serious, with that comic pedagoguish expression that betokened, in Appleby, complete sincerity.

'I'll back my instinct over trouble in the fleet . . .' Drinkwater looked up sharply.

'Go on,' he said, content to let Appleby have his head for once.

'Look, Nat, this cutter's an exception, small ships usually are, but you are well aware to what I refer, the denial of liberty, the shameful arrears of pay, the refusal of many captains to sanction the purchase of fresh food even in port and the general abuses of a significant proportion of our brother officers, these can only have a most undesirable effect.

'Take the current rate of pay for an able seaman, Nathaniel. It is twenty-four shillings, twelve florins for risking scurvy, pox, typhus, gangrene, not to mention death itself at the hands of the enemy . . . d'you realise that sum was fixed in the days of the Commonwealth . . .' Appleby's indignation was justly righteous. To be truthful Drinkwater did not know that, but he had no time to acknowledge his ignorance before Appleby continued his grim catalogue of grievances.

'To this you must add the vast disparity of prize money, the short measure given by so many pursers that has added the purser's pound of fourteen ounces to the avoirdupois scale; you must add the abatement of pay when a man is sick or unfit for duty, even if the injury was sustained in the line of that duty; you must add deductions to pay for a chaplain when one is borne on the books, the deductions for Greenwich Hospital and the Chatham Chest . . .' Appleby was becoming more and more strident, counting the items off on his fingers, his chins quivering with passion.

'And if that were not enough when a man is gricomed by the whores that are the only women he is permitted to lie with, according to usage and custom, he must *pay me* to cure him whilst losing his pay through being unfit!

'The families of seamen starve in the gutters while their men-folk are incarcerated on board ship, frequently unpaid for years and when they do return home they are as like to be turned over to a ship newly commissioning as occasion demands.

'I tell you, Nathaniel, these are *not* facts that lie comfortably with the usual canting notions of English liberty and, mark me well, if this war is protracted there will be trouble in the fleet. You cannot fight a spirited enemy who is proclaiming Liberty, Equality and Fraternity with a navy manned by slaves.'

Drinkwater sighed. Appleby was right. There was worse too. As the prime seamen were pressed out of homeward merchant ships the Lord Mayor's men and the quota men filled the Press Tenders, bringing into the fleet not hardened seamen, but the misfits of society, men without luck but not without intelligence; demagogues, lower deck lawyers; men who saw in the example of France a way to power, to overturn vested interest in the stirring name of the people. With a pot so near the boil, was the purpose and presence of Capitaine Santhonax at Sheerness to stir it a little? The proximity of Sheerness to Tunbridge occurred to him. A feeling of alarm, of duty imperfectly performed, swept over him.

'Aye, Harry. Happen you are right, though I hope not. It might be a bloody business . . .'

'Of course, Nat! *When* it comes, not "if"! *When* it comes it could be most bloody, and the authorities behave with crass stupidity. See how they handled that *Culloden* business,' Drinkwater nodded at the recollection but Appleby was still in full flood.

'Half the admirals are blind. Look how they ridiculed John Clerk of Eldin because he was able to point out how to win battles. Now they all scrabble to fight on his principles. Look how the powdered physicians of the fleet ignored Lind's anti-scorbutic theories, how difficult it was for Douglas to get his cartridges taken seriously. Remember Patrick Ferguson's rifle? Oh, the list of thinking men pointing out the obvious to the establishment is endless . . . what the deuce are you laughing at?'

'Your inconsistent consistency,' grinned Nathaniel

'What the devil d'you mean?'

'Well you are right, Harry, of course, these things are always the same, the prophet unrecognised in his own land.'

'So, I'm correct. *I* know that. What's so damned amusing?'

'But you yourself objected to Sir Sydney Smith meddling in your sick bay, and Sir Sydney has a reputation for an original mind. You are therefore inconsistent with your principles in your own behaviour, whilst being comfortingly consistent with the rest of us mortal men.'

'Why you damned impertinent puppy!'

Drinkwater dodged the empty tankard that sailed towards his head.

Thus it was that they rubbed along together while things went from bad to worse for British arms. Sir John Jervis evacuated the Mediterranean while Admiral Morard de Galles sailed from Brest with an army embarked for Ireland. That he was frustrated in landing General Hoche and his seasoned troops was a piece of luck undeserved by the British. The south-westerly gale that ruined the enterprise over Christmas 1796 seemed to the Irish patriot, Wolfe Tone, to deny the existence of a just God, while in the British fleet the gross mismanagement of Lord Bridport and Sir John Colpoys only reduced the morale of the officers and increased the disaffection of the men.

Again only the frigates had restored a little glitter to tarnished British laurels. And that at a heavy price. Pellew, now in the *razée Indefatigable*, in company with *Amazon* off Brest, sighted and chased the *Droits de l'Homme* returning from Ireland. In a gale on a lee shore Pellew forced the French battleship ashore where she was wrecked. *Indefatigable* only escaped by superlative seamanship while *Amazon* failed to claw off and was also wrecked.

In the North Sea, action of even this Pyrrhic kind was denied Admiral Duncan's squadron. Maintaining his headquarters in Yarmouth Roads, where he was in telegraphic communication with London, Duncan kept his inshore frigates off the Texel and his cutters in the gattways through the Haakagronden, as close as his lieutenant-commanders dared be. Duncan's fleet was an exiguous collection of old ships, many of sixty-four guns and none larger than a third rate. The admiral flew his flag in the aptly named *Venerable*.

The Dutch, under Vice-Admiral de Winter, were an unknown force. Memories of Dutch ferocity from King Charles's day lingered still, forgotten the humiliation of losing their fleet to a brigade of French cavalry galloping over the ice in which they were frozen. For like the Spanish they were now the allies of France, but unlike them their country was a proclaimed republic. Republicanism had crossed the Rhine, as Drinkwater had predicted, and the combination of a Franco-Dutch fleet to make

117

another attempt on Ireland was a frightening prospect, given the uneasy state of that unhappy country.

Then, as the wintry weather gave way to milder, springlike days, news of a different kind came. The victory of St Valentine's Day it was called at first, then later the Battle of Cape St Vincent. Jervis had been made an earl and the remarkable, erratic Captain Nelson, having left the line of battle to cut off the Spanish van from escape, had received a knighthood.

The air of triumph even permeated *Kestrel*'s crowded little cabin as Griffiths read aloud the creased copy of the Gazette that eventually reached the cutter on her station in the Schulpen Gat. Drinkwater received an unexpected letter.

Mr Dear Nathaniel, he read,

I expect you will have heard the news of Old Oak's action of St Valentine's Day but you will be surprised to hear your old friend was involved. We beat up the Dons thoroughly, though I saw very little, commanding a battery of 32's on Victory, into which ship I exchanged last November. You should have been here, Nat. Lord, but what a glorious thing is a fleet action. How I envied you Rodney's action here in '80 and how you must envy us ours! Our fellows were so cool and we raked Salvador del Mundo wickedly. The Dons fought better than I thought them capable of and it was tolerably warm work . . .

Drinkwater *was* envious. Envious and not a little amused in a bitter kind of way at Richard White's mixture of boyish enthusiasm and sober naval formality. There was a good deal more of it, including the significant phrase *Sir John was pleased to take notice of my conduct*. Drinkwater checked himself. He was pleased for White, pleased too that his old friend, now clearly on the path to success, still considered the friendship of an obscure master's mate in an even more obscure cutter worth the trouble of an informative letter. So Drinkwater shared vicariously in the euphoria induced by the victory. The tide, it seemed, had turned in favour of British arms and the Royal Navy reminded her old antagonists that though the lion lay down, it was not yet dead.

Then one morning in April *Kestrel* rounded the Scroby Sands and stood into Yarmouth Road with the signal for despatches at her masthead. Coming to her anchor close to *Venerable* her chase guns saluted the blue flag at the flagship's main masthead. A moment or so later her boat pulled across the water with Lieutenant Griffiths in the stern.

When Griffiths returned from delivering his message from the frigates off the Texel he called all the cutter's officers into the cabin.

Drinkwater was the last to arrive, late from supervising the hoisting of the boat. He closed the lobby door behind him, aware of an air of tense expectancy. As he sat down he realised it was generated by the frigid gleam in Griffiths's eyes.

'Gentlemen,' he said in his deep, clear voice. 'Gentlemen, the Channel Fleet at Spithead is in a state of mutiny!'

A Flood of Mutiny

'Listen to the bastards!' said Jessup as *Kestrel*'s crew paused in their work to stare round the crowded anchorage. The cheering appeared to come from *Lion* and a ripple of excitement ran through the hands forward, several staring defiantly aft where Jessup, Drinkwater and Traveller stood.

Yarmouth Roads had been buzzing as news, rumour, claim and counter-claim sped between the ships anchored there. The red flag, it was said had been hoisted at the Nore and Duncan's ships vacillated between loyalty to their much respected admiral and their desire to support what were felt to be the just demands of the rest of the fleet.

The cheering was enough to bring others on deck. Amidships the cook emerged from his galley and the knot of officers was joined by Appleby and Thompson. 'Thank God we're anchored close to the flagship,' muttered the surgeon. His apprehensions of mutiny now having been confirmed, Appleby feared the possibility of being murdered in his bed.

Kestrel lay anchored a short cannon shot from *Venerable*. The battleship's guns were run out and the sudden boom of a cannon echoed flatly across the anchorage. A string of knotted bunting rose up her signal halliards to jerk out brightly in the light breeze of a May morning.

'Call away my gig, Mr Drinkwater,' growled Griffiths emerging from the companionway. Admiral Duncan was signalling for his captains and when Griffiths returned from the conference his expression was weary. 'Call the people aft!'

Jessup piped the hands into the waist and they swarmed eagerly over the remaining boat on the hatch. 'Gentlemen,' said Griffiths to his officers, 'take post behind me.'

The officers shuffled into a semi-circle as ordered, regarding the faces of the men. Some open, some curious, some defiant or truculent and all aware that unusual events were taking place.

'Now hark you all to this, do you understand that the fleets at Spithead and the Nore are in defiant mutiny of their officers . . .' He looked round at them, giving them no ground, despite his inner sympathy. 'But if any man disputes my right to command this cutter or proposes disobeying my orders or those of one of my officers,' he gestured behind him, 'let him speak now.'

Griffiths's powerful voice with its rich Welsh accent seemed to come from a pulpit. His powerful old body and sober features with their air of patriarchy exerted an almost tangible influence upon his men. He appeared to be reasoning with them like a firm father, opposing their fractiousness with the sure hand of experience. 'Look at me,' he seemed to say, 'you cannot rebel against me, whatever the rest of the fleet does.'

Drinkwater's palms were damp and beside him Appleby was shaking with apprehension. Then they saw resolution ebb as a sort of collective sigh came from the men. Griffiths sent them forward again.

'Get forrard and do your duty. Mr Jessup, man the windlass and inform me when the cable's up and down.'

It was the season for variable or easterly winds in the North Sea and Duncan's preoccupation was that the Dutch fleet would leave the Texel, taking advantage of the favourable winds and the state of the British squadrons. The meeting to which Griffiths had been summoned had been to determine the mood of the ships in Duncan's fleet. The small force still off the Texel was quite inadequate to contain De Winter if he chose to emerge and it was now even more important to keep him bottled up. There was a strong possibility that the mutinous ships at the Nore might attempt a defection and this was more likely to be to the protestant Dutch than the catholic French, for all the republican renunciation of formal religion. A demonstration by De Winter to cover the Nore Squadron's exit from the Thames would be all that was necessary to facilitate this and strengthen any wavering among the mutineers. It was already known at Yarmouth that most of the officers had been removed from the warships with the significant exception of the sailing masters. They were held aboard the *Sandwich*, the 'flagship' of the self-styled admiral, Richard Parker.

For a few days *Kestrel* remained at anchor while Duncan, who had personally remonstrated with the Admiralty for redress of many of the men's grievances and regarded the mutiny as a chastisement and warning to the Admiralty to mend its ways, waited on events.

The anonymous good sense that had characterised the affair at Spithead was largely responsible for its swift and satisfactory conclusion. Admiral Howe was given special powers to treat with the delegates who knew they had 'Black Dick's' sympathy. By mid-May, amid general rejoicing, fireworks and banquets the Channel Fleet, pardoned by the King, returned to duty.

There was no evidence that foreign sedition had had anything to do with it. The tars had had a case. Their cause had been just, their conduct exemplary, their self-administered justice impeccable. They had sent representatives to their brethren at the Nore and it would only be a matter of days before they too saw sense.

But it was not so. The Nore mutiny was an uglier business, its style aggressive and less reasonable. By blockading trade in the Thames its leaders rapidly lost the sympathy of the liberal middle-class traders of London and as the Government became intransigent, Parker's desperation increased. The tide in favour of the fleet turned, and as the supplies of food, fuel and merchandise to the capital dwindled, troops flooded in to Sheerness and the ships flying the red flag at the Nore felt a growing sense of isolation.

At the end of May there arrived in Yarmouth an Admiralty envoy in the person of Captain William Bligh, turned out of the *Director* by his crew and sent by the authorities to persuade Duncan to use his ships against Parker's. He also brought news that four delegates from the Nore had seized the cutter *Cygnet* and were on their way to Yarmouth to incite the seamen there to mutiny.

Duncan considered the intelligence together with the mooted possibility of Parker defecting with the entire fleet to Holland or France. In due course he ordered the frigate *Vestal*, the lugger *Hope* and the cutter *Rose* to cruise to the southward to intercept the visitors. If Parker sailed for the Texel or Dunquerque then, and only then, would the old admiral consider using his own ships against the mutineers. In the meantime he sent *Kestrel* south into the Thames to guard the channels to Holland and to learn immediately of any defection.

'By the mark five.'

Drinkwater discarded the idea of the sweeps. Despite the fog there was just sufficient wind to keep steerage on the cutter and every stitch of canvas that could be hoisted was lily responding to it.

'I'll go below for a little, Mr Drinkwater.'

'Aye, aye, sir.' Their passage from Yarmouth had been slow and Griffiths had not left the deck for fear the men would react, but they were too tired now and his own exhaustion was obvious. Grey and lined, his face wore the symptoms of the onset of his fever and it seemed that the elasticity of his constitution had reached its greatest extension. Drinkwater was glad to see him go below.

Since the news of the Spithead settlement the hands had been calmer, but orders to proceed into the Thames had revived the tension. In the way that these things happen, word had got out that their lordships were contemplating using the North Sea squadron against the mutineers at the Nore, and Bligh was too notorious a figure to temper speculation on the issue.

The chant of the leadsman was monotonous so that, distracted by larger events and the personal certainty that the Nore mutiny was made the more hideous by the presence of Capitaine Santhonax, Drinkwater had to force himself to concentrate upon the soundings. They were well into the estuary now and should fetch the Nubb buoy in about three hours as the ebb eased.

'By the deep four.'

'Sommat ahead, sir!' The sudden cry from the lookout forward.

'What is it?' He went forward, peering into the damp grey murk.

'Dunno sir . . . buoy?' If it was then their reckoning was way out.

'There sir! See it?'

'No . . . yes!' Almost right ahead, slightly to starboard. They would pass very close, close enough to identify it.

''s a boat, sir!'

It was a warship's launch, coming out of a dense mist a bowsprit's length ahead of them. It had eight men in it and he heard quite distinctly a voice say, 'It's another bleeding buoy yacht . . .', and a contradictory: 'No, it's a man o'war cutter . . .'

Mutually surprised, the two craft passed. The launch's men lay on their oars, the blades so close to *Kestrel*'s side that the water drops from their ends fell into the rippling along the cutter's waterline. Curiously the Kestrels stared at the men in the boat who glared defiantly back. There was a sudden startled gasp, a quick movement, a flash and a bang. A pistol ball tore the hat from Drinkwater's head and made a neat hole in the mainsail. There was a howl of frustration and the mutineers were plying their oars as the launch vanished in the fog astern.

'God's bones!' roared Drinkwater suddenly spinning round. The men were still gaping at him and the vanished boat. 'Let go stuns'l halliards! Let go squares'l halliards! Down helm! Lively now! Lively God damn it!'

The men could not obey fast enough to satisfy Drinkwater's racing mind. He found himself beating his thighs with clenched fists as the cutter turned slowly.

'Come on you bitch, come *on*,' he muttered, and then he felt the deck move beneath him, ever so slightly upsetting his sense of balance, and another fact struck him.

He had run *Kestrel* aground.

Kestrel lay at an alarming angle and her sailing master was still writhing with mortification. Used as he had been to the estuary while in the buoy yachts of the Trinity House the situation was profoundly humiliating.

Lieutenant Griffiths had said nothing beyond wearily directing the securing of the cutter against an ingress of water when the tide made. It was fortunate that they had been running before what little wind there was and their centre plates had been housed. The consequences might have been more serious otherwise. An inspection revealed that *Kestrel* had suffered no damage beyond a dent in the pride of her navigator.

Below, Griffiths had regarded him in silence for some moments after listening to Drinkwater's explanation of events. As the colour mounted to Drinkwater's cheeks a tired smile curled Griffiths's lips.

'Come, come, Nathaniel, pass a bottle from the locker . . . it was no more than an error of judgement and the consequences are not terrible.' Griffiths threw off his fatigue with a visible effort. 'One error scarcely condemns you, *bach*.'

Drinkwater found himself shaking with relief as he thrust the sercial across the table. 'But shouldn't we have pursued sir? I mean it *was* Santhonax, sir. I'm damned sure of that.' In his insistence to make amends, not only for grounding the cutter but for his failure earlier to report the presence of the French agent, the present circumstances gave him his opportunity. For a second he recollected that Griffiths might ask him how he was so 'damned sure'. But the lieutenant was not concerned and pushed a full glass across the table. He shook his head.

'Putting a boat away in this fog would likely have embroiled us in a worse tangle. Who ambushes whom in this weather is largely a matter of who spots whom first,' he paused to sip the rich dark wine.

'The important thing is what the devil is Santhonax doing in a warship's launch going east on an ebb tide with a crew of British ne'er-do-wells?'

The two men sat in silence while about them *Kestrel* creaked as the first of the incoming tide began to lift her bilge. Was Santhonax a delegate from the Nore on his way to Yarmouth? If he was he would surely have used the Swin. Their own passage through the Prince's Channel had been ordered to stop up the gap not covered by *Vestal*, *Rose* or *Hope*. And it was most unlikely that a French agent would undertake such a task.

If Santhonax's task was to help suborn the British fleet he had already achieved his object by the open and defiant mutiny. So what was he doing in a boat? Escaping? Was the mutiny collapsing? Or was his passage east a deliberate choice? Of course! Santhonax had attempted to kill Drinkwater. Nathaniel was the only man whose observation of Santhonax might prejudice the Frenchman's plans!

'There would seem to be only one logical conclusion, sir . . .'

'Oh?' said Griffiths, 'and what might that be?'

'*Santhonax must be going to bring aid to the Nore mutineers* . . .' He outlined his reasons for presuming this and Griffiths nodded slowly.

'If he intends bringing a fleet to support the mutiny or to cover its defection does he make for France or Holland?'

'The Texel shelters the largest fleet in the area, sir. Given a fair wind from the east which they'd need to get up the Thames with a fair certainty of a westerly soon afterwards to get 'em all out together . . . yes, I'll put my money on the Texel, anything from Brest or the west'll have the Channel to contend with.'

'Yes, by damn!' snapped Griffiths suddenly, leaning urgently forward. 'And our fellows will co-operate with a fleet of protestant Dutch and welcome their republican comrades! By heaven Nathaniel, this Santhonax is a cunning devil! *Cythral*! I'll lay gold on the Texel . . .'

The two of them were half out of their chairs, leaning across the table like men in heated argument. Then Griffiths slumped down as *Kestrel* lurched a little nearer the upright.

'But our orders do not allow me discretion. Santhonax has escaped, in the meantime we must do our duty.' He paused, rubbing his chin while Drinkwater remained standing. 'But,' he said slowly, 'if we could discover the precise state of the mutiny . . . if, for instance there were signs that they were moving out from the Nore, then, by God, we'd know for sure.'

Drinkwater nodded. He was not certain how they could discover this without running their heads into a noose, but he could not now tell Griffiths of the encounter in Sheerness and the premonitions that were consuming him at that very moment. For the time being he must rest content.

Two hours later they were under way again. The breeze had come up, although the fog had become a mist and the warmth of the sun could be felt as *Kestrel* resumed her westward passage. It was late afternoon when a cry from forward caught the attention of all on deck.

'Sir!'

'What is it?' Drinkwater scrambled forward.

'Sort of smashing sound,' the man said, cocking one ear. They listened and Drinkwater heard a muffled bang followed by crashes and the splintering of timber. He frowned. 'Swivel gun?' He turned aft. 'Call all hands! Pass word for the captain! Clear for action!' He was damned if he was going to be caught a second time.

In a few moments the lashings were cast off the guns and the men were at their stations. Griffiths emerged from the companionway pale and drawn. Drinkwater launched into an explanation of what they had heard when suddenly the fog lifted, swept aside like a curtain, and bright sunshine dappled the water.

'What the devil . . .?' Griffiths pointed and Drinkwater turned sharply, then grinned with relief.

'It's all right, sir, I recognise her.'

Ahead of them, a cable distant, lay an ornate, cutter-rigged yacht, decorated aft like a first rate, with a beak head forward supporting a lion guardant. Alongside the yacht the painted bulk of the Nubb buoy was being systematically smashed by axes and one-pound swivel shot.

'Trinity Yacht ahoy!' Faces looked up and Drinkwater saw her master, Jonathan Poulter, direct men aft to where she carried carronades. He saw the gunports lift and the muzzles emerge.

'Hold your fire, damn your eyes! We're a King's cutter,' then in a lower voice as they closed the yacht, 'Heave to, Mr Drinkwater, while we speak him.'

The two cutters closed, their crews regarding each other curiously. 'Do you have news of the Nore fleet, is there any sign of them moving?'

A man in a blue coat stood beside Poulter and Drinkwater recognised Captain Calvert, an Elder Brother of Trinity House.

'No, sir,' Calvert called, 'and they'll find it impossible when we've finished. All the beacons are coming down and most of the buoys are already sunk. Another night's work will see the matter concluded . . . is that Mr Drinkwater alongside of you?'

Drinkwater stood on the rail. 'Aye sir, we had hopes that you might have news.'

'They had a frigate down at the Middle flying the red flag yesterday to mark the bank and the fear is they'll try treason . . . they've gone too far now for anything else . . . my guess is they'll try for France or Holland. Are you from Duncan?'

'Aye,' it was Griffiths who spoke now. 'Are you sure of your facts, sir?'

'Aye, sir. We left Broadstairs yesterday. The intelligence about the frigate we learned from the buoy yacht *Argus* from Harwich; I myself called on Admiral Buckner at Sheerness on my way from London.'

Griffiths reflected a moment. 'And you think they'll try and break out?'

'It's that or starve and swing.'

Griffiths eyed the pendant. 'Starboard tack, Mr Drinkwater,' then in a louder voice as *Kestrel* turned away, 'Much obliged to you, sir, God speed.'

The two cutters parted, *Kestrel* standing seawards again. Griffiths came aft to where Drinkwater was setting the new course.

'Black Deep, sir?'

'Aye if she'll hold the course.' Griffiths shivered and wiped the back of his hand across his forehead.

'She'll hold it, sir, with the centre plates down. I take it we're for Yarmouth?'

Griffiths nodded. 'Mr Drinkwater . . .' He jerked his head

sideways and walked to the rail, staring astern to where, alongside the Trinity Yacht, the Nubb buoy was sinking. In a low voice he said, 'It seems we have our proof, Nathaniel . . .' His white eyebrows shot up in two arches.

'Aye sir. I'd come to pretty much the same conclusion.'

After *Kestrel* the admiral's cabin aboard *Venerable* seemed vast, but Admiral Duncan was a big man with a broad Scots face and, even seated, he dominated it. There was a story that he had subdued *Adamant*'s crew by picking up one of her more vociferous seamen and holding him, one armed, over the side with the sarcastic comments that the fellow dared deprive him of command of the fleet. The general laughter that followed this spectacle had ensured *Adamant*'s loyalty.

As Griffiths, unwell and sweating profusely, strove to explain the significance of their news, Drinkwater examined the other occupants of the cabin in whose august company he now found himself. There was Captain Fairfax, Duncan's flag-captain, and Captain William Bligh. Drinkwater regarded 'Bounty' Bligh with ill-concealed curiosity. The captain had a handsome head, with a blue jaw and firm chin. The forehead was high, the hairline balding and his grey hair drawn back into a queue. Bligh's eyes were penetrating and hazel, reminding Drinkwater of Dungarth's, the nose straight and flanked with fine nostrils. Only the mouth showed anything in the face that was ignoble, a petulance confirmed by his voice which had a quality of almost continuous exasperation. The remaining person was Major Brown, summoned by telegraph from London and still eating the chicken leg offered him on his arrival.

'Now I'm not quite clear about the significance of this Santhonax,' frowned the admiral, 'if I'm losing my ships do I really have to bother about one man?'

'If he's the man we think, sir,' put in Bligh in his high-toned voice, 'I consider him to be most dangerous. If he is the man said to have been seen aboard several of the ships at the Nore as this gentleman,' Bligh indicated Brown, 'seems to think, then I'd rate him as the most seditious rascal among the clutch of gallowsbirds. They deserve to swing, the whole festering nest of them.'

'Thank ye, captain,' said Duncan, with just a touch of irony. 'Major Brown?'

The major always seemed to be called on for explanations in

the middle of a mouthful, thought Drinkwater as he pricked up his ears to hear what news Brown had brought.

'It seems certain, gentlemen, that this man was indeed Capitaine Santhonax, a French agent whose current duty seems to be to suborn the Nore fleet. There were reports of him in connection with the *Culloden* affair. One of the sailing masters held aboard *Sandwich* recognised him as a Frenchman and smuggled word ashore by a bumboat. Apparently they had fought hand to hand off Trincomalee in the last war,' he explained, 'and a number of other reports,' here he paused and inclined his head slightly towards Drinkwater and Griffiths, 'have led us to take an interest in him . . . it would appear he has been the *eminence grise* behind Richard Parker.'

Bligh nodded sharply, 'And behind the removal of myself and my officers from my ship!'

'But he has escaped us now,' soothed Duncan, 'so where's all this leading us?'

Brown shrugged, 'Captain Fairfax tells me you captured the Nore delegates on their way here.'

'Aye, Major, *Rose* took *Cygnet* off Orfordness so our friend is not coming here.'

Drinkwater looked desperately round the circle of faces. Did none of them see what was obvious to him? He looked at Griffiths but the lieutenant had drifted into a doze.

'Excuse me sir.' Drinkwater could hold his tongue no longer.

'Yes, what is it Mr, er, Drinkwater?' Duncan looked up.

'With respect, sir, may I submit that I believe Santhonax was in the boat on passage to Holland . . .' he paused, faltering before the gold lace that appeared to take heed of him for the first time.

'Go on, Mr Drinkwater,' encouraged Brown, leaning forward a half-smile on his face.

'Well sir,' Drinkwater doggedly addressed the admiral, 'I believe from all the facts I know, including the news from the Trinity Yacht relative to the movements of the Nore ships, that a defection of the fleet was ripe. Santhonax was bound for Holland to bring out Dutch ships . . .'

'To cover the defection of the Nore squadron, by heaven!' Fairfax finished the sentence.

'Exactly, sir,' Drinkwater nodded.

'But that smacks of conspiracy, gentlemen, of collusion with a foreign power. Och, I don't believe it, man.' The admiral looked for support to Fairfax who, with the discretionary latitude of a flag-captain said gently, 'Your good-nature, sir, does you credit but I fear Mr Drinkwater may be right. Jack Tar is not always the easy-going lion the populace likes to imagine him . . .' They all looked at the old admiral until Brown's voice cut in.

'We have a woman in Maidstone Gaol that would support Mr Drinkwater's theory, sir.'

'A woman, sir! What in God's name has a woman to do with a fleet mutiny?'

Drinkwater's pulse had quickened as he realised Brown knew more than he had so far admitted. He was eager to ask the woman's identity but he already knew it.

'That, Admiral Duncan, is something we'd very much like to know.'

'Well has the woman told ye anything?'

Brown smiled. 'She is not the type to go in for confessions, sir.'

'But she is not beyond sustaining a conspiracy, sir,' put in Drinkwater with a sudden vehemence.

'So you ken the woman, Mr Drinkwater?' The admiral's brows showed signs of anger. 'There seems to be a deal about this matter that is known to the masters of cutters and denied to commanders-in-chief. Now, sir,' he rounded on Brown, 'd'ye tell me exactly who and what this woman is, what her connection is with our French agent and what it's all to do with my fleet.'

'*Kestrel* brought Mlle Montholon, the woman now in custody, out of France, sir . . .' Brown went on to outline the incidents that had involved the cutter. Drinkwater only half listened. So Hortense was in prison now. His suspicions had been confirmed after all. He wondered if Santhonax knew and doubted it would have much effect on him if he did. Hortense would not have confessed, but he guessed her pride had made her defiant and she had let slip enough. He wondered how Brown's men had eventually taken her and was satisfied in his curiosity as the major concluded: '. . . and so it seemed necessary to examine the young woman more closely. A theft of jewellery was, er, traced to a footman attending the Dowager Comtesse De Tocqueville and in the resulting search of her house a number of interesting documents and a considerable sum of gold was discovered.' He paused to sip from a glass of wine and ended with that curiously Gallic shrug. 'And so we had her.'

When he had finished Duncan shook his head. 'It's all most remarkable, most remarkable. She must be a she-devil . . .'

Beside Drinkwater Griffiths stirred and growled in Welsh, '*Hwyl*, sir . . . she has *hwyl*, the power to stir men's bowels.'

'But it is not the woman that concerns us now, Admiral Duncan,' said Brown. 'The man Santhonax is the real danger. Mr Drinkwater is right and we are certain he intends to bring out the Dutch. He has been in close consultation with Parker and if the mutiny is wavering De Winter must come out at the first opportunity or be more securely shut up in the Texel. If, on the other hand, he emerges to cover the Thames and the Nore ships join him, I leave the consequences to your imagination. Such a force on the doorstep of London would draw the Channel fleet east uncovering Brest, leaving the road clear for Ireland, the West Indies, India. Whichever way you look at it to have the Dutch at sea, *mutiny or not*, would put us in a most dangerous situation. Add the complication of an undefended east coast and a force of republican mutineers in the Thames, then,' Brown spread his hands and shrugged again in that now familiar gesture that was a legacy of his sojourns amongst the Canadians and the French. But it was supremely eloquent for the occasion.

Duncan nodded. 'Those very facts have been my constant companions for the past weeks. I begin to perceive this Santhonax is something of a red hot shot.'

'What is the state of your own ships, Admiral?' asked Brown.

'That, Major, is a deuced canny question.'

Admiral Duncan's fleet deserted him piecemeal in the next few days. Off the Texel Captain Trollope in the *Russell*, 74, with a handful of cutters, luggers and a frigate or two, maintained the illusion of blockade. Five of his battleships left for the Nore.

On the 29th May Duncan threw out the signal to weigh. His remaining ships stood clear of Yarmouth Roads until, one by one, they turned south-west, towards the Thames. Three hours after sailing only *Venerable*, 74, *Adamant*, 50 and the smaller *Trent* and *Circe*, together with *Kestrel*, remained loyal to their admiral.

The passage across the North Sea was a dismal one. In a way Drinkwater was relieved they were returning to the Texel. Wearying through blockade duty was, he felt instinctively that that was where they should be, no matter to what straits they were reduced. Brown thought so too, for after sending a cipher by the telegraph to the Admiralty, he had joined the cutter with Lord Dungarth's blessing.

'I think, Mr Drinkwater,' he had said, 'that you may take the credit for having set a portfire to the train now and we must wait patiently upon events.'

And patiently they did wait, for the first days of June the wind was in the east. De Winter's fleet of fourteen sail of the line, eight frigates and seventy-three transports and storeships were kept in the Texel by the two British battleships, a few frigates and small fry who made constant signals to one another in a ruse to persuade the watching Dutch that a great fleet lay in the offing of which this was but the inshore squadron.

But would such a deception work?

Chapter Thirteen

No Glory but the Gale

The splash of a cannon shot showed briefly in the water off *Kestrel*'s starboard bow where she lay in the yeasty waters of the Schulpen Gat, close to the beach at Kijkduin.

'They have brought horse artillery today, Mr Drinkwater,' said Major Brown from the side of his mouth as both men stared through their telescopes.

Drinkwater could see the knot of officers watching them. One was dismounted and kneeling on the ground, a huge field glass on the shoulder of an orderly grovelling in front of him.

'That one in the brown coat, d'you know who he is?'

Drinkwater swung his glass. He could see a man in a brown drab coat, but it was not in the least familiar. 'No sir.'

'That,' said Brown with significant emphasis, 'is Wolfe Tone . . .'

Drinkwater looked again. There was nothing remarkable about the man portrayed as a traitor to his country. *Kestrel* bucked inshore and Drinkwater turned to order her laid off a point more. 'I'll give them the usual salute then.'

'Yes—no! Wait! Look at the man next but one to Tone.' Brown was excited and Drinkwater put up his glass again to see a tall figure emerge from behind a horse. Even at that distance Drinkwater knew the man was Santhonax, a Santhonax resplendent in the blue and gold of naval uniform, and it seemed to Drinkwater that across that tumbling quarter mile of breakers and sea-washed sand that Santhonax stared back at him. He lowered the glass and looked at Brown. 'Santhonax.' Brown nodded.

'You were right, Mr Drinkwater. Now give 'em the usual.'

Drinkwater waved forward and saw Traveller stand back from the gun. The four-pounder roared and the men cheered when the ball ricochetted amongst the officers. Their horses reared in fright and one fell screaming on broken legs.

'Stand by heads'l sheets there! Weather runner! Stand by to gybe! Mind your head, Major!' Drinkwater called to Brown who had hoisted himself on to Number 11 gun to witness the fall of shot. 'Up helm . . . mainsheet now, watch there! Watch!'

Kestrel turned away from the shore as the field-gun barked again. The shot ripped through the bulwarks on the quarter and passed between the two helmsmen. The wind of its passage sent them gasping to the deck and Drinkwater jumped for the big tiller. Then the cutter was stern to the beach and rolling over in a thunderous clatter of gybing spars and canvas. 'Larboard runner!' Men tramped aft with the fall of the big double burton and belayed it, the sheets were trimmed and *Kestrel* steadied on her course out of the Schulpen Gat to work her way round the Haakagronden to where Duncan awaited her report.

The admiral was on *Venerable*'s quarterdeck when Drinkwater went up the side. He saluted and made his report to Duncan. The admiral nodded and asked, 'And how is Lieutenant Griffiths today?'

Drinkwater shook his head. 'The surgeon's been up with him all night, sir, but there appears to be no improvement. This is the worst I've known him, sir.'

Duncan nodded. 'He's still adamant he doesn't want a relief?'

'Aye sir.'

'Very well, Mr Drinkwater. Return to your station.'

The strange situation that Duncan found himself in of an admiral almost without ships, compelled him to tread circumspectly. He did not wish to transfer officers or disrupt the delicate loyalties of his pitifully small squadron. Griffiths was known to him and had indicated the professional worth of *Kestrel*'s sailing master. The admiral, astute in the matter of personal evaluation, had formed his own favourable impression of Drinkwater's abilities.

As the week of easterly winds ended, when the period of greatest danger seemed to be over, Duncan received reinforcements. Sir Roger Curtis arrived with some units of the Channel Fleet. *Glatton*, the curious ex-Indiaman armed only with carronades, had mutinied, gone to the Downs and cooled her heels. There her people resolved not to desert their admiral and returned to station. Other odd ships arrived including a Russian squadron under Admiral Hanikov. Then, at the end of June, the Nore mutiny had collapsed and Duncan's ships returned to him. At full strength the North Sea squadron maintained the blockade through the next spell of easterly winds at the beginning of July.

Kestrel made her daily patrols while Griffiths lay sweating in his cot, Appleby a fretful shadow over him. They saw no more of Santhonax and still the Dutch did not come out. Major Brown became increasingly irritated by the turn of events. Santhonax had shot his bolt. The Nore mutiny had collapsed and the French captain had failed, just as he had failed on the *Culloden*. Now, if he was still at the Texel, Santhonax had failed to coerce De Winter.

'A man of action, Mr Drinkwater, cannot sit on his arse for long. This business of naval blockade is the very essence of tedium.'

Drinkwater smiled over his coffee. 'I doubt you would be of that opinion, sir, if the conduct of the ships were yours. For us it is a wearing occupation, requiring constant vigilance.'

'Oh I daresay,' put in Brown crossly, 'but I've a feeling that De Winter won't shift. When we next report to the admiral I shall transfer to the flagship and take the first despatch vessel to Yarmouth. No, Mr Drinkwater, that train of powder has gone out.'

'Well sir,' answered Drinkwater rising from the table and reaching for his hat, 'perhaps it was a little longer than you expected.'

Major Brown stared after the younger man, trying to decide if he had been the victim of impertinence or perception. Certainly he bridled at Drinkwater's apparent lack of respect for a major in His Majesty's Life Guards, but he knew Nathaniel was no fool, no fool at all. Brown remembered the dinner at the Fountain and Drinkwater's insistence that the presence of the uniforms, charts and money indicated the *Citoyenne Janine* held a secret. He also remembered that he had been less than frank about what he had discovered at Tunbridge Wells.

It was true, as he had said to Lord Dungarth, that he had not *found* anything. But where the wolf has slept the grass remains rank. That much he had learned from the Iroquois, and he was no longer in doubt that Santhonax lay frequently at Tunbridge, in enviable circumstances too. A refuge in Hortense's arms was typically Gallic, and if Santhonax had not persuaded her to flee from France in the first place he had turned that fortuitous exit to his own advantage.

But Brown could not admit as much to Dungarth before *Kestrel*'s officers. He had lain a trap and until Santhonax sprung it the hunter remained silent. He had learned that too from the painted men of the Six Nations.

Whether Dungarth had guessed as much when he had ordered surveillance of the Dowager Comtesse's household mattered little. Santhonax had eluded Brown just as Brown had escaped from Santhonax in Paris.

The major bit his lip over the recollection. Had the girl detected him? As he had seen her on the arm of her handsome naval lover in Paris, had she perhaps seen Brown himself some time during the negotiations with Barrallier and De Tocqueville? That would have revealed his true allegiance, and Etienne Montholon had been a party to the arrangements. He tried to recollect if she might have discovered him with Santhonax during his spell as a clerk in the Ministry of Marine. Then he shrugged, 'It's possible . . .'

Santhonax had reached the coast before him, had nearly cut off *Kestrel* but for Madoc's skill and young Drinkwater's timely rescue. It brought him full circle. Was Drinkwater right and Santhonax still trying to bully Jan De Winter into sailing? Brown knew Santhonax to be ruthless. He was certain the man had had De Tocqueville assassinated in London, the more so as it removed a threat to his occupancy of Hortense's bed. And the officer commanding the naval forces at Roscoff had been shot for his prudence in strengthening a convoy escort by the addition of the *Citoyenne Janine*. His mistake was in requisitioning Santhonax's own lugger. Brown's reflection that that meant one less Frenchman to worry about begged the pressing question. It pecked at his present frustration, counselling caution, caution.

Was Santhonax still at the Texel? Was Drinkwater right? Did the train of powder still sputter here, off the Haakagronden? Was De Winter under French pressure?

'It's possible,' he repeated to himself, 'and there is only one way to find out.'

And he shuddered, the old image of geese over a grave springing unbidden into his mind.

Drinkwater was very tired. The regular swing of the oarsmen had a soporific effect now that they had run into the smoother water of the Zeegat van Texel. Astern of them in the darkness the curve of sand dunes and marram grass curled round to Kijkduin and the Schulpen Gat, where *Kestrel* lay at anchor. It was late before full darkness had come and they had little time to execute their task. Drinkwater pulled the tiller slightly to larboard, following the coast round to the east. He steadied it again, feeling the bulk of the man next to him.

Major Brown, wrapped in a cloak under which he concealed a small bag of provisions, had insisted that he be landed. From his bunk Griffiths had been powerless to prevent what he felt to be a hopeless task. He did not doubt Brown's abilities but the gleaning of news of De Winter's intentions was a desperate throw. Griffiths had therefore instructed Drinkwater to land the agent himself. Johnson, the carpenter, had contrived a pair of clogs and they had been carefully scuffed and dirtied as Brown prepared himself in the seamen's cast-offs as a grubby and suitably malodorous fisherman.

Drinkwater turned the boat inshore and whispered 'Oars'. The men ceased pulling and a few moments later the bow of the gig grounded with a gentle lift. Brown shrugged off the cloak and scrambled forward between the pairs of oarsmen. Drinkwater followed him on to the beach and walked up it with him to discover a landmark by which they might both return to the spot. They found some fishing stakes which were sufficient to answer their purpose.

'I'll be off then, Mr Drinkwater.' Brown shouldered his bag and a dimly perceived hand was thrust uncertainly out in an uncharacteristic gesture. 'Until two days hence then. Wish me luck . . . I don't speak Dutch.'

As he turned away Drinkwater noticed the carriage of confidence was missing, the step unsure. Then he jeered at his qualms. Walking in clogs was bad enough. Doing it in soft sand damned near impossible.

On the afternoon of the day on which they were due to recover Major Brown, *Kestrel* sailed into the Schulpen Gat, taking the tide along the coast on her routine patrol. When the masts of the Dutch fleet had been counted over the intervening sand dunes and attempts made to divine whether De Winter had advanced his preparations to sail, which all except Drinkwater were now beginning to doubt, she would retire seawards until her midnight rendezvous with the agent.

As she stood inshore towards the battery at Kijkduin, Drinkwater scanned the beach. The usual officer and orderly were observing their progress. He slewed the telescope and caught in its dancing circle the rampart of the battery. Then he saw something that turned his blood cold.

A new structure had been erected above the gun embrasures, gaunt against the blue of heaven and terrifying in its sinister outline. And from the gibbet, unmistakable in the faded blue of *Kestrel*'s slops, swung the body of Major Brown.

Drinkwater lowered the glass and called for Jessup. The bosun came up immediately aware of the cold gleam in Drinkwater's grey eyes. 'Sir?'

'See if Lieutenant Griffiths is fit enough to come on deck.' Drinkwater's voice was strangely controlled, like a man compelled to speak when he would rather weep.

'Nat, what the deuce is this . . .?' Appleby came protesting out of the companionway.

''Vast that, Harry!' snapped Drinkwater, seeing Griffiths following the surgeon on deck, the flutter of his nightgown beneath his coat.

Without a word Drinkwater handed the telescope to Griffiths and pointed at the battery. Even as he watched the lieutenant for a sign of emotion Drinkwater heard the dull concussion of the first cannon shot roll over the sea. He did not see the fall of shot, only the whitening of the already pallid Welshman and when he lowered the glass Griffiths, too, spoke as though choking.

'Our friend Santhonax did that, Mr Drinkwater, put the vessel about upon the instant.' Griffiths paused. 'That devil's spawn is here then,' he muttered, turning aft.

Drinkwater gave orders and watched Griffiths stagger back to the companionway, a man who looked his years, sick and frail. The battery fired again, Shot rained about them and they were hulled once. Running south with the wind free and his back to the gibbet, Drinkwater imagined he could hear the creaking of the contraption and the laughter of the gunners as they toiled beneath their grim trophy.

The death of Major Brown had a desolating effect on *Kestrel*. The enigmatic army officer had become almost one of themselves and the cramped cabin was a sad place without him. For Madoc Griffiths the loss was more personal, their friendship one of long standing. In the twilit world of their professions strange and powerful bonds drew men together.

'Brown was not his real name,' Griffiths had muttered, and it was all the epitaph the Major ever had.

It seemed that his death extinguished the powder train whose extent he had been so eager to determine. Whatever Santhonax's achievements in the apprehension of spies it was apparent to the watching British that he had failed to persuade De Winter to sail.

Yet Duncan, and in a lesser way Nathaniel Drinkwater too, persisted in their belief that the Dutch might yet sally; or at least must be prevented from so doing. As the summer waned and turned to autumn the routine blockade wore down men and ships. Much of the time the line of battleships lay anchored, weighing and standing offshore, even sheltering in Yarmouth Roads when the weather became too boisterous. Hovering on the western margins of the Haakagronden the inshore squadron, the frigates *Beaulieu* and *Circe* and the sloop *Martin*, maintained the visual link between the admiral and those in close contact with the enemy, the lieutenants in command of the little flotilla of cutters and luggers working inside the Haak Sand.

The cutters *Rose, King George, Diligent, Active* and *Kestrel* kept their stations through the long weeks, assisted by the luggers *Black Joke* and *Speculator*. The last two named provided endless witicisms as to predicting whether the Dutch would, or would not, emerge. When *Speculator* was on an advanced station the chances were said to be better than when the sardonically named *Black Joke* was inshore.

These small fry fell into a routine of patrolling the gatways, acting as fleet tenders and advice boats. It was exhausting work that seemed to be endless. Scouting through the approaches to the channels, counting the mastheads of the enemy, determining which had their topmasts up and yards across, constantly worrying about the shoals, the state of the tide and whether a change of wind might not bottle them up in range of a field gun or battery.

Griffiths's health improved and he reassumed effective command of *Kestrel*. But the Dutch did not come out. As week succeeded week, expectancy turned to irritation and then to grumbling frustration. In the fleet, officers, still suspicious after the mutiny, watched for signs of further trouble as the quality of rations deteriorated with the passing of time. Imperceptibly at first, but with mounting emphasis, discipline was tightened and a return 'to the old days' feared on every lower deck. Among the men the triumph of the mutiny was lost in petty squabblings and resentments. Men remembered that executions had followed the suppression of the Nore affair, that they still had had no liberty, that the pursers were not noticeably more generous or their pay more readily available.

Then the weather worsened with the onset of September and the admiral, taking stock of the condition of his fleet, decided that he must return to Yarmouth to refit, replenish stores and land his sick. For scurvy had broken out and no admirals as considerate of his men as Adam Duncan could keep the sea under those circumstances. Yet, in the leaking cabin of *Venerable* he still fretted as to whether the Dutch, supine for so long, might not still take advantage of his absence.

Drinkwater peered into the screaming darkness, holding on to the weather shrouds and bracing himself against the force of the westerly gale. *Kestrel*, hard reefed with her centre plates down, stood north-west, beating out of the Molen Gat, clawing to windward for sea-room and safety. Somewhere to the south of her, across the roaring fury of the breakers on the Haakagronden, *Diligent* would be thrashing out of the Schulpen Gat while *Rose* should have quitted the West Gat long since.

Drinkwater rubbed his eyes, but the salt spray inflamed them and the fury of the wind made staring directly to windward impossible. He had hoped to see a lantern from *Circe* but he had difficulty seeing further than the next wave as it rose out of the darkness to larboard, its rolling crest already being torn to shreds by the violence of the wind.

Kestrel's bow thumped into it, the long line of her bowsprit disappearing. Water squirted inboard round the lips of her gun-ports and a line of white foam rose to her rail but she did not ship any green water. Drinkwater was seized with a sudden savage satisfaction in the noble way the cutter behaved. In the tense moments when they could do nothing but hang on, trusting to the art of the Wivenhoe shipwrights who had built her, she never failed them.

He turned and cautiously moved aft, his tarpaulin flapping round him. When he had checked the course, he secured himself by the larboard running backstay, passing a turn of its tail around his waist.

Tregembo approached, a pale blur in the darkness. 'You sent for me sir?'

'Aye, Tregembo. An occasional cast of the lead if you can manage it.' He sensed rather than saw the Cornishman grin.

They must not go aground tonight.

Drinkwater adjusted himself against the big stay's downhaul. He could feel the trembling of the top-hamper transmitted down to the hull as a gentle vibration that transferred itself to his body, so that he felt a part of the fabric of the cutter. It was a very satisfying feeling he concluded, a warm glow within him defying the hideous howl of the gale. For a time the image of Brown in his gibbett was dimmed.

Drinkwater noted the helm relieved, the two men leaving the tiller, flexing their arms with relief and seeking shelter beneath the lee gig. A sea crashed against the hull and foamed brutally over the rail, sluicing the deck white and breaking in eddies round the deck fittings. They would be clearing the Molen Gat now, leaving the comparative shelter of the Haakagronden.

Again he peered to windward seeking a light from the frigate. Nothing.

The Dutch would never come out in weather like this, thought Drinkwater. It was going to be a long, dirty night for the British blockaders and there was little glory in such a gale.

They reached the admiral at ten in the morning. The gale was at its height, a low scud drifting malignantly across the sky reducing the visibility to a monotonous circle of grey breaking waves, streaked with white spindrift that merged at its margins with the lowering clouds. In and out of this pall the pale squares of reefed topsails and the dark shapes of hulls streaming with water were all that could be seen of the blockading battleships. Even the patches of the blue ensigns of Duncan's squadron seemed leeched to the surrounding drab.

Kestrel had come up under *Venerable*'s lee quarter like a leaping cork, or so it seemed to the officers on the flagship's quarterdeck, and the admiral had had his orders sealed in a keg and thrown into the sea.

With great skill Griffiths had manoeuvred in the flagship's wake to recover the keg. 'Orders for the fleet, Mr Drinkwater, excepting for *Russell, Adamant, Beaulieu, Circe, Martin* and two cutters, ah, and *Black Joke*, the fleet's for Yarmouth Road.'

'And we're to tell 'em?'

Griffiths nodded. 'Very good, sir, we'll bear away directly.'

Dipping her ensign in acknowledgement of her instructions *Kestrel* turned away.

As she steadied on her course Drinkwater returned to Griffiths's side. 'What about us, sir?'

'*Active* and *Diligent* to remain, the rest of us for Yarmouth.'

Drinkwater nodded. The nagging notion that they had unfinished business off the Texel caused him to catch Griffiths's eye. Griffiths held his gaze but said nothing. Both of them were thinking of the shrivelling body of their friend.

They were running downwind now, closing Vice-Admiral Onslow in the *Monarch*. Passing their message they reached down the line of Onslow's division, watching the lumbering third rates, *Powerful, Montagu* and *Russell*, the smaller sixty-four's *Veteran* and *Agincourt* with Bligh's *Director*. Next they passed word to the obsolete old *Adamant*, she that so gallantly supported Duncan's deception off the Texel. They found *Circe* and *Beaulieu* and both the luggers hanging on to the frigates like children round their mother's skirts. It was dark before they returned to *Venerable* and sent up a damply fizzing blue rocket as a signal to the admiral.

Drinkwater scrambled below, jamming himself into a corner of the cabin and gratefully accepted a bowl from Merrick. The skillygolee was all that could be heated on the galley stove but it tasted excellent laced with molasses and he wolfed it, aware that Appleby was hovering in the doorway.

'D'you want me, Harry?' Drinkwater asked, nodding to Traveller who was groping his way into the cabin, bracing himself against the violence of the cutter's motion, also in search of something to eat.

Appleby nodded too. 'A word, Nat, if you've a moment . . .' He plucked at Drinkwater's sleeve and drew him towards his own cabin.

'By God, that skilly was good . . . Hey! Merrick! D'you have any more?' Fresh from the deck and very hungry Drinkwater found Appleby irritated him.

'Nat, for heaven's sake, a moment of your time. Listen, while you and Griffiths have been busy on deck I have been increasingly aware of unrest in the ship . . . nothing I can pin down, but this miserable blockade duty at a season of the year when no self-respecting Dutchman is going to emerge into the North Sea when he has a bed ashore, is playing the devil with the men. No, don't dismiss me as a meddling old fool. I have observed glances, mutterings, listened to remarks dropped near me. Damn it, Nat, you know the kind of thing . . .'

'Oh come now Harry, I doubt now that we're going back to Yarmouth that anything will materialise,' Drinkwater bit off a jibe at Appleby's increasing preoccupation with mutiny. Blockade duty in such a small vessel was playing on all their nerves, even those of the men, and it was doubtless this irritation had manifested itself to Appleby. 'What seaman doesn't grumble, Harry? You are worrying for nothing, forget it . . .'

There was a thumping crash and the bulkhead behind them trembled. From the lobby outside a torrent of Welsh oaths mixed with Anglo-Saxon expletives ended the conversations. Appleby threw open the door to reveal Lieutenant Griffiths lying awkwardly at the foot of the ladder. His face contorted with pain.

'My leg, doctor . . .By damn, I've broken my leg!'

A Private Insurrection

'Can you manage the cutter, Mr Drinkwater?'

Drinkwater looked at the admiral. Duncan's eyes were tired from a multitude of responsibilities. He nodded. 'I believe so, sir.'

'Very well. I will have an acting commission made out immediately. You have been acting before, have you not?'

'Yes sir. Twice.'

Duncan nodded. 'Good. If you discharge your duty to my satisfaction I shall see that it is confirmed without further ado . . . now sit down a moment.' Duncan rang a bell and his servant entered the cabin. 'Sir?'

'My secretary, Knapton, and my compliments to Captain Fairfax and will he bring in his lordship,' he turned to Drinkwater. 'It'll not hurt you to know what's in the wind, Mr Drinkwater, as you are to occupy an advanced station. Were you not part of the prize crew that brought in *Santa Teresa* to Gibraltar in '80?'

'Yes sir. She was commanded by Lieutenant Devaux, Lord Dungarth as is now, sir.'

'Aye, I remember your name now, and here is his lordship,' Duncan rose stooping under the deckhead to motion Lord Dungarth and Captain Fairfax to chairs.

Drinkwater covered his astonishment at the earl's sudden appearance with a bow. He remained standing until the admiral motioned him to sit again.

'Now gentlemen, Mr Drinkwater is to remain. Under the circumstances he ought properly to be informed of our deliberations and can convey their substance to Trollope. I have given him an acting commission. Now, my Lord, what have you to tell us?'

'You could not have made a better choice, Admiral,' put in Dungarth, smiling at Drinkwater. 'Now when are you able to sail?'

The old admiral passed a hand over his face. 'I *must* have a few more days to recruit the fleet. Yes what is it?' Duncan paused at the knock on the door. A large man with a saturnine face entered. He was in admiral's uniform. 'Ah, Richard, come in, you know Fairfax of course, this is Lord Dungarth, from the Admiralty . . .' Onslow's eyebrows lifted, '. . . and this is Lieutenant Drinkwater of *Kestrel*.'

Drinkwater rose and bowed. 'Your servant, sir.'

'What happened to Griffiths?'

Duncan said, 'Broke his leg and I've promoted Drinkwater, he kens the crew and I'm not one to be fussing about with officers on other ships with the situation as delicate as it is now . . .' He looked significantly at Onslow who nodded his agreement. Drinkwater realised there were doubtless a score of passed midshipmen who might regard their claim on the first available commission as better than his own.

'Congratulations, Mr Drinkwater,' said Onslow. 'Are you familiar with Psalm 75? No? "Promotion cometh neither from the east, nor from the west, nor from the south, but God is the judge; he pulleth down one and setteth up another."'

The little group chuckled. Onslow was well-known for his Biblical references so that signals midshipmen had to keep a copy of the Bible alongside Kempenfelt's code.

'Most apposite. But to business. My Lord?'

'Well, gentlemen, since the regretted loss of Major Brown,' Dungarth paused and there was a deferential murmur as death passed his grim shadow across their council, 'I have learned from our people in Paris that Capitaine Santhonax has been seen there. However, his stay was not long and he was seen in The Hague last month. It is confidently expected that he is now back at the Texel breathing down De Winter's neck. We were under the impression that enthusiasm for another attempt upon Ireland has dwindled since the death of General Hoche. But Austria has reached an accommodation with this new General Buonaparte at Leoben and it seems likely that troops will be available for other enterprises.' He paused and accepted a glass of wine from Knapton who appeared with silent ease, bearing tall glasses on a silver salver.

'Most of you will know of the Director's raid last February on Fishguard. It was American led . . .' a murmur of anger went round the listeners. 'Although it was an ignominious failure the Directory learned that it was perfectly possible to land on our soil.

'Whether the target is Ireland or the mainland we do not know. However it seems certain that the Directory, in the person of Santhonax, will exert great pressure upon De Winter to sail. If he prevaricates he will be superseded and possibly more will be struck down than his flag. Jan De Winter is a convinced republican but a soldier by training. I think Santhonax is at his elbow to overcome his misgivings. So you see, gentlemen, De Winter *must come out* and you *must stop him*. A junction with the Brest squadrons would be disastrous for us on all fronts.'

There was an awkward shuffling of feet as Dungarth finished. The collection of ships that made up the North Sea squadron was far from the crack units of the Channel fleet, the Grand Fleet as it was commonly called.

'I must have a few more days,' said Duncan, looking anxiously at Onslow for support.

'I agree Adam. You'll have to inform Government, my Lord, we must have time, this squadron is cranky enough. Look, even its commander-in-chief has to endure this sort of thing . . .' Onslow pointed to the strategically located buckets in Duncan's cabin that had been placed to catch water from the leaks in the deckhead.

Drinkwater listened to the deliberations of his seniors with one ear and turned over Dungarth's news in his mind. So, his instinct had been right. They were not yet finished with the Texel. And he was not yet finished with Santhonax. He began to see that Ireland was probably the key. At least the paralysis of the British Fleet and combination of the republican navies for some expedition had been the mainspring of Santhonax's actions. And Brown had taken an interest in Wolfe Tone on the beach at Kijkduin. Yes, Santhonax's actions were clear now: the suborning of the British Fleet that had so nearly succeeded, the urgency to get Dutch support before the collapse of Parker's resolve. When that failed a last thrust from Brest with the combined fleets to force aside a Royal Navy weakened by mutiny, and then a descent on the naked coasts of Britain by a French army under this new general, said to be more brilliant than Hoche or Moreau, this General Buonaparte . . .

'Mr Drinkwater? . . . Mr Drinkwater!'

He came to with a start. 'I beg your pardon, sir. I, er, I was just digesting the implications of Lord Dungarth's . . .' he tailed off flushing scarlet.

'Yes, yes,' said Duncan testily, 'I will have written orders within the hour, please make yourself at home in the wardroom.

You will convey my despatches to Trollope then station yourself as close to Kijkduin as ye can. I want to know the moment the Dutch move. D'ye understand, man?'

Drinkwater rose. 'Aye sir. Thank you for taking me into your confidence. Your servant gentlemen.' He bowed and made his way back on deck.

'You two are in collusion, damn you both,' Griffiths muttered, sweat standing out on his pale forehead, his pupils contracted by the opiate administered by Appleby.

'No sir,' said Drinkwater gently, 'that is really not the case at all. Admiral Duncan's orders, sir. If you will permit us we will have you ashore directly and into the hospital.' He motioned Short and a seaman into the cabin to lift Griffiths on to the stretcher. As they struggled through the door Appleby mopped his forehead.

'Phew! He took it from you like a lamb, Nat my boy. He's been tearing the seat out of my breeches this hour past.'

'Poor old fellow,' said Drinkwater, 'will his leg mend?'

Appleby nodded. 'Yes, if he keeps off it for a while, his constitution is remarkable considering the Gambia fever.'

'He'll miss his bottle in hospital.' They followed the stretcher up on deck where Jessup was preparing to lower the lieutenant into the waiting boat.

'Mr Drinkwater,' croaked Griffiths, trying to raise his head.

'Sir?' Drinkwater took the extended hand.

'Good luck to you Nathaniel *bach*, this may be your opportunity, see. Be vigilant and success will be within your grasp. Good luck now. Lower away you lubbers and handsomely, handsomely.'

Drinkwater saw the old man, wrapped in his wood and canvas shroud, pulled away from the cutter. He watched the gig curve away for the shore and found his eyes misting. He dismissed sentiment from his mind and turned his attention inboard.

'Mr Jessup!'

'Sir?'

'Pipe the hands aft.'

His heart beat with a mixture of excitement and apprehension. His elevation to command might only be that of an officer 'acting', unsubstantive and very temporary, but for as long as it lasted he held power over the men who crowded round the remaining gig amidships, and was accountable for every movement of the cutter, the duty and mistakes of his subordinates. He reached into his pocket and withdrew the roll of paper.

When silence fell he began to read himself in.

At the conclusion of the solemnly formal words he added a sentence of his own. 'I trust you will do your duty for me as you did for Lieutenant Griffiths. Very well Mr Jessup, we will weigh directly the boat returns, you may heave short now.' Jessup shouted and the men turned away to make preparations. Drinkwater called to Hill. 'Mr Hill! Mr Hill, I am rating you master, do you take the first watch in my place.'

While the cutter's sails were cast loose he slipped below. Merrick, fussing like an old hen, was lugging the last of Drinkwater's gear out of the little cabin and settling it in the lieutenant commander's. It was a trifle larger than his own but in the rack for glass and carafe, Drinkwater wrily noted, the two objects were in place. As he hung the little watercolour he thought of Elizabeth. They had been separated for eighteen months now. It was a pity he had had no time to let her know of his promotion and Duncan's promise. A knock on the door interrupted his privacy. It was Appleby.

'Nat, er, sir,' Appleby rubbed a large, pudgy hand across his several chins.

'What is it?' asked Drinkwater, settling his books.

'I'm damned glad to see you promoted, Nat . . . sir . . . but believe me it is imperative you are circumspect with the men. They are still in an ugly mood. Orders for the Texel will do nothing to ameliorate that. It's nothing specific,' Appleby hurried on before Drinkwater could interrupt, 'but I anticipate that they will try you now Griffiths is gone, that's all . . .'

'You seem,' said Drinkwater passing a lashing round his quadrant box, 'to have let sedition, mutiny and all manner of lower deck bogeys infect your otherwise good sense, Harry.'

'For God's sake, Nat, damn it, sir, take my warning lightly and you do so at your peril.'

Drinkwater felt anger rising in him. To be thwarted now filled him with horror and Appleby's defeatism galled him. He mastered himself with difficulty.

'Look Harry, we have been weeks on this tedious blockading, we are all worn with it, sick of it, but it is our duty and now, more than ever, there exists a need for cruisers off the Texel. D'you cease this damned cant at once.'

'For God's sake man, this command nonsense has gone to your head!'

'Have a care Harry,' said Drinkwater with low and furious menace in his voice. He pushed past the surgeon in search of the fresh air of the deck.

Bulman met him at the companionway. 'Mr Hill's compliments, Mr Drinkwater, and the anchor's underfoot and the gig approaching.'

Drinkwater nodded and strode to the rail, grasping it with trembling hands. Damn Appleby and his pusillanimous soul. He wanted to clear his mind of such gloomy thoughts to concentrate on his duty.

They recovered the gig and weighed, heading south east for St Nicholas Gat and the passage south of the Scroby Sands.

Forward the last lashings were being passed over the gig, the last coils of the halliards turned on to their pins and the taut sheets belayed. Hill had the cat stoppers clapped on and was passing the shank painter to secure the anchor against its billboard. Already two men had buckets over the side and were sluicing the mud of Yarmouth Road off the planking. Traveller was walking round the guns, checking their breechings. All was reassuringly normal. He relaxed and checked the course. Ahead of him lay the challenge of the Texel.

At midnight Appleby's apprehensions were fulfilled. When Hill turned the deck over to Jessup the men demanded to be paid. It was an odd and impossible request but had ranked as a grievance for many months. It was now that those who influenced the grumblings of the fo'cs'le chose to make it manifest itself. *Kestrel*'s complement had not been paid for over a twelvemonth. Their recent period at anchor had been marred by a refusal of further credit by James Thompson, the purser, largely because that gentleman had himself run out of ready cash. This denial had led to the men being unable to make purchases from the bumboats of Yarmouth. The consequent lack of small comforts exacerbated the already strong resentment of the hands. By an irony several bottles of liquor had found their way on board and the consumption of these in the first watch had led to the midnight revolt.

Drinkwater was called and sleepily tumbled from his cot. But his dreams were quickly displaced by anger at the news Jessup brought him. For a minute, as he dressed while Jessup spoke he

149

fulminated against the men, but he forced himself to acknowledge their grievance and that his own anger was unlikely to get him anywhere. But to pay them was not merely out of the question, it was impossible.

'Who's behind this, then, Mr Jessup, come on, there must be a ring-leader?'

Jessup shrugged. 'Not that I know of . . . here I'll do one of those.' He took one of the pistols that Drinkwater had taken out of their case. They belonged to Griffiths and Drinkwater thought furiously as he slipped the little ramrod back into its socket. 'Can I count on you Mr Jessup?'

'O' course, sir,' said Jessup indignantly.

'Very well, you keep that pistol then. Where are the men now?'

'On deck waiting for you.'

'Call all the other officers.'

'I did that on my way to you, ah, here's Mr Appleby . . .'

Appleby pushed into the cabin. 'I told you, Nat, I warned you . . .' His face was grey with worry and his nightgown increased his girth where it protruded from hastily drawn on breeches.

'To the devil with your premonitions, Harry. Are you armed?'

'Of course,' he held up a brace of heavy pistols. 'I've had these loaded and ready for a month.'

'Have you checked the primings then,' snapped Jessup and Appleby withered him at a glance.

'Right gentlemen. Let's go!' Traveller joined them in the lobby and they went on deck.

It was a clear night with a quartering wind and sea driving them east at a spanking rate. Patches of cloud obscured the stars. As his eyes adjusted to the darkness he could see Bulman had the helm and a blur of faces amidships showed where the hands waited to see what he would make of their action. Drinkwater knew that he must act with resolution and he turned briefly to the officers behind him.

'I expect your support. To the utmost if need be.'

Then he turned forward until he was no more than a yard from the waiting men. A cold and desperate feeling had settled on him. He would not be diverted from his orders now, nor from the one chance providence had so parsimoniously offered him. Instinctively he felt no man would offer him bodily harm. He was less sure of his own restraint.

He drew his hanger with a rasping flourish and noted the involuntary rearward movement, heard the sharp intake of breath.

'Now my lads, I know your grievance but this is not the time to air it. We are on urgent service and you'll all do your duty.' He let the words sink in.

'Bollocks,' came a voice from the rear of the crowd and he saw grins in the darkness.

He whipped the pistol from his belt and held it suddenly and terribly against the skull of the nearest seaman.

'Mr Jessup! Mr Appleby! Your weapons here upon the instant!'

Again he felt the will of the men waver: resolution from the rear, weakening from those in front. 'I will shoot this man if you do not disperse at once. I beg you not to force me to this extremity . . .' The man's eyes were enlarged with fear, the whites clear in the gloom.

'Jesus mates,' he whispered.

'Get fucked, Mr Drinkwater, you can't bluff us, we want our money.' A murmur of supporting approval greeted this sentiment.

With a click Drinkwater pulled the pistol hammer back to full cock. 'I'm not bluffing.' He ranged his eyes over the men. Behind him Appleby spoke, 'Mr Drinkwater has a reputation for courage, lads, I most earnestly recommend you not to strain his patience . . .'

'Aye, lads, Mr Appleby's right, remember that Froggy lugger . . .' It was Tregembo's voice and Drinkwater held his tongue, aware of the deadly little melodrama being played out. He did not know of the grisly reputation he had acquired for hand to hand fighting, of how it was said that he cleared the deck of the *Citoyenne Janine*, of how, in the American War, Mr Drinkwater killed the French officer of *La Creole* and still carried the dead man's sword to prove it.

Drinkwater felt the tide turn. 'I will count to five. If the watch below isn't off the deck by then I'll shoot. Otherwise we'll let the matter drop and I'll personally apply to the admiral for your pay. One . . . two . . .' The man beside him was trembling uncontrollably. Drinkwater brought the muzzle up. 'Three.'

A rearward surge went through the men. 'Four.'

Murmuring to themselves they went forward.

Drinkwater lowered his pistol. 'Carry on,' he said quietly to the frightened man beside him who trembled with reaction.

The mutiny was over. It was just one bell in the middle watch.

'Time for bed, gentlemen,' said Drinkwater in a tone taken for coolness by those who heard, but redolent with relief to his beating heart.

'Four bells, sir.'

Drinkwater stirred, swimming upwards from the depths of sleep to find Merrick bent over him and the aroma of coffee in his nostrils. Swinging his legs over the edge of the cot he took the mug while Merrick put a glim to his lantern. Drinkwater shivered in the predawn chill and felt a dull ache in his right arm. The pain reminded him of the events of the night and he was suddenly wide awake.

Merrick turned from adjusting the lantern. 'Mr Traveller said to tell you 'e expects to sight the squadron at first light, sir.'

'Then why didn't you say so when you called me?' Drinkwater felt a peevish irritation rising in him, together with a flood of loneliness that combined with the bitter realisation that in addition to a heavy responsibility to Duncan, he had to contend with a disobedient crew. He did not listen to Merrick's mumbling excuse and experienced a mean delight when the man fled.

While he shaved he calmed himself, shaking off resentment as the coffee scoured his mouth and cleared his head. Duncan's task was not impossible. Griffiths had been right, this could be his opportunity and he was damned if he was going to lose it now. Wiping the lather from his face he completed dressing and went on deck.

Exchanging courtesies with Traveller he walked to the weather rail. The north westerly breeze had held during the night and the eastern horizon was becoming more clearly defined against the coming daylight. For a moment he drank in the cold air of the morning then called to Traveller.

'Mr Drinkwater?'

'All quiet?'

'Not a peep. Begging your pardon, Mr Drinkwater, but I'd say as how you'll have no more trouble with this lot.' Drinkwater looked at the gunner.

'Let us hope you are right, Mr Traveller,' he replied as coolly as he could.

'We should sight the squadron very soon, sir. She was making nine knots at four bells.'

Drinkwater nodded and walked forward as far as the boats. Surreptitiously he shot a glance at the two helmsmen. They were intent on the compass. He had cowed them, it seemed, and with an effort he stopped twisting his hands nervously behind his back. He set his mind to preparing what he would say to Trollope in an hour or two.

'Wind's dying,' Hill said. They were well up into the Schulpen Gat, the battery at Kijkduin broad on the bow, just out of cannon shot. Mercifully the gibbet was no longer there. Against the south going tide they were making no headway and Drinkwater gave the order to anchor. Already the sun was westering and the night's chill could be felt in the air. Drinkwater looked at the sky. The cloud was clearing, the dunes, mills and churches of the Dutch coast had a sharpness that owed more to a drying of the air than the sinking of the sun.

'A shift of wind to the east, I think, Mr Hill.'

'Aye sir, happen you are right.'

Drinkwater waited until the hands had the sails down and stowed. Then he ordered a spring clapped on the cable, the charges drawn and the guns reloaded. While the men bustled round he ascended the rigging to the hounds. Securing himself he levelled his glass to the eastward.

He recalled the words of William Burroughs, first lieutenant of *Russell*, who had entertained him while Trollope digested his orders. 'I envy you that cutter, so will a number more, I don't wonder, once they hear old Griffiths is laid up. At least you set eyes on the squareheads, all I've seen is a few mastheads over the dunes. Trying to make an intelligent guess at the number of ships they represent is like . . . is like,' Burroughs had searched for a simile and failed with a shrug. 'Well you know it's damned impossible. Yes, I do envy you that. It gets deuced boring out here week after week, it's not the Mediterranean, don't you know, no blue seas and snow-capped sierras to moon over, just acres and acres of dung coloured water and a lot of squareheaded Dutchmen sitting on their arses laughing at us, eh?' It was a sentiment commonly expressed in the fleet. But Burroughs's farewell had been less flippant. 'Good fortune, m'dear fellow, we will all be relying most heavily upon you.'

Well, he must do better than Burroughs. Wiping his eye on his sleeve he replaced the glass and concentrated.

The dreary coast extended far to the south in wave after wave of dunes and marram grass. Here and there the cluster of habitations huddled round the conspicuous spires of churches. Shreds of smoke rose into the tranquil air. In the circle of the glass he picked up a lone horseman riding along the tideline keeping an eye on them. He swung left to where the parapet of the battery fronted the cottages of Kijkduin. The Dutch tricolour hung limply above the dun coloured rampart and here too he could see men, the flash of light on a bayonet or telescope. Beyond Kijkduin the coast trended away into the anchorage where the black masts of ships could be seen. He felt his heart skip as he realised that most of the ships had their yards crossed. Preparations for sailing were well advanced. Lord Dungarth was right! He counted twenty ships at the least. He swept the glass to the north. On the far side of the Zeegat van Texel the island of Texel faded into the far distance. A Dutch yacht lay in the channel. De Winter's eyes, as he was Duncan's.

Northwards in the Molen Gat he could see a little dark shape that was *Diligent* while to the westwards the three masts of *Black Joke*, one time advice boat to Earl Howe, lay anchored in the West Gat. Between them a flat expanse of sand, fringed with the curl of shallow breakers, the Haakagronden, covering as the tide rose. To the west the sun sank redly, the sea a jade green except where the sun laid a golden bar upon its rippled surface.

He returned to the deck, prepared the signal 'Enemy has yards crossed,' hoisted it and fired a gun. As the sun set *Black Joke* acknowledged it and Drinkwater could just see where she repeated it to Trollope's innermost ship, the sloop *Martin*. Drinkwater smiled to himself with self-satisfaction. Elizabeth would think him very pompous just at the moment.

'Did you see the way Mr Drinkwater smiled just now,' muttered Tregembo to another seaman leaning on the rail beside him, 'I reckons as how us'll be seeing some action afore long, my handsome.'

The light airs had died completely by midnight and a glassy calm fell on the black water the rudder creak and the tiller kick gently in the tackles.

'Good tide running now, we'll get under way with the centre

plates down and sweep her up to the north a little, Mr Jessup. Call the hands.'

Drinkwater had no desire to work the men unnecessarily but one mile to the north they would command a much better view of the Dutch fleet at anchor, still out of dangerous gunshot of the battery. The centre plates would give them ample warning of going around on such a quiet night and the labour at the sweeps would keep the men busy, giving them little time to reflect on their grievances, imagined or otherwise.

The steady clunk of pawls tripping on whelps told where the windlass was manned, while down the cutter's side the carpenter and his mate were knocking the poppets out of the sweep row-locks. A muffled thudding in the darkness amidships indicated the hands were getting the ungainly lengths of the sweeps from their stowage between the gigs into position. Two men came aft and cast off the tiller lashings. They stood ready to execute Drinkwater's orders.

From forward came the low cry, 'Up and down,' and after a little, 'Anchor's aweigh.'

'Hard a-starboard.' The two men pushed the tiller over. 'Give way together, Mr Jessup.'

The sweeps came to life, swinging awkwardly across the deck, splashing alongside while the men got into their stride and Jessup belaboured them with rhythmic obscenities, curiously inflected with emphatic syllables so that they gradually came into unison. *Kestrel* gathered way, turning to bring the tide under her while Jessup intoned his meaningless invective in the ingenuous way of the British seaman. Drinkwater steadied the cutter on course and half an hour later they re-anchored.

'Get a spring on the cable, Mr Jessup, then send the watch below. We'll clear for action at dawn just in case that Dutch yacht has moved.'

'Aye, aye, sir.' Jessup moved off giving orders. Drinkwater was pleased with himself. The centre plates had not touched once. They should be in the position he wanted. Wrapping himself in his cloak and kicking off his shoes he threw himself on to his cot and was soon asleep.

He was called at six. Five minutes later he was on deck. The wind was sharp and from the east. At five bells he called all hands and the men tumbled up to draw and reload the guns. Alternate lashings were cast off the mainsail and the halliards prepared for rapid hoisting, their falls faked out along the deck in case daylight revealed them too close to the battery. Daylight came with a mist.

An hour later Drinkwater stood the men down and went below to shave and break his fast. The skillygolee and molasses warmed him and only his new found dignity as commander prevented him from chaffing Appleby who was making a half-hearted protest that the creaking of the sweeps had kept him awake. The fact that the wind was from the east had set Drinkwater in a state of tension that would not let him relax.

He returned to pacing the deck while he waited for the mist over the land to lift. If they had anchored in the wrong place they might have to cut and run before being caught in the cross fire of the yacht and the heavier guns at Kijkduin. He tried to calm himself, to stay the prickling sweat between his shoulder blades and forget the fine, fire-eating phrase that kept leaping unbidden into his mind: *morituri te salutant* . . .

'Mist's clearing, Mr Drinkwater.' It was Traveller, anxious to fire his precious guns.

'Thank you Mr Traveller.' Drinkwater went forward and began climbing the mast. From his perch he could see the mast trucks of the Dutch fleet rising from the white shroud that enveloped the town of Den Helder. In the foreground the land was already clear and the solitary boom of a gun echoed seawards where the battery ranged them. The Dutch yacht still lay in the fairway, some eight cables away, and beyond her, now emerging dramatically from the evaporating vapour, lay the Dutch fleet.

Movement was clearly discernible. There were men aloft and he started to count as the ships began to warp themselves clear of the buoys. At noon *Black Joke*, beating skilfully up through the West Gat, came alongside. By agreement it was she that ran out to Trollope during the afternoon of the 7th October to inform him that the Dutch were on the move. There was every prospect that if the wind held east, Admiral De Winter would sail.

Late afternoon came and still the breeze was steady. Drinkwater kept the deck, not trusting himself to go below. The weary months of blockade duty had screwed him to a pitch that cried out for the release of action. What was true of him was true of all of *Kestrel*'s people. He looked round the deck. Men lingered half hoping, half dreading that the Dutch would come out. He looked away to the east. The yacht remained at her anchor, like a dog at the door of his master's hall, and beyond . . .

Drinkwater reached for his glass. One of the ships had sail set and a bone in her teeth. He hastened forward and levelled the glass, steadying it against a stay.

It was a frigate, coming down the fairway under topsails. Would she re-anchor or was she leading the fleet to sea? Drinkwater mouth was dry, his back damp and his heart hammered. The frigate was still heading seawards. He stared at her for perhaps ten minutes then relaxed. He saw her topsails shiver and her hull lengthen as she turned into the wind to anchor. She was to act as guardship then, weighing first and sweeping the puny opposition outside from the path of De Winter's armada. Drinkwater found himself shaking with relief. He was about to turn aft when a movement beside the frigate caught his eye. A boat had put off from her side and was being pulled seawards, towards the yacht.

As the sun dropped *Kestrel* made the signal 'Enemy in an advanced state of preparation' to *Black Joke* five miles to the west. They saw her repeat it and a few minutes later received a reply from Trollope. It was a distance signal of three square flags and a black ball and it meant 'I am unsupported.'

Duncan had not arrived.

Drinkwater turned east once more. They would have to run before the enemy then. The boat had left the yacht and was pulling back for the frigate. He wondered what orders the commander of the yacht had received. Positive sailing instructions, he concluded. And then he noticed something else. Something that made the muscles of his stomach contract and his whole body tense.

The Dutch yacht had hoisted a flag to her masthead.

A black, swallow-tailed pendant.

Chapter Fifteen 8th–11th October 1797

Camperdown

Sleep eluded Nathaniel Drinkwater that night. When he heard four bells struck in the middle watch he rose and entered the cabin, opening the locker where Griffiths kept his liquor. His hands closed round the neck of the first bottle and he drew it out, pulling the cork and pouring cognac into his throat. The smell of it reminded him of the night off Beaubigny and the eyes of Hortense Montholon. He had a strong sensation of events coming full circle. 'This is witchery,' he muttered to himself, and drew again at the bottle, shuddering from the effect of the raw spirit. He shifted his mind to Elizabeth, deliberately invoking her image to replace that of Hortense as a man touching a talisman; as he had done years ago in the swamps of South Carolina. But Elizabeth was distant now, beyond the immense hurdle of the coming hours, obscured by the responsibilities of command. Somehow his old promise of circumspection to Elizabeth now seemed as pompously ridiculous as that of doing his duty to Duncan.

He hurled the bottle from him and it shivered to pieces against the far bulkhead.

'Damned witchery,' he repeated, heading for the companionway. Up and down he strode, between the taffrail and the gigs, the anchor watch withdrawing from his path. From time to time he paused to look in the direction of Kijkduin. Santhonax *had* to be at Kijkduin. Had to be, to feed the cold ruthlessness that was spreading through him. If his chance lay in the coming hours he must not lack the resolution to grasp it.

Vice-Admiral De Winter ordered his fleet to sail on the morning of October 8th. The frigate that Drinkwater had watched the previous afternoon stood seawards at first light, catching up the yacht in her wake. *Kestrel* weighed too, standing seawards down the West Gat, firing her chasers and flying the signal for an enemy to windward. *Black Joke* caught the alarm, wore round and stood in her grain, hoisting the same signal.

For an hour *Kestrel* ran ahead of the Dutch fleet as ship after ship rounded the battery at Kijkduin, turning south for the Schulpen Gat. The cutter, diverging towards Trollope, observed them, her commander making notes upon a tablet.

They rejoined the squadron at noon, closing the commodore for their orders.

'What d'you make of them?' Trollope called through his speaking trumpet.

'Twenty-one ships, sir, including some ship-sloops and frigates, say about fifteen of the line. There are also four brigs and two yachts . . . I'd say his whole force excepting the transports . . .'

'So Ireland's out.'

Drinkwater shook his head. 'No sir, they could come out next tide or wait until he's dealt with us, sir.' He saw Trollope nod.

'Take station on my lee beam. I'm forming line, continue to repeat my signals. Good luck!'

'And you sir.' He exchanged a wave with Burroughs, then turned to Hill.

'Mr Hill, our station is the commodore's lee beam. Do you see to it.'

'Aye, aye, sir.'

'You may adjust sail to maintain station and watch for any signals either general to the squadron for repeating, or particular to us.'

Drinkwater felt a great burden lifted from his shoulders. It was good to be in company again, good to see the huge bulk of *Russell* a cannon shot to windward. He suddenly felt very tired but there was one thing yet to do. 'Mr Jessup!'

'Sir?'

'Call the hands aft!'

'Now my lads,' began Drinkwater, leaping up on to the breech of one of the three pounders when they had assembled. 'I'm not one to bear a grudge, and neither are you. We are now in the presence of an enemy force and disobedience to an order carries the penalty of death. I therefore rely absolutely upon your loyalty. Give me that and I promise I will move heaven and earth to have you paid the instant we return to Sheerness.' He paused and was pleased to find a murmur of approval run through the men.

'Carry on, Mr Jessup, and pipe up spirits now . . .'

Drinkwater jumped down from the gun. 'Mr Hill, you have the deck. Call me if you need me.' He went gratefully below, passing through the cabin where light through the skylight had exorcised the spectres of the preceding night.

'Spirit ration, Mr Thompson,' said Jessup to the purser. James Thompson nodded and indicated the guns of *Russell* half a mile to windward. They were a dumb but powerful incentive to obedience.

'He chooses his moments for exhortatory speeches, don't he, Mr Jessup?'

Jessup had only the vaguest idea of what an exhortatory speech was, but the significance of *Russell*, surging along, sail set to the topgallants as she stood south to maintain station with De Winter, was not lost on him.

'Aye, Mr Thompson, he's a cool and calculating bastard,' muttered Jessup, unable to keep the admiration out of his voice.

Captain Trollope formed his squadron into line with the sloop *Martin* ahead and to larboard, keeping De Winter in sight as he edged south along the coast. Then, as the day wore on and his rear cleared the Schulpen Gat De Winter altered more to the west.

Trollope's main body consisted of the *Beaulieu*, a frigate of forty guns, following by the faithful fifty *Adamant* and his own *Russell*. In her wake came the smaller frigate *Circe* of twenty-eight guns. *Kestrel* and *Active*, cutters, lay to leeward of the line and *Black Joke* had long since been sent to Duncan to inform him the enemy was out.

Towards evening the wind fell away then backed round to the south west. De Winter tacked in pursuit of Trollope who drew off, while the Dutch, unable to catch the British, stood south again, confirming Drinkwater's theory that they intended to force the Straits of Dover.

During the following two days the wind hauled more steadily into the west and De Winter's fleet began to beat to windward, closing the English coast in the vicinity of Lowestoft with Trollope just ahead, covering his communications with Yarmouth.

'What d'you make of it, Nat?' asked Appleby confidentially at dinner. 'D'you still hold to your idea that they're bound for Brest, then Ireland?'

Drinkwater nodded, wiping his mouth with the crumpled napkin. 'He's covering Duncan while the troopships and store-ships get out of the Texel. They'll get south under the cover of the French coast and the De Winter'll follow 'em down Channel.'

Appleby nodded in uncharacteristic silence. 'It seems we've been wasting our time then,' he said.

On the morning of the 10th October Trollope despatched *Active* to find Duncan with the latest news of De Winter. At this time De Winter had learned from a Dutch merchant ship that Duncan had left Yarmouth and had been seen standing east. Alarmed for his rear De Winter turned away and, with the wind at north-west stood for the Dutch coast in the vicinity of Kampenduin.

Meanwhile Duncan, having left Yarmouth in great haste on seeing *Black Joke* making furious signals for an enemy at sea while still to seaward of the Scroby Sands, had indeed headed east for the Texel.

Trollope, though inferior in force, had hung on to the windward position chiefly because the shallow draughted Dutch ships were unable to weather him. He was still there on the morning of the 11th when officers in the Dutch fleet saw his ships throw out signals from which they rightly concluded Duncan was in sight of the main body of the British fleet. De Winter headed directly for the coast where he could collect his most leeward ships into line of battle and stand north for the Texel in the shallow water beloved by his own pilots. About twelve miles off the coast De Winter formed his line heading north under easy sail and awaited the British.

Admiral Duncan, having first reconnoitred the Texel and discovered the troop and storeships were still at their moorings, collected *Diligent* and turned south in search of his enemy. During the forenoon Trollope's detachment rejoined their admiral. Duncan's ships were indifferent sailors and he had neither time nor inclination to form line. De Winter's fleet was dropping to leeward into shoal water by the minute and the old admiral accepted their formal challenge with alacrity. Duncan hoisted the signal for 'general chase' and the British, grouped together into two loose divisions, Duncan's to the north and Onslow's slightly advanced to the south, bore down on the Dutch.

The increase in the westerly wind with its damp air had brought about a thickening of the atmosphere and the battle that was now inevitable seemed to be marred by disorder amongst the British ships. Just before noon Duncan signalled that his intention was to pass through the enemy line and engage from leeward, thus denying the Dutch escape and ensuring all the windward batteries of the British ships could be used. The signal was repeated by the frigates and cutters. At noon they hoisted that for close action.

Thirty minutes later Onslow's *Monarch* opened the action by cutting off De Winter's rear between the *Jupiter* and *Harlem*, ranging up alongside the former, raked by the heavy frigate *Monikendaam* and the brig *Atalanta* forming a secondary line to leeward of the Dutch battleships. Amid a thunder of guns the battle of Camperdown had begun.

Kestrel, in common with the other cutters as a repeating vessel, was not a target. Stray shot might hit her but in general the conventions of a fleet action were observed. The British cutters and Dutch yachts were expected to render assistance to the wounded where they could be found clinging to fallen spars and continue to repeat their admirals' signals. *Kestrel* had formed part of Onslow's division and Drinkwater found himself in a confusing world of screaming shot, choppy seas and a strong wind. Smoke and mist enveloped the combatants as gun flashes began to eclipse the dull daylight.

Within minutes Drinkwater had lost sight of *Monarch* behind the Dutch line and he altered to the north to maintain contact with *Russell*, but Trollope, too, cut through the line and *Kestrel* found herself passing under the stern of the Dutch seventy-four *Brutus*, bearing the flag of a rear-admiral at her mizen.

Through the rolling clouds of smoke a brig was seen to lee-ward and her commander did not extend the courtesy or disdain of his bigger consorts. Shot whistled about *Kestrel* and a shower of lancing splinters from the starboard rail sent one man hopping bloodily below in agony to where Appleby had his gruesome instruments laid out on the cabin table.

'Down helm!' roared Drinkwater, his eyes gleaming with concentration now the final, cathartic moment of action had arrived. 'Haul the sheets there!' the cutter bore away from her overlarge opponent and headed north, passing *Brutus* as the latter turned to assist De Winter ahead, now being pressed by several British ships tearing pell-mell into battle.

Suddenly ahead of them loomed a Dutch sixty-four, fallen out of line with her colours struck. For a moment Drinkwater contemplated putting a prize crew on board for it seemed unlikely that her antagonist, *Triumph*, engaged to larboard by a frigate and the seventy-four *Staten General*, had had the opportunity. But a sudden crash shook the cutter. One of the crew of Number 12 gun fell dead, cut clean in half by a ball that destroyed the jolly boat and the handsome taffrail. The brig which had fired on them had set her topgallants and was coming up fast in pursuit.

Drinkwater looked wildly round him. 'Down helm! Harden in those sheets there, put her on the wind, full and bye! Down centre plates! And throw that,' he indicated the faintly twitching lumps that a moment before had been a living man, 'overboard, for God's sake!'

Kestrel pointed up into the wind, escaping as she had done off Ushant, heeling to the hardening of her sails. Spray whipped over the rail and tore aft. Drinkwater looked astern.

'Well I'm damned,' he said aloud and beside him Hill whistled. The brig, unable to continue the chase so close to the wind, had come up with her consort, the surrendered sixty-four *Wassanaer*. Seeing her shameful plight the brig opened fire into her. In a few moments the Dutch tricolour jerked aloft again and snapped out in the wind.

'This ain't like fighting the Frogs, Mr Drinkwater. Look, there's hardly a mast down, these bloody squareheads know how to fight by Jesus . . . The bastards are hulling us. Christ! There'll be a butcher's bill after this lot . . .'

Russell loomed up ahead and *Kestrel* wore round in her wake.

'Ahead of you, sir,' Drinkwater bellowed through the speaking trumpet, 'a seventy-four. Yours for the taking . . .' He saw Trollope wave acknowledgement.

For a moment or two they kept pace with the battleship, huge, majestic and deadly, as she ran down her quarry. Her sides were already scarred by shot, several of which could be clearly seen embedded in her strakes. Seamen grinned at them from a jagged hole where adjacent gunports had been amalgamated. Thin streaks of blood ran down her sides.

'Spill some wind, Mr Hill. We'll drop astern.' *Russell* drew ahead, driving off the brig with one, apocalyptic broadside. *Wassanaer* surrendered again.

Kestrel crossed *Russell*'s wake. To larboard two or three ships lay rolling, locked in a death struggle. One was the *Staten General*.

Suddenly, from behind the hard-pressed Dutchman, leapt a

small but familiar vessel. Her bowsprit stabbed at the sky as her helm was put over and her course steadied to intercept the British cutter. At her masthead flew the black swallowtail pendant.

Drinkwater had no idea how Santhonax had persuaded De Winter to allow him the use of the yacht. She flew the Dutch tricolour from her peak but there was no mistaking the significance of that sinister weft at the masthead. Drinkwater thought of the corpse of Major Brown, of the hanged mutineers of the *Culloden*, of the scapegoats of the Nore and of the collusion between Capitaine Santhonax and the red-haired witch now in Maidstone Gaol. He was filled with a cold and ruthless anger.

'Larboard battery make ready!'

The yacht was on the larboard bow, broad-reaching to the north-east and closing them. For a few minutes they both ran on, lessening the range.

'Ease her off a point,' then in a louder voice, 'fire when you bear, Mr Bulman!'

Almost immediately the first report came from forward and Number 2 gun recoiled inboard, its crew fussing about it reloading. A ragged cheer broke from the Kestrels as they opened a rolling fire. Holes appeared in the yacht's sails. She was trying to cross *Kestrel*'s bow to rake and Drinkwater had a sudden idea.

'Down helm! Headsail sheets! Hard on the wind!' *Kestrel* turned, presenting her bow for the raking broadside but at a time of her own choosing and too quickly for Santhonax to take full advantage. Only two balls from his broadside came near and they struck harmless splinters from the starboard gig. 'Starboard guns! Starboard guns!'

Traveller held his hand up in acknowledgement, as if coolly assuring his commander that no last minute manoeuvre would rob Jeremiah Traveller of his moment. He had all the quoins out and the guns at full elevation as they made to cross the yacht's stern.

But Santhonax rose to the occasion. The yacht turned now, spinning to starboard so that the two vessels passed on opposite courses at a combined speed of nearly twenty knots. Doggedly they fired gun for gun, time permitting them one shot from each as they raced past. Drinkwater saw huge sections of the yacht's rail shivered into splinters. Jeremy Traveller had double shotted his guns.

Then the whine of shot, the impact, thumps and screams of the yacht's fire turned *Kestrel*'s deck into a shambles of wounded and dead men who fell back from their cannon. Aft, Drinkwater laid his pistol at a tall man near the yacht's tiller and squeezed the trigger. The ball missed its mark and the fellow coolly raised his hat and smiled. Drinkwater swore but he was cold as ice now, lifted on to a terrible, calculating plane that was beyond fear. He had surrendered to providence now, was a hostage to the capricious fortune of war and had long forgotten his earnest promises to Elizabeth. Elizabeth was of another world that had no part in this dull and terrible October afternoon. For this was not the Nathaniel known to Elizabeth, this was a man who had taken the French lugger and quelled incipient mutiny. This was an intelligent man butchering his fellows, and doing it with consummate ability.

'Up helm! Stand by to gybe!'

There was a scrambling about the decks as Jessup, aware of Drinkwater's intentions, whipped the shocked men to their stations. He had not yet felt the pain of the splinter in his own leg. *Kestrel* swung round in pursuit of the yacht, heeling violently as her huge boom, barely restrained by its sheet, flew across the deck. The unsecured guns of the starboard battery rolled inboard to the extent of their breechings and those of the larboard thumped against the rail, their outboard wheels in the water that drove in through the open gunports. They steadied after the yacht. Across her stern they could see her name; *Draaken*. Shot holes peppered her sails as they did their own, and frayed ropes' ends streamed to leeward from her masthead.

Drinkwater never removed his eyes from his quarry, gauging the distance. It was closing, the yacht with her leeboards sagging down to leeward as *Kestrel* came up on her larboard quarter. He was aware of, rather than saw, Jessup clapping a set of deadeyes on a weather shroud, wounded in the action, that had parted under the sudden strain of that impetuous gybe. And beneath his feet there was a sluggishness that told of water in the hold. Even as his subconscious mind identified it he heard too the clanking of the pumps where Johnson was attending to his duty.

'Mr Traveller!' There was no answer, then Jessup called 'Jem's bought it, sir . . .' There was a pause, eloquent of eulogy for a friend. 'I'll do duty if it's the starboard guns you'll be wanting . . .' There was a high, strained quality of exaggerated emphasis in Jessup's voice, also present in his own. He knew it for the voice of blood-lust, a quality that made men's words memorable at such moments of heightened perception.

It's the starboard battery I want, right enough Mr Jessup,' he confirmed, and it seemed that a steadying influence ran along *Kestrel*'s deck. The wounded had been pulled clear of the guns from where Meyrick and his bearers could drag the worst of them below, to Appleby.

The surrounding battle had ceased to exist for Drinkwater. His whole being was concentrated on overhauling the *Draaken*, attempting to divine Santhonax's next move. Jessup came up to him.

'I've loaded canister on top o'ball, sir, in the starboard guns, an' the larbowlines will be ready to board.'

With an effort Drinkwater directed his attention to the man beside him. There was the efficiency he had first noted about Jessup, paying dividends at last. He must remember that in his report. If he lived to write it.

'Thank you, Mr Jessup.' His eye ran past the boatswain. Forward he could see James Thompson checking the priming in a pistol and taking a cutlass from Short. Short, a kerchief round his grimy head, was lovingly caressing a boarding pike. By the companionway Tregembo was thumbing the edge of another pike and glancing anxiously aft at Drinkwater. All along the starboard side the starbowlines knelt by their guns as if at gun drill. He could see the red beard of Poll pointed at the enemy.

A wave of emotion seized Drinkwater for a terrible moment. It seemed the cutter and all her people were in the grip of some coalescing of forces that stemmed from his own desire for vengeance. They could not have caught the same madness that led Drinkwater in hot pursuit of Santhonax, nor all be victims of the witchcraft of Hortense Montholon.

He shook his head to clear it of such disturbing thoughts. It was merely the result of discipline, he reassured himself. Then he cast all aside as ahead of them *Draaken* luffed.

Unable to escape, she would stand her ground while she had a lead, lie athwart *Kestrel*'s bow, rake her and run north, delivering a second broadside as she did so.

'Lie down!' Drinkwater commanded, lending his own weight to the tiller and turning *Kestrel* a quarter point to starboard, heading directly for the yacht.

166

The cutter staggered under the impact of *Draaken*'s broadside. The peak halliard was shot through and the mainsail sagged down. Splinters rose in showers from the forward rails and a resonating clang told where at least one ball had ricochetted off a bow chaser. Someone screamed and one of the helmsmen dropped into eternity without a sound, falling against Drinkwater's legs. Then *Draaken* completed her turn and began to pass the cutter on the opposite tack, no more than twenty yards to windward.

'Now Jessup! Now!' Scrambling up from their prone positions the men gathered round the starboard guns.

Draaken drew abeam. 'Fire!'

Drinkwater saw the bulwarks fly as smoke from the yacht's own fire rolled down over *Kestrel*. As it cleared he saw her sails flogging uncontrolled. Santhonax had let fly his sheets and *Draaken* was dropping to leeward. With her shallow draught she would drive down on top of the cutter as *Kestrel* lost way, her mainsail hanging in impotent folds, the gaff shot through and her jib blowing out of the bolt ropes through shot holes.

'Let fly all sheets! Boarders stand by!'

All along her side *Kestrel*'s gunners poured shot after shot into the yacht as fast as they were able. It was murder and the cracking sails added to the screams of wounded men and the roar of the cannon. Then, in the smoke and confusion, *Draaken* was on top of them, her mast level with *Kestrel*'s tiller.

'Boarders aft here!' Drinkwater roared, lugging a pistol from his belt and drawing his hanger. Through the smoke he saw Tregembo and Short and James Thompson and half a dozen other faces familiar as old friends.

Kestrel shook as *Draaken* ground into her and the Dutchmen passed lashings over anything prominent. The wind whipped the last shreds of smoke from the now silent guns and as it cleared they saw their enemy.

They were poised to board, round red faces hedged with the deadly spikes of cutlass, axe and pike. Drinkwater sought vainly for Santhonax and then forgot him as the Dutchmen poured over the rail. The Kestrels were flung back, swept from their own deck as far as the gigs in a slithering, sliding *mêlée* of hacking stabbing and murdering. Drinkwater thrust, twisted and thrust with Tregembo grunting and swearing on his right hand and James Thompson on his left. He felt himself step on a body that still writhed. He dared not look down as he parried a clumsy lunge from a blond boy with the desperate look of reckless terror in his eyes. The boy stabbed again, inaccurately but swiftly in short defensive reflexes. Drinkwater hacked savagely down at the too-extended forearm. The boy fell back, unarmed and whimpering.

Briefly Drinkwater paused. He sensed the Dutch attack falter as the British, buttressed by the solid transoms of the gigs, found their defence was effective.

'Come on the Kestrels!' Drinkwater's scream cracked into a croak but about him there was a hefting of pikes, a re-gripping of cutlasses and then they were surging forward, driving the Dutch before them. Over a larboard gun leapt Short, a maniacal laugh erupting from him as he pitched a man overboard then drove two more before him into the larboard quarter. They were disarmed and with his pike Short tossed them both over the shattered transom like stooks on to a rick.

Drinkwater swung himself left, across to the starboard quarter where the enemy were in retreat. 'Board the bastard, James, board the bastard!' he yelled, and next to him Thompson grinned.

'I'm with 'ee, Mr Drinkwater!' Tregembo's voice was still there and here was Hill, and Bulman with the chasers' crews, having fought their way down the starboard side. Then they were up on the rail and leaping down on to *Draaken*'s deck, their impetus carrying them forward, men made hard and ruthless by months of blockade carried with them a more vicious motivation than the Dutch, torn from comfortable moorings and doing the bidding of foreign masters.

Opposition fragmented, lost its edge and above it all Drinkwater could hear the furious oaths in a fairer tongue than the guttural grunts of dying Dutchmen.

With careless swathes of the hanger Drinkwater slashed aft. A Dutch officer came on guard in front of him and instinct made him pause and come into the same pose but he was passed by Short, his face a contorted mask of insane delight, his pike levelled at the officer. A pistol ball entered Short's eye and took the back of his skull off. Still the boatswain's mate lunged and the Dutch lieutenant crashed to the deck, pierced by the terrible weapon with Short's twitching corpse on top of him.

Drinkwater stepped aside and faced the man who had fired the pistol.

It was Edouard Santhonax.

The Frenchman dropped the pistol and swiped downwards with his sword in the *molinello* he had used at Sheerness. Drinkwater put up his hanger in a horizontal parry above his head and the blades crashed together. Then Tregembo was beside him his pike extended at Santhonax's exposed stomach.

'Alive, Tregembo! Take him alive!' and on the last word, with a final effort Drinkwater twisted his wrist, disengaged and drew his blade under Santhonax's uncovered forearm.

Santhonax, attacked by two men, took greater terror from the levelled pike and tried to push it aside even as Tregembo obeyed Drinkwater and brought it up. The vicious point entered the Frenchman's face and ripped his cheek in a bloody, disfiguring wound and he fell back, covered in blood.

Drinkwater turned to see the deck of *Draaken* like a butcher's shambles. Lolling on the yacht's companionway James Thompson was holding his entrails, staring with disbelief. Drinkwater turned away, appalled. A kind of hush fell on them all, the moaning of the wind rising above the groans of the wounded. Then Hill said, 'Flag's signalling, sir . . . Acts 27 verse 28 . . .'

'For Christ's sake . . .'

All along the line of ships the smoke had cleared away. Admiral De Winter had surrendered and those of Onslow's commanders still with men on their quarterdecks able to open bibles obeyed their chief. They sounded and found, not fifteen fathoms, but nine. In great peril the British fleet secured their prizes.

Among them, her decks cluttered with corpses, her gear wounded, her bulwarks riven by shot, plunged the King's cutter *Kestrel*.

Chapter Sixteen October 1797

Aftermath

'How is he, Mr Appleby?' In the swaying lamplight *Kestrel*'s cabin had the appearance of an abbatoir and Appleby, grey-faced with exhaustion, was stained by blood, his apron stiff with it. They stared down at the shrunken body of James Thompson, the purser, his waist swathed in bloody bandages.

'Sinking fast, sir,' said the surgeon, his clipped formality proper in such grim circumstances. 'The livid colour of the lips, the contraction of the nostrils and eyebrows an indication of approaching death . . . besides he has lost much blood.'

'Yes.' Drinkwater felt light-headed, aware of a thousand calls on his time, unable to tear himself away from the groans and stench of the cabin as though by remaining there he could expiate himself for the murder they had been doing a few hours earlier. 'Yes,' he repeated, 'I am told he supported me most gallantly in boarding.'

Appleby ignored the remark.

'You are giving him an opiate?' Appleby lacked the energy to be indignant. He nodded.

'He is laced with laudanum, Mr Drinkwater, and will go to his maker in that state.' There was reproach in his voice.

Drinkwater left the cabin and returned on deck, passing the cabin, his own former hutch, where Santhonax lay, sutured and waxen, his hands bound. The rising wind had reached gale force and the British fleet clawed offshore, each ship fending for itself. In the howling blackness, lurching up and down the plunging deck, Drinkwater calmed himself before he could lie down and submit to the sleep his body demanded.

Rain came with the wind, driving over the wavecaps with a greater persistence than the sheets of spray that lashed the watch. Out in the night an occasional lantern showed where one of the battleships struggled to windward and twice he heard Bulman caution the lookouts to exert themselves.

Drinkwater knew he had not escaped the brutalising of his spirit that had begun so many years ago in the cockpit of *Cyclops*, nor escaped the effects of the events in the swamps of Carolina. The savagery he displayed in battle was a primaeval quality that those events had dragged out of the primitive part of him. But such ferocity could not be sustained against the earlier influence of a gentle home and in reaction he veered towards sentiment, like so many of his contemporaries.

He took refuge in the satisfaction of a duty acquitted and an increased belief in providence. As fatigue tamed the feelings raging in him since the battle, numbing his recollections, he felt better able to trust himself to write his report.

. . . *the vessels were laid board and board*, Drinkwater wrote carefully, *and after a sharp engagement the Draaken, despatch vessel, was carried.*

I have to inform you that the enemy defended themselves with great gallantry and inflicted severe losses on the boarders. All of the latter, however, conducted themselves as befitted British seamen and in particular James Thompson, Purser, Edward Jessup, Boatswain and Jeremiah Traveller, Gunner, who died in the action or of mortal wounds sustained therein.

He paused, reflecting on the stilted formality of the phraseology. One final piece of information needed to be included before this list of dead and wounded.

He began to write again. *Among those captured was a French naval officer, Capitaine de frégate Edouard Santhonax, known to your Honour to have been an agent of the French Government. Among his papers were found the enclosed documents relative to a proposed descent upon Ireland.* Drinkwater carefully inscribed his signature.

When he had appended the butcher's bill he went on deck. The frightful casualties inflicted on their number could not damp the morale of the crew. The Kestrels shared a common sense of relief at being spared, and a corporate pride in the possession of the *Draaken*, following astern under the command of Mr Hill, whose gashed arm seemed not to trouble him.

Drinkwater could not be offended at the mood of the crew. Of all the Kestrels he knew he and Appleby were alone in their sense of moral oppression. It was not callousness the men displayed, only a wonderful appreciation of the transient nature of the world. Drinkwater found he envied them that, and he called them aft to thank them formally, for their conduct. It all sounded unbelievably pompous but the men listened with silent attention. It would have amused Elizabeth, he thought, as he watched the cautiously smiling seamen. He felt better for those smiles, better for thinking of Elizabeth again, aware that he had not dared contemplate a future since the Dutch showed signs of emerging from the Texel. The grey windy morning was suddenly less gloomy and the sight of *Adamant* out of the corner of his eye was strangely moving.

He completed his speech and a thin cheer ran through the men. Drinkwater turned to the grey bundles between the guns. There were thirteen of them.

He had murdered and harangued and now he must bury his dead in an apparently meaningless succession of contradictory rituals.

From the torn pocket of his grubby coat he took the leather prayer book that had once belonged to his father-in-law and began to read, 'I am the resurrection and the life, saith the Lord . . .' and overhead the bright bunting snapped in the wind.

Duncan's fleet anchored at the Nore to the Plaudits of Parliament and the gratitude of the nation. At first the strategic consequences of the battle were of secondary importance to the relief of ministers. Despite the mutiny the North Sea fleet was unimpaired in efficiency. The seamen had vindicated themselves and the Government had been justified in its intransigence. Vicarious glory was reflected on all parties, euphoria was the predominating emotion and honours were heaped upon the victors. Admiral Duncan's earlier ambition of quiet retirement with an Irish peerage was eclipsed by his being made a baron and viscount of Great Britain, Onslow was made a baronet, Trollope and Fairfax knights and all the·first lieutenants of the line of battleships were promoted to commander. Medals were struck, swords presented and the thanks of both Houses of Parliament voted unanimously to the fleet. The latter was held to be, as Tregembo succinctly put it, of less use than his own nipples.

Before reporting to Duncan, Drinkwater interviewed Santhonax. The Frenchman could only mutter with difficulty, his lacerated mouth painfully bruised round the crude join Appleby had made of his cheek. He had given his name after prompting, using English, but Drinkwater had troubled him little after that, too preoccupied with managing the damaged cutter with half his crew dead or wounded.

But on the morning they anchored at the Nore, Santhonax was a little better and asked to see Drinkwater.

'Who are you?' he asked, through clenched teeth but in an accent little disfigured by foreign intonation.

'My name, sir, is Drinkwater.'

Santhonax nodded and muttered 'Boireleau . . .' as if committing it to memory then, in a louder voice, 'you are not the commander of this vessel?'

'I am now.'

'And the old man . . . Griffiths?'

'You know him?' Drinkwater was surprised and lost his chill formality. Santhonax began to smile but broke off, wincing.

'The quarry always knows the hunter . . . your boat is well named, *La Crécerelle*.'

'Why did you hang Brown?'

'He was a spy, he knew too much . . . he was an enemy of the Revolution and of France.'

'And you?'

'I am a prisoner of war, M'sieur Boireleau . . .' This time Santhonax crinkled the skin about his eyes. Stung, Drinkwater retorted, 'We have evidence to hang you. We have Hortense Montholon in custody.'

Santhonax's sneer was cut short. He looked like a man unexpectedly whipped. What colour he had, drained from his face.

'Take him away,' snapped Drinkwater to Hill, standing edgily behind the prisoner, 'and then have my gig made ready.'

'Drinkwater, good to see you, my word but what a drubbing we gave 'em and what a thundering good fight they put up, eh?' Burroughs met him at *Venerable*'s entry port, bubbling with good spirits and new rank. He gestured round the fleet, 'hardly a spark knocked down among the lot of us but hulls like colanders . . . by heaven but I'm glad we did for 'em, damned if I'd like another taste of that . . . not a single prize that's worth taking into service . . . except perhaps yours, eh?'

'Aye, sir, but it's already cost a lot.'

Burroughs became serious. 'Aye, indeed. Our losses were fearful, over a thousand killed and wounded . . . but come, the admiral wants a word with you, I was about to send a midshipman to fetch you.'

Drinkwater following Burroughs under the poop and was swept past the marine sentry. 'Mr Drinkwater, my Lord.' Burroughs winked at him and left. Drinkwater advanced to where

Duncan was writing at his desk, its baize cloth lost under sheaves of paper.

'Sit down,' said the admiral wearily, without looking up, and Drinkwater gingerly lowered himself on to an upright chair, still stiff from the bruises and cuts of Camperdown. He felt the chair had suffered the repose of many backsides in the last twenty-four hours.

At last Duncan raised his head. 'Ah, Mr Drinkwater, I believe we have some unfinished business to attend to, eh?'

Drinkwater's heart missed a beat. He felt suddenly that he had made some terrible mistake, failed to execute his orders; to repeat signals. He swallowed and held out a packet. 'My report, my Lord . . .'

Duncan took it and slit the seal. Rubbing tired eyes he read while Drinkwater sat silently listening to the pounding of his own heart. The white paintwork of the great cabin was cracked and flaking where Dutch shot had impacted the *Venerable*'s side and in one area planks had been hastily nailed in place. A chill draught ran through the cabin and a faint residual stain on the scrubbed deck showed where one of *Venerable*'s men had bled.

He heard Duncan sigh. 'So you've taken a prisoner, Mr Drinkwater?'

'Yes, my Lord.'

'You'd better have him transferred over here immediately. I'll have a marine detachment sent back with you.'

'Thank you, my Lord.'

'The conduct of Captain Trollope's squadron, of which you were a part, was most gratifying and I have here a paper for you.' He held out a document and Drinkwater stood to take it. It was a commission as lieutenant.

'Thank you, my Lord, thank you very much.'

Duncan had already bent to his papers again and he said, without looking up, 'It's no more than you deserve, Mr Drinkwater.'

Drinkwater had his hand on the door handle when he recollected something. He turned. Duncan was immersed in the details of his fleet. There was talk of a court martial on Williams of the *Agincourt*. Drinkwater coughed.

'My Lord?'

'Uh?' Duncan continued writing.

'My people are long overdue for their pay, my Lord, might I

ask you for an order to that effect?'

Duncan laid his pen down and looked up. The admiral was too experienced a sea-officer not to know something lay behind the request. He smiled faintly at the earnest young man. 'See my clerk, Mr Drinkwater, see my clerk,' and the old admiral bent once again to his work.

Kestrel lay a week in Saltpan Reach while they did what they could to patch her up. Drinkwater was confirmed in command until they decommissioned for extensive repairs and he gave a dinner for those of his officers still alive. It was a modest affair at which they were served by Merrick and Tregembo who volunteered for the task and accomplished it with surprising adroitness. Afterwards he sought out Drinkwater.

'Begging your pardon, zur,' he began awkwardly, shuffling from one foot to the other and finally swallowing his diffidence. 'Ar damnation, zur, I ain't one for beating about, zur, but seeing as how you're promoted I'd like to volunteer for your cox'n, zur.'

Drinkwater smiled at the Cornishman. 'I'm only promoted lieutenant, Tregembo, that ain't quite post-captain, you know.'

'We've been shipmates a year or two now, zur . . .'

Drinkwater nodded, he felt very flattered. 'Look Tregembo, I can pay you nought beyond your naval pay and certainly not enough to support you and your future wife . . .' he got no further.

''tis enough, zur, your prize money'll buy you a handsome house, zur an' my Susan can cook, zur.' He grinned triumphantly. 'Thank 'ee, zur, thank 'ee . . .'

Taken aback Drinkwater could only mutter 'Well I'm damned,' and stare after the retreating seaman. He remembered Tregembo's Susan as a compact, determined woman and guessed she might have some part in it.

He had better write to Elizabeth and tell her he had a commission and she, it appeared, had a cook.

The Puppet Master

'Orders, sir.' Hill passed the oiled packet that the guard boat had just delivered. Drinkwater pushed the last bottle of Griffiths's sercial across to Appleby and opened the bundle on the table.

As he read the frown on his brow deepened. Silently Appleby and Hill searched their commander's face for some indication of their fate. Eventually Drinkwater looked up.

'Mr Hill, we drop down to the Nore with the ebb this after-noon and I will require a boat to take me to the Gun Wharf at five of the clock . . .' He looked down again at the papers.

Hill acknowledged his instructions and left the cabin. 'What is it?' enquired Appleby.

Drinkwater looked up again. 'Confidential I'm afraid, Mr Appleby,' he said with chilly formality. But it was not Appleby's curiosity that had set Drinkwater on edge. It was the signatory of his orders. They had not come from Admiral Duncan but from Lord Dungarth.

It was the earl who descended first from the carriage that swung to a halt on the windy quay. Drinkwater advanced to greet him as he turned to assist the second occupant out of the carriage. The hooded figure was obscured in the gathering dusk, but there was something about the newcomer that was vaguely familiar.

'So,' she said, looking about her, 'you are going to deport me, no? Not shoot me after all?'

Drinkwater recognised Hortense Montholon as Dungarth replied 'Aye ma'am against both my judgement and inclination, I do assure you.' He turned to Drinkwater. 'Good evening, Lieutenant.' Dungarth gave a thin smile of congratulation.

'Good evening, my Lord.'

Lord Dungarth turned to the woman and removed a pair of handcuffs from his coat pockets. 'Be so kind as to hold out your right wrist.'

'Must you practise this barbarity,' she said frowning and shooting Drinkwater a look full of pathetic helplessness. He avoided her gaze.

'We are men, not saints sweet lady,' quoted his lordship as he handcuffed himself to the prisoner then led her towards the waiting boat.

Kestrel weighed and carried a favourable westerly breeze out of the Thames. Drinkwater came below at midnight to find Lord Dungarth sitting in the lamplit cabin with Hortense Montholon asleep on the leeward settee.

Silently Drinkwater brought out a bottle. He poured two glasses and passed one to Dungarth. The wheel had come full circle now, the cutter's cabin that had been the scene of its beginning witnessed its end. Dungarth raised his glass.

'To your cockade, Nathaniel, you have earned it.'

'Thank you, my Lord.' His eyes strayed to the woman. The auburn hair tumbled about her shoulders and a slight emaciation of her face due to her incarceration lent her a saintly, martyr-like quality. Something of her effect on Drinkwater was visible on his face.

'She is as dangerous as poison,' said Dungarth in a low voice and Drinkwater turned guiltily away.

'What is to be done with her?'

Dungarth shrugged. 'Were she a man we would have shot her, were she an English woman in France the regicides would have guillotined her. As it is she is allowed her freedom.' The cynical way in which Dungarth made his remarks clearly indicated he did not approve of the decision.

'Her brother has some influence in emigré circles and pressure was brought to bear upon Government,' he sighed. 'Would that poor Brown had had such an advocate.'

'Aye my Lord . . .' Drinkwater thought of the gibbet hanging over the battery at Kijkduin. 'And what of Santhonax?'

'Ah,' Dungarth grunted with greater relish, a cruel smile crossing his mouth. 'We have *him* mewed up close, very close. You ruined his looks Nathaniel, tch, tch.' Drinkwater passed the bottle as *Kestrel* lurched into a wave trough. Dungarth waved it towards the sleeping woman. 'She does not yet know of his apprehension. It is going to be something of a disappointment to her when she arrives home.' He smiled and sipped his wine.

Drinkwater looked at Hortense again. She stirred as *Kestrel* butted another wave and her eyes opened. She sat up puzzled, then shivered and drew the cloak round her in a curiously childish way. Then her eyes recognised the company and her circumstances and an expression close to satisfaction settled upon her face.

'Watch her well, Nathaniel,' said Dungarth, 'she is an old deceiver, a veritable Eve. It was a pity Jacobin sentiment, undiscriminating though it is, had not been a little more zealously employed at Carteret and saved us the trouble of rescuing such a viper.'

'Can you believe such a face could betray her betrothed, eh?'

Drinkwater saw Hortense frown, uncomprehending. He remembered poor De Tocqueville and his unrequited passion.

'What do you mean?' she asked, 'betray . . .'

'Do not mock me ma'am, your lover Santhonax had De Tocqueville cut down in the gutters of London and well you know it.'

'No, no . . . I knew nothing of that.' For a moment she digested the news then held up her head. 'I do not believe you. You lie . . . you lie to protect yourself, you are fools, already your navy is crippled by the brave republicans, soon the Dutch will come to help and then all the ships will join those of France and the greatest navy in the world will be at our command . . .' Her eyes blazed with the conviction of one who had sustained herself in prison with such thoughts. 'Even now you have spared me to use me in your plight.'

Beside him Drinkwater heard Dungarth begin to laugh. Quietly Nathaniel said, 'The mutiny in our navy is over, ma'am. The Dutch are not coming, their fleet is destroyed.'

'You see,' put in Dungarth, 'your plan has gravely misfired. Command of the Channel is ours and Ireland is safe.'

'Ireland is never safe,' snapped Hortense, a gleam of rekindled fire in her eyes which died abruptly as Dungarth replied, 'Neither is Santhonax.'

Hortense caught her breath in alarm, looking from one to another and finding no comfort in the expressions of her captors. 'He is in France,' she said uncertainly.

'He *was* in Holland, madam, but Mr Drinkwater here took him prisoner in the recent battle with the Dutch fleet.'

She opened her mouth to protest they were bluffing but read the truth in their eyes. Drinkwater had not baited her, Drinkwater did not deal in words and intrigue. She recollected him probing De Tocqueville's wound here, in this very cabin, an age ago. He was a man of deeds and she knew Santhonax had been taken, immured like herself by these barbarian English.

178

'And I believe his face was much disfigured by a pike,' Dungarth said abstractedly.

Both Dungarth and Drinkwater went ashore in the gig. Above them the height of Mont Jolibois rose into the night, its summit shrouded in a light mist that the breeze rolled off the land. The sea was smooth under the mighty arch of the sky.

Between the two of them the hooded figure remained obscured from the oarsmen. The gig was run on to the beach and Drinkwater lifted Hortense into his arms, splashing ashore and setting her down on the sand.

'There madam,' said Dungarth pointedly, 'I hope we never meet again.'

Hortense caught Drinkwater's eyes in the gloom. Hers were openly hostile that this nondescript Englishman had taken her lover and disfigured his beaut;. Then she turned and made off over the sand. Drinkwater watched her go, oblivious of Dungarth beside him until the pistol flashed.

'My Lord!' He stared after Hortense, feeling Dungarth's hand restraining him from rushing forward. She stumbled and then they saw her running, fading into the night.

He stood staring with Dungarth beside him. Behind them he heard the boat's crew murmuring.

'It wasn't loaded,' said Dungarth, 'but she'll run the faster.'

He smiled at Drinkwater. 'Come, come, Nathaniel, surely you are not shocked. She had even half-seduced you.' He chuckled to himself. 'Why sometimes even a puppet-master may pull a wrong string.'

They turned and walked in silence back to the boat.

Out of the pain and glory – a memorable
and classic novel of men at war

SOLDIERS

WALTER WINWARD

Some were little more than teenagers, fleeing from the dole
queues. Others were seasoned campaigners of the Falls Road.
But, between the euphoria of their departure and the grim
killing grounds of Goose Green, something happened to the
Commandos in their green berets, the Paras in their red ones and
the infantry in their blue – the Rainbow soldiers of Daddy
Rankin's crack battalion. Something which gave them the
courage and character to fight, to win the war that no one really
wanted – and to die.

RAINBOW SOLDIERS is a magnificent and moving account
of men at war, men caught up in one of the most extraordinary
conflicts of recent years.

'WELL RESEARCHED . . . WELL DONE'
IRISH TIMES

'ILLUMINATES IMPORTANT ASPECTS OF THE CONFLICT'
TIMES LITERARY SUPPLEMENT

'A MOVING AND READABLE STORY'
COVENTRY EVENING TELEGRAPH

0 7221 9199 5   GENERAL FICTION   £3.50

A selection of bestsellers from Sphere:

FICTION

THE SECRETS OF HARRY BRIGHT	Joseph Wambaugh	£2.95 ☐
CYCLOPS	Clive Cussler	£3.50 ☐
THE SEVENTH SECRET	Irving Wallace	£2.95 ☐
CARIBBEE	Thomas Hoover	£3.50 ☐
THE GLORY GAME	Janet Dailey	£3.50 ☐

FILM & TV TIE-IN

INTIMATE CONTACT	Jacqueline Osborne	£2.50 ☐
BEST OF BRITISH	Maurice Sellar	£8.95 ☐
SEX WITH PAULA YATES	Paula Yates	£2.95 ☐
RAW DEAL	Walter Wager	£2.50 ☐

NON-FICTION

URI GELLER'S FORTUNE SECRETS	Uri Geller	£2.50 ☐
A TASTE OF LIFE	Julie Stafford	£3.50 ☐
HOLLYWOOD A' GO-GO	Andrew Yule	£3.50 ☐
THE OXFORD CHILDREN'S THESAURUS		£3.95 ☐
THE MAUL AND THE PEAR TREE	T. A. Critchley & P. D. James	£3.50 ☐

All Sphere Books are available at your local bookshop or newsagent, or can be ordered direct from the publisher. Just tick the titles you want and fill in the form below.

Name_____

Address_____

_____

Write to Sphere Books, Cash Sales Department, P.O. Box 11, Falmouth, Cornwall TR10 9EN.

Please enclose a cheque or postal order to the value of the cover price plus:
UK: 60p for the first book, 25p for the second book and 15p for each additional book ordered to a maximum charge of £1.90.
OVERSEAS & EIRE: £1.25 for the first book, 75p for the second book and 28p for each subsequent title ordered.
BFPO: 60p for the first book, 25p for the second book plus 15p per copy for the next 7 books, thereafter 9p per book.
Sphere Books reserve the right to show new retail prices on covers which may differ from those previously advertised in the text elsewhere, and to increase postal rates in accordance with the P.O.